DEMONCHASER IV

David Berardelli

DEMONCHASER IV

"Still kicking demon butts and still wearing great shoes"

GRAVESTONE PRESS

A GRAVESTONE PRESS PAPERBACK

ISBN: 978 1 78695 668 2

Gravestone Press
is an imprint of Fiction4All
www.fiction4all.com

This Edition
Published 2021

Cover Art: Linda York

DAY ONE - "HOMECOMING"

CHAPTER 1

Vicki would never forget the first time she saw the angel.

At first, she didn't know if the lady was an angel at all. Angels just weren't something a thirteen-year-old girl thought much about these days. In fact, she'd never thought much about angels at all before that afternoon. All Vicki had been thinking about was taking Toby, her three-year-old West Highland terrier, down the street for his afternoon walk. School would start in just a few days, and she wanted to spend as much time as she could with her furry little friend before summer vacation ended.

However, things quickly changed, and her mind went all sorts of crazy once the nightmare happened. Her whole world seemed to break apart in just a second or two, the moment the van slammed into Toby, and everything slowed down and stopped from that point on. It was almost like in a movie, when the camera stops right in the middle of an important scene and everything turns into one of those weird three-dimensional photos.

Moms had always told her to be careful when taking Toby out for his walk. "People drive like idiots," she'd told Vicki over and over. "They don't slow down for dogs, cats, or even other people. They text each other and don't watch where they're going. They talk on the phone and zone out, and the last thing they think of is their driving, or what's ahead of them on the highway. I've seen women applying their makeup. Some even comb their hair at the same time. Some of the people driving on the roads are drunk, while others are on drugs. You've got to be extra careful, baby, and don't give them a reason to do anything stupid because they really don't need much of one at all…"

Because of what Moms had told her, Vicki promised herself to keep really close to Toby whenever she took him for his walk. She knew to be careful when they went down to the end of the driveway to get the mail and when they went down the street for a longer walk to exercise his short little furry legs. They lived in a quiet subdivision in a quiet neighborhood, but people still drove down their street much too fast—especially the ones using it as a detour to get to the main highway faster.

"Always hold on tight to his leash," Moms told her, time after time. "Always make sure his collar is fastened to the clasp on the leash, and never forget to keep your end looped around your wrist so it doesn't slip."

This had never been a problem—except for just a moment ago, when she gave a slight tug and suddenly realized that the other end of the leash had been dragging behind her on the sidewalk. It took her only a moment to discover what had just happened, another moment to wonder why it happened, and one last terrifying instant for reality to kick in and send the panic ripping violently through her.

But by then, it was too late. The moment she realized that she'd really and truly messed up, she heard a sickening *thump*! behind her. At the same time, a horrible high-pitched squeal was abruptly cut off. By the time she'd spun around, Toby was already lying on his side by the curb, his back legs twitching.

"*Toby*!" Her heart had climbed up her throat the moment she broke into a run. Her limbs were tingly and her head felt like it had been shoved into a vat of hot water, but she forced herself to keep moving. The white van that had slammed into her beloved dog had already reached the end of the block and zipped right through the stop sign, but all she could focus on was the tiny white furry body lying on the grass just off the curb.

Toby suddenly stopped twitching and lay motionless. The sight of him lying there like that tore through her like barbed wire, and she was certain she could feel her heart crumbling into tiny pieces. Toby was her puppy, her friend. Her partner. He was her Christmas present nearly two years earlier and hadn't left her side except for the time she spent at school. She'd taught him how to fetch the tiny squeaking rubber bone Moms had bought last summer and bring it back so Vicki could toss it again. She remembered how Toby had wagged his tiny nub of a tail the day she'd given him his first treat—a tiny piece of crispy bacon she'd smuggled from the breakfast table. Toby knew to cuddle her when she felt bad or sick…and how not to jump up in her lap when she was doing her homework. He knew to be quiet when she and Moms were sleeping, and how to patiently wait in the kitchen, underneath the pegboard next to the refrigerator, where his leash hung, to let someone know he had to go to the bathroom. He was her bright spot on a rainy day and never failed lifting her spirits whenever she was depressed.

Now her best friend lay next to the curb, and it was her fault. The clasp on the leash had broken, but it was still her fault. She should have noticed. She should have kept her attention on him instead of watching for traffic at the end of the block. She should have felt the leash coming apart.

But she hadn't. She'd been wrapped up in her own little world, and because of it, she'd just lost her very best friend.

"*Oh, Toby!*" She knelt down close to him and bent over him. She wanted to touch him but was afraid to. She didn't want to feel cold coming from him. She wanted him to be warm and furry as always, panting, licking her face, rubbing his head against her. Her tears filled her eyes, and she didn't care one bit if another van roared down the street and hit her as well. She'd lost her very best friend and wanted to go with him, wherever that was, and the only thing that mattered was that Toby was dead and she didn't want to go on without him.

Then, in the midst of her agony, a soft voice somewhere behind her startled her, pulling her out of her nightmare.

"Would you mind very much if I looked at your friend? I might be able to help."

The voice was soft and warm, but Vicki was overcome with grief and was frightened that she could be imagining things. However, she realized that if she *had* heard a voice, and if this voice had actually said what she *thought* it said, maybe the person who'd said it could help her somehow.

But how could anyone help Toby? Her friend was dead, and it was all her fault.

"He's...*dead*..." That last word hurt. For a moment she thought a sliver of glass had torn out of her throat. *Toby. Dead.* Two words Vicki had never *ever* wanted to put together.

"I'd still like to see if I can help," the soft voice said.

Vicki took a breath and tried her best to collect herself. She still could not bear to pull her gaze away from her little friend. "Toby...he's...my best friend..." She gently touched the little dog's pointed ear, hoping to see it twitch. It always had whenever she touched the tip. But now it didn't—which conveyed the dreaded message even more completely.

She sniffed and shuddered when she took her next breath. "Some bastard in a white van...hit him...and *didn't even stop!*" The anger gushed out, making her hot and tingly all over. She wanted to find whoever was driving that van so she walk right up to them, tell them she'd seen what they'd done, then claw their eyes out, push them down onto the pavement and jump on them, over and over, until their guts splashed out onto the sidewalk.

But once again, some inner feeling told her she should listen to the voice behind her.

Taking a deep breath, she turned.

A very beautiful lady stood a couple of feet behind her, looking down at her with the kindest, warmest expression Vicki had ever seen. The lady was young, maybe just a handful of years older than Vicki, actually. She had the most beautiful face and the softest blue eyes Vicki had ever seen. The lady's hair was a honey-blonde, covering her shoulders with shimmering curls, and when the sun hit it, tiny silver stars appeared, winking at her. The lady wore a bright-red short-sleeve tank top and dark blue Capri's. Her shoes were opened-toed white sandals with two-inch heels and tiny glittering blue diamonds arranged in wavy rows on the sides. Vicki had never seen shoes like that before and wondered where the lady had found them.

But that wasn't important right now. Toby was what mattered, and this nice lady wanted to help. Vicki had no idea why, but the feelings she'd had since she'd first heard the lady's soft, soothing voice suggested that things might not be as horrible as she'd originally thought. She had no idea why, but as this lady drew closer, Vicki felt warm, content and safe. A strong sense of hope urged her to comply with this lady's wishes.

"People are not very nice nowadays," she said, and Vicki could feel both sadness and anger coming from the lady when she'd said it. "They don't care about hurting others."

Vicki felt even more hot, stinging anger sliding down her back. "They hit him and *didn't stop!* They *kept on going!*" The fresh tears welling in her eyes blurred her vision.

"I'd still like to see if I can help." Her smile returned quickly—as if it had never left her face.

Her smile was very bright, and Vicki felt even warmer and more content. The lady's smile seemed to make the anger—as well as the hatred she'd felt for the driver of the van—go away. But reality quickly intervened, and she couldn't stop wondering how anyone could possibly help Toby.

"Toby's…gone," she whispered. She didn't want to say the d-word again. But even so, she choked down more tears. "How can you help?"

"I'd like to try. Will it be all right?"

Still skeptical, Vicki felt herself nodding.

The lady knelt down on the other side of Toby. She smelled sweet, like flowers, and when Vicki gazed into the woman's eyes, she saw sunshine and felt even more warmth…and this was when she first suspected that this woman was very, very special. Vicki had read all sorts of fantasy stories she'd bought online and remembered the fairy tales Moms had read to her years ago, when Vicki was little. She strongly felt that this lady had somehow come out of a fairy tale. Vicki's feelings of warmth and hope told her she was in the presence of someone truly special.

Vicki couldn't help it; she began shivering.

"Are you all right?"

"I'm…fine." Vicki tried to stop shivering but quickly found that she could not. "I'm just…I'm…this is just too—"

Without a word, the lady placed her hand on Vicki's shoulder.

A rush of warmth ran down Vicki's arm, and in seconds her whole body felt warm and tingly. It reminded her of the time she got off the rollercoaster last summer. But this was much different. This time, she had no idea why it was happening, and when she realized it was because this special lady had touched her, she shivered even worse.

"Please…let me see if I can help."

"Do you really think you can?" Vicki asked in a soft voice.

"We won't know till we try."

Before Vicki could reply, the lady bent and began gently stroking Toby's ruffled white fur. "He's very soft," she said, smiling.

"I…I brushed him…*brush* him…every day." Vicki nearly choked on the words and was surprised that they'd come out right. She wanted to tell this nice lady just how much Toby meant to her. Vicki knew she would understand.

"You've done a fine job." The lady smiled at her. Then she reached down with her other hand and began stroking Toby very gently with both hands.

Vicki couldn't understand what was happening. The lady was stroking Toby's fur—just as Vicki herself had done a million times before. Her friend was gone—how could a little stroking change anything?

"Miss?" She couldn't keep it inside her any longer. She needed to know what was going on—

what this woman was doing and why she was doing it.

"*Sshhh…*" She continued stroking Toby.

Vicki pressed her lips tightly together. Although she had no idea what was going on, she knew better than make this worse than it already was.

Then it dawned on her, and she instinctively placed her hand on her shoulder. *Warm.* The lady's touch. It was so special…so strange...

So *magical…*

She touched me, and I felt warm and comfortable inside…

Could *this* be what she was doing to Toby? This lady obviously had a special touch. Could this actually help Toby? Would she be able to—

Suddenly…incredibly…Toby began to stir.

The lady continued stroking his fur, but more vigorously. Toby shifted, stretched his short furry white legs and rolled his head as if he'd just awakened from a nap. A moment later, he yawned. Then he turned his head toward Vicki and began panting.

"He's…he's…" Vicki found that she was much too choked up to finish her statement.

"I think he'll be okay now." The lady stopped stroking Toby and sat back. Squirming, the little dog sat up. After looking around, he shook himself, panted some more and without warning, leaped into Vicki's arms.

Vicki squeezed her friend tightly. Toby squirmed in her arms, licking her face and wagging his little nub of a tail. More tears filled her eyes.

This time, they were tears of joy. She couldn't believe what had just happened. Only moments ago, Toby was dead… But now he was alive and acting just like he was before all this happened…

He *was* dead, wasn't he?

Did it matter? Did it really?

Maybe he wasn't dead at all. Maybe he was just stunned.

That sounded more likely, didn't it? You couldn't bring back someone from the dead, could you?

No one could…*could* they?

She realized that none of this mattered at all. As she hugged and kissed Toby's face and head, she glanced at the lady and saw something in those beautiful blue eyes she'd never seen before. She couldn't explain it. All she could think of was a bright rainbow, and when Vicki closed her eyes, she saw herself and Toby running around in a beautiful field of flowers beneath a bright, cloudless sky.

And this was when Vicki was convinced that the lady was an angel. She had to be, because nothing else made any sense. And even though Vicki didn't know much about angels, she knew that only an angel could have done what this lady had just done.

But although this in itself was the most fantastic thing that had ever happened to her, she knew that it wasn't the most wonderful thing that had happened in the last few minutes. Toby licked her nose, bringing her right back to reality, and in that one amazing moment, her world had become fun and exciting again.

"Toby, Toby…you're back! *You're back*!" She hugged him even harder, stroking his head and belly and kissing him all over as he licked her face, her nose and her chin. She bathed herself in the incredible moment, clutching her beloved friend, closing her eyes and enjoying the unbelievable feeling that Toby had miraculously been brought back to her…

And when she finally opened her eyes again, she discovered that she and Toby were alone.

The lady was no longer there.

Clutching Toby tightly, Vicki jumped up and spun around.

The lady was walking away. But now she wasn't alone. A skinny little guy with wild red hair was walking beside her. Just as they reached the curb on the other side of the street, her companion bent and, without missing a step, grabbed a clump of grass, put it in his mouth and began eating it.

Strange. Really, really strange.

Vicki couldn't help wondering where the lady's friend had come from. It occurred to her that he might have been standing behind the lady while she tended to Toby.

That didn't matter, did it? Not at the moment, anyway. It didn't matter at all because there was something much more urgent that Vicki had to address.

She wasted no time. Still clutching Toby tightly in her arms, she trotted across the street, until she reached the two of them. "Excuse me! Miss?"

They both stopped. The lady turned around and smiled. "Yes?"

"I-I don't know how to…how to…to thank…to tell you how much I—"

"It's all right. I understand. Just don't let it happen again. And if I were you, I'd buy a new leash. That clasp broke, you know."

"Probably made in China," her friend said, frowning.

"*Please* tell me something…"

"Yes?"

Vicki didn't know how to say it. She swallowed, took a breath and opened her mouth, but nothing came out. *I need to ask. I really need to find out. I don't know how this lady can possibly know, but I have this strange feeling that she does. I think she knows a lot of things, and if I'm right, she probably knows if Toby will be okay.*

It was almost as if the woman had just read her mind. Smiling, she said, "Toby's back with you. That's all you need to know."

That sounded exactly right—but what about everything else? Toby was hit by a van. There wasn't any blood, but that didn't mean he hadn't been severely hurt. There were probably injuries no one could see. Internal injuries. Those were the ones that didn't show, the ones that were really bad.

Yet the furry little guy squirming in her arms and licking her face seemed just fine.

"He's perfectly healthy," the lady said. "Just take him home and love him and give him a special treat. I have a feeling he likes chicken."

How on earth did she know that?

Vicki's cheeks flushed. "H-How did…how did you—"

"Just a lucky guess." The lady smiled. Then she waved. "'Bye, Toby."

Toby turned his furry white head and gazed at the lady. Then, wagging his tail furiously, he sent over a soft, *"Woof..."*

As the lady and her friend began walking away, Vicki wanted her to know what this truly meant to her. She wanted her to know that Toby was her very best friend…and that just moments ago, she'd wanted to die because Toby had been hit by a van. She wanted to find some way of thanking her properly. She wanted her to know that she'd never ever forget her.

I don't even know her name...

All she knew was the woman was young and beautiful…and kind…and had the brightest blue eyes she'd ever seen …

Most of all, she'd brought Toby back to life.

"Toby's back with you. That's all you need to know."

There was much more to it than just that. There had to be. Toby was dead. This sweet, wonderful lady had somehow brought him back.

And Vicki didn't even know her name.

"I really would like to thank you," she said.

"It's all right. I'm glad I was able to help."

"Please…at least tell me your name…"

"I'm Tiffany."

Tiffany. It figured. Tiffany was a beautiful name. It fit her. Vicki remembered the Tiffany lamp her mother had seen in a fashion magazine and loved so much. The lamp was beautiful and bright and dazzling to the eye. But it was so expensive that there was no way Moms could afford it. It was only right that this beautiful lady should have a name like that.

"My name is Vicki." She wanted her to know her name as well. "Vicki Shannon."

"Nice to meet you, Vicki. You and Toby go home now, and stay safe. And remember what I said about buying him a new leash, okay? And, of course, his special treat. But don't give him too much. You don't want him to get fat. It's not good for him."

Are you an angel?

Vicki couldn't help wondering. She'd wanted to ask it out loud, but something told her not to. Something told her to keep it to herself. She didn't know if it was because she didn't want to sound silly or because she wasn't prepared to hear the answer. But no matter how tightly she kept her lips together, the thought squirmed its way out of her head anyway.

Just then, she knew she was right.

Tiffany didn't say anything. She didn't have to. Her eyes closed for a moment. When they opened again, they seemed even brighter. Another wave of warmth passed through Vicki, and she shivered again. It must have passed through Toby, too. He suddenly stopped squirming and relaxed for a moment. He uttered another soft, "*Woof,*" and continued squirming and wagging his little nub.

Vicki wanted to say something else but couldn't find the words. She didn't want Tiffany to leave, but she just couldn't think of anything else to say. Before she realized it, Tiffany gave her one last smile, waved, then turned and began walking down the street with her strange-looking friend.

CHAPTER 2

Munching on a plug of grass, Chip glanced at Tiffany as they went down the street. She was walking her normal gait and gave no indication of what she'd just done. That made things a tad more serious. He thought it was time to discuss this.

"Think that was wise, Tifferoo?"

They'd reached the end of the block. She gave him one of her clueless expressions.

He could tell she had no idea what he was talking about. Tifferoo didn't play games. Her expression suggested that she honestly had no idea what was going on.

"What are you talking about?"

He was relieved she hadn't pulled her mind thingy by going inside his head to find out what he was thinking. He didn't like her doing that; it made him nauseous.

"Bringing that dog back to life," he said flatly. "What else could we be talking about? You haven't worked any other miracles since we got off the bus, have you? We just got into town an hour ago. I've been right beside you ever since. Unless you did something phenomenal and breathtaking while I wasn't looking, I'd say it's safe to focus on the dead dog thingy."

"Didn't you see the look on that little girl's face? She was devastated."

"I could tell she was more than slightly upset, yeah…"

"Then what's the problem? I didn't know you hated dogs."

"I don't hate dogs, Tiffers. In fact, I love the furry little guys. They're warm and cuddly and make you feel all kindsa good and honorable inside. You can do the world's worst, most godawful thing, but a dog won't care. It'll treat you like you're the greatest thing in the universe. I had a little dog when I was a kid a few centuries back, when I was still alive. His name was Poco, and he used to steal things from my sister's underwear collection when she wasn't around."

Tiffany blinked. "They wore underwear back then?"

"All kinds of scarves and sheets and lacy things to cover the really good parts."

"And your dog went through her things? All on his own?"

Chip smiled sheepishly. "I kinda showed him the ropes—so to speak."

"That's disgusting."

"Whaddya expect? I was a little shit before I grew up, matured, fell down a well, died, went to the Dark Place and was turned into a flower for Olivier's rock garden."

Tifferoo rubbed her temples. "Let's try and stay on the subject, okay?"

"You know me, Princess. I never make promises I can't keep."

"Just tell me what's so wrong about helping out a little girl..."

Chip swallowed another plug of dirt and tried to put his thoughts into words. It was going to be tough, no matter how he phrased it. He sure didn't want to upset Tifferoo. She was a delight to be with most of the time, but when she was pissed off, things tended to get scary.

But this was important. This was something that had been on his mind ever since it happened. They'd been half a block away and had both seen everything. The van slammed right into the furry little guy and kept on moving. The dog bounced off the bumper like a tennis ball and landed twenty feet away. Chip couldn't be positive, but was reasonably certain the dog had been slightly more than stunned. And if he was right, and the dog was actually dead, this meant one thing, and it scared him.

Tifferoo had brought a dead creature back to life.

This made no sense at all. Tifferoo could do a shitload of impressive things, true…but bringing a dead dog back to life?

"Well? What's so wrong about this?"

She was watching him. He knew that if he didn't say something soon, she'd do her mind thingy. With her, it was no biggie; she just stared, crawled into his head and looked around.

"Why are you stalling? It isn't like you at all."

"Me? Stall?"

"You know what I'm talking about."

"Tifferoo—"

"You're still stalling."

"I'm merely getting my thoughts together in a more organized fashion so I don't confuse you."

"Then tell me what's wrong…and why you're acting like this…and why you didn't think I should have helped that girl—even though you just said you love dogs."

"Um, which part should I answer first, Tifferoosky?"

"You're stalling again."

He bent and snatched another plug of grass out of the ground. This wasn't going to be easy at all.

"You're still stalling."

"I know."

She crossed her arms. "Are your thoughts organized yet?"

"I'm working on it as we speak…"

"*We're* not speaking. *I'm* speaking. You're *stalling.*"

"As I just said—"

"Oh, stop this nonsense and just tell me what's bothering you!"

"All righty-rooty. It's like this. In plain, simple language, you're scaring the living shit out of me, Tifferoo."

"How?"

He spat out an earthworm and shrugged. "You brought that dog back."

"As I told you, that little girl—"

"I'm not talking about the little girl, Tifferoo. I'm talking about something that both you and I know should be, well, way the hell out of our job description."

She didn't say anything, but he could tell she knew what he was talking about.

"You brought a dog back, Tifferoosky. A *dead* dog. You brought it back. From the dead."

Tifferoo was silent, just watching him.

He knew exactly what was going on. *She's gonna downplay this. She doesn't want to make me think she's somehow gone a few hundred clicks or so above the level of a subordinate demon and might now be drifting dangerously close to the super category.*

"First of all, I'm not really sure the dog was actually dead."

"Tifferoo, I was right there, too. I saw—"

"He might have just been stunned, you know."

He didn't reply. Despite his suspicions, he knew she could actually be right. It was highly unlikely, but he had to admit that there was that one tiny possibility. He wanted to believe that because he didn't want to fear Tifferoo. Anyone who could bring back the dead was definitely someone to fear.

"Well?"

"Well what?"

"What if he *was* just stunned? All I did was massage his coat. It apparently stimulated him enough to bring him back."

"Tifferoo—"

"It's possible, isn't it?"

He just sighed.

"Well? Isn't it?"

"Yeah. It's possible."

"What about it, then?"

"What if you're wrong? What if the dog *wasn't* just stunned? What if it was really stone-cold?"

Tifferoo didn't reply.

"Admit it, Precious. You might have actually made a dead dog alive again."

"As I've been trying to say—"

"What if *I'm* the one who's right this time? I know I'm not right very much, so maybe it's time for me to nail one out of the park. So, to repeat myself: What if you actually *did* bring a dead dog back to life?"

"What if it was just dangerously close to death? It doesn't really matter, does it? I made the little girl very happy. I like making people happy. I've always been that way. I'm not a *demon*, you know…"

She still wasn't getting it—which told him he'd been right all along. Tifferoo had no idea that her powers had gone through the roof.

"Tifferoo, we've got to face facts. If the dog was dead, it isn't anymore. You *brought it back*."

"I don't know exactly what happened. And neither do you. Neither of us is a doctor, you know…"

"Babykins, I saw the little guy bounce off the bumper of a speeding van. I saw it sail through the air like a spitball and land twenty feet away. I just think something like that would make it slightly more than stunned."

"We can't be sure of that, can we? As I just said, neither of us is a doctor, and neither of us brought along a stethoscope."

"Listen to me, Tifferoo, and try and understand…"

"I know what you're gonna say, but it doesn't matter anymore, does it?"

"It does matter, Princess, so let me put it this way. If the dog was just stunned, you're right, it ain't a big deal. But if it wasn't—if it was actually dead—then it *is* a big deal. *I* can't do something like that, and I don't know of *anyone else* who can do something like that. I don't think the best vet in the world could've managed bringing it back. Not in this world, and certainly not in the one we escaped. The only dude who could actually do that did it more than two thousand years ago, and there hasn't been anyone to take his place since."

Tifferoo didn't reply. Chip could tell she was thinking it over. He could also tell she had no idea what she'd been doing while she was doing it. He could see serious confusion in those big baby blues. He also saw fear. He'd seen this before. It happened in Florida, when she discovered she could do certain things she'd never imagined she could ever do before. He'd also seen it in Pittsburgh, when her powers had grown even more, enabling her to communicate mentally with a magician halfway across town.

But this was different. This was the big-time, and there was no way either of them could logically explain what Tifferoo had actually done.

Even so, they needed to discuss this before anything else happened. Tiffany had to be reminded that they couldn't get the wrong people sniffing after them. As far as they both knew, the super demon Braithwaite was still operating from Central Florida. However, he had a long reach and was only a phone call away from the big boys in Peoria—or wherever the Diocese hung out.

"Well?" he asked. "Any ideas?"

She did her usual hair-thing—taking a thick strand of it and flipping it over her shoulder. She always did that when she didn't know what to say. That told him he wasn't going to get a meaningful morsel of an idea out of her.

She proved him right a moment later. "Not a one." Then she turned and began moving quickly down the walk.

"That's it?"

She spun around. "I can't tell you what I don't know!"

"You brought a dog back, Tifferoo. Maybe it was stunned, maybe it wasn't. You're trying to convince us both that it was just stunned because you don't want to consider the fact that you might have the power to bring something back from the dead. Isn't that about it in a nutshell?"

"Even if it is, it doesn't tell us what happened, does it?"

"All I know is that ever since we came up here from the Dark Place to look for the wolf guy, your powers have grown by leaps and bounds, while mine haven't budged. In case you haven't figured it out by now, it's beginning to give me a complex."

"I'm sorry."

"I know."

"I'd tell you how I did it if I knew."

"I know that, too."

"Then why are you so upset?"

"Because you don't know why any of this is happening."

"That doesn't make any sense."

"Tifferoo, have you forgotten who you're talking to?"

She sighed. "Sorry."

"Why don't we just take this one step at a time?"

"And just how do we do that?"

"First of all, tell me what you did."

"When?"

Frowning, Chip reached up and pulled a clump of red hair from his scalp.

"Didn't that hurt?" Tiffany asked.

"Well, yeah…"

"Then why'd you do it?"

"It was the only thing I could think of that would kill my frustration right now."

"Well? Did it work?"

"Not even slightly…"

"What's next, then?"

He bent, replaced the hair on his head and sighed. "Tell me what you did when you touched the dog. How's that for getting back on the subject?"

"Better."

"Then please answer my heartfelt inquiry!"

She was silent for a few moments. "I stroked his fur."

"I know. I was there. I saw you do it."

"Then why'd you ask?"

"I wanna know what else you did."

She shrugged. "That was it."

"That was *all* you did?"

She nodded.

"In other words, a dog was killed—"

"*Or* stunned…"

He sighed tiredly. "A dog was killed—*or* stunned. You stroked his fur, and suddenly he was alive and well and happy again?"

"More or less."

He groaned. "Muffin, this isn't working for me."

"That's all I can tell you."

"What were you thinking when you were stroking the dog?"

"I was thinking, "You're a nice dog, a really sweet dog, and you need to come back, because this little girl is falling apart and will probably never be the same until you're back with her."

"That was it?"

"That's all I can tell you."

Chip gazed into her eyes. She was definitely telling him the truth. He knew that for a fact. Tifferoo was true-blue. The only time she'd ever lied to him was in Florida, when she'd suddenly developed the ability to enter people's thoughts and carry on secret conversations with them. She hadn't told him about it at first and said that the only reason she'd kept it from him was because she was talking girl stuff with their friend the Ashley babe and didn't want to hurt his feelings.

"You believe me, don't you?" she asked.

He nodded.

"If I knew anything else, I'd surely tell you. We're buds, aren't we?"

"Affirmativo."

"So…why would I hide something from you?"

"You wouldn't."

"All right, then."

Silence.

"So...can we *please* drop this and focus?"

"On what?"

She closed her eyes. "On why we're here—what else?"

"That sounds like a nifty okey-dokie. Let's try that for a change."

Tifferoo just sighed.

Chip could tell she was falling into one of her dark moods. After all, they'd just arrived in Peoria. This was where she was born and raised. This was the place she'd escaped just a few years ago, not long after her stepdad started doing things to her that she could not possibly tolerate or endure. This was also the place she'd left for Hokeywood, where she went to become an actress.

Lastly and most important of all, this was where she'd left her mother. The sadness in Tifferoo's eyes suggested that she really hadn't wanted to come back.

But he knew she had to because she never got to say good-bye to her mom before she died.

He just hoped her mother was still here.

"You gonna be okay, Tiffers?"

She was silent for a moment. "I have to be, don't I?"

"Cheer up. You had a good start back there. Things might not be so bad."

"You really think so?"

"How can things go downhill once you've brought a furry little guy back to life?"

"I wish you'd phrased that differently."

He grinned. "I'm not exactly the poster child for subtlety, you know."

"You're not doing your usual silly routine of quips and one-liners. What's wrong? Not enough grass in your diet? You're not constipated, are you?"

"For your information, I just had two big plugs of fresh Illinois weed and a slice of earthworm for good measure. I'm good, thanks."

"Then why the concern?"

"We're in Peoria, Princess. Ever since you died and came back up with me, you've wanted to come back. Well, you're back, but you're all pouty and tragic and messed up."

"I can't help it. I've got issues."

"Tifferoo, *I'm* the one with the issues. How many times have you saved my bacon?"

"What does that have to do with anything?"

"Your issues aren't of your own making, Princess. Mine are."

"I can't help that, can I?"

"I'm just saying things might not go so badly here."

She frowned, suggesting that he'd said the wrong thing. "My mother married an abuser who forced me to leave my own home when I was still in my teens."

"I know, Princess."

"I went to Hollywood."

"I know that, too. I also know you died a couple of years later."

"I never got to see my mom again. Now I'm dead, but I've been able to come back. I now have to face that cold-hearted moron and see what he's done to her. How fantastic do you think things are going to be?"

Chip knew better than reply. He just smiled sheepishly and wiggled his ears.

"Wiggling those ears isn't doing a thing for me right now."

He shrugged. "I figured it was worth a try."

"Maybe later, if things aren't so bad...and I need a laugh."

"How about tomorrow? I'm not doing much. Or maybe Saturday. Saturday's always been a good day for me. I could set aside a few minutes this Saturday afternoon for a quick session of ear-wiggling—"

"The humor isn't working, either."

"You really do need a boost, Tifferoosky."

"Like I said, I've got issues—old ones as well as new ones. Even after all we've done and have been through, I still miss Lou. And don't forget Pittsburgh. I'm still trying to cope with losing Ashley and saying good-bye to Jimmy Russo. You'd think that you wouldn't have to keep saying good-bye to people you love once you're dead..."

"I know, Tiffers. But we've got to move on. Don't forget, all we have to do is attract the wrong attention. Braithwaite will hear about it and be on us like flies on road kill."

"You could have picked a much less offensive metaphor, by the way."

"Best I could do on the spur of the moment, Muffin. I can't help it. I get a little stale when I'm bored."

"Why are you bored?"

"Well, for openers, we've been standing here the last twenty minutes, arguing about things that don't matter anymore."

"For openers?"

"The other thing, I hope, will eventually resolve itself."

"What other thing?"

"The fact that we're standing here when we should be looking for the house you once lived in."

Tiffany went silent and stayed that way. She stared at him, then lowered her head and regarded the walk at her feet. She didn't move. He could tell something was bothering her.

"Tifferoo?" he whispered. "Everything all right?"

She still didn't speak. A few moments later, she sighed, raised her head and looked him squarely in the eye. "We really don't need to be looking much longer."

"Howzat?"

Taking a breath, she turned slowly to the big two-story brick house sitting at the end of the block. When she finally spoke again, her voice had become a whisper. "We've already found it."

CHAPTER 3

Keenan V. Durant stepped up to the intersection and waited for passing traffic. As the flow went past, he adjusted his faded white helmet to shield his sensitive chestnut eyes from the glare of the afternoon sun. Then he gently nudged his round-rimmed glasses a quarter of an inch up his nose to gawk at the stunning young blond woman gazing at the Reynolds house at the end of the block.

Standing close beside her, a short, slight guy with wild red hair eyed the house as well. He was chewing on something he'd picked up from the ground. From the back he looked like a cartoon character, but Keenan found that he didn't care. He couldn't take his eyes off the blonde. She wore a bright-red tank top, dark-blue Capri's and white pumps. She had the kind of body that belonged in a Victoria's Secret commercial, or Miss Universe pageant. What she was doing with such a weird-looking guy was anyone's guess.

Pulling his canvas sack to sit more comfortably on his narrow shoulders, Keenan crossed the street. He'd been doing his job for ten years and was able to keep his gaze on the two of them as he performed his daily routine. Since he always spent the first hour of his workday sorting the mail before setting out to deliver, the bulk of his task was simple. He merely stuck each rubber-banded bundle into the appropriate box as he shuffled down the street, stopping only a few moments for each. No boxes today; delivery would be a snap.

Back to the blonde…

He had no idea what he'd say to her once he'd reached the Reynolds house. She was stunning, growing even more so as he drew closer. Keenan had never been a hit with the ladies. Being short, slight, near-sighted and ordinary-looking, no one gave him a second glance. This suited him nicely for the important stuff, of course, making it much easier to perform his *main* job, which earned him the really big bucks. But when a beautiful lady came into the picture, he had to ramp up the game plan so he could watch them without arousing suspicion.

He couldn't do that now, of course. One of his customers might see what he was doing and ask questions, and it would go down from there very quickly. He knew this neighborhood well. Like most, it had its share of window-watchers. You just never knew who could be looking out at any given time. Keenan had learned many years ago that people were predictable only because they were so unpredictable. They paid attention when you didn't want them to and paid no attention whatsoever when you needed them to notice you or what you were doing. Anyway, this wasn't the time for foolishness. He needed to keep his mind on his work. Otherwise, everything would quickly go down the tubes.

Maybe later on…

But only if he could meet up with her when no one was watching…

Once he clocked out and got back into his civvies, he could find out where this beauty lived or hung out. Then he could find some way of watching her without being obvious.

He wondered who she was, what she was doing with the redhead. They didn't look like your average couple; she was *way* out of his league. They were probably just friends.

A couple of minutes later, he'd reached the Reynolds house.

"Help you folks?" He put on his friendly postman's smile and tipped his helmet.

She turned and smiled. The moment their eyes met, he felt a sense of warmth and excitement. She was even sexier and more beautiful close-up. "Hi. My friend and I…we were just looking. I grew up in this house." She was smiling, but he could tell she was uncomfortable.

He'd been assigned this route for the last six years. He would have remembered a beautiful lady like her living here. She'd obviously moved away and had recently come back. "You grew up in the Reynolds house?"

She blinked, and he could tell he'd just said something that shocked her. "The *Reynolds* house?"

"The Phillips family moved out two, maybe three years ago."

The brightness vanished from her eyes the instant he'd uttered the name. So did her smile. She'd apparently just heard something very distressing. She pushed some golden hair away from her face and began staring at the sidewalk.

"Miss? Did I say something…have I—"

"No. It's all right. I just…I guess I just wasn't expecting to hear such news."

"I take it you've been gone a while?"

She nodded.

"Did you know the Phillips?"

A shadow drifted across her eyes. She crossed her arms and began shifting her weight. Her voice sounded different when she spoke again. It was softer, weaker. "My mother remarried…not long after my father died."

Something very bad had obviously happened to her family. He wanted to hear more but knew it would be awkward to ask too many questions, especially with the weird-looking redhead standing there. She might clam up and walk away. The less said, the better. But he thought she should at least have an idea of what happened. "I remember Jack Phillips. He—"

"That was him." The shadow in her eyes grew darker.

He tried to read her expression. The only thing he could tell for sure was that something extremely unpleasant had happened while this girl was living in that house.

"They moved?" she asked in a soft voice.

"Actually, I believe they split up."

She blinked. "Split…up?"

"Divorced. I remember her mail being forwarded to a duplex on the other end of town. I think she changed her name back to what it was before. Was it…Sedarski?"

"*Yes.*" The shadow had lightened somewhat. She uncrossed her arms; her luscious body became less tense. She took a breath; the valley between those perfect breasts deepened. "Can you tell me where…can you please give me the address—"

He reached into his pocket. "Would you like to know where she's living right now?"

"*Please...*"

He pulled out his notepad, opened it up to his address book, scanned it and gave her the new address.

"Thank you *so* much..." The brightness returned to her eyes, and her smile reappeared in all its glory.

"No problem."

"One other thing."

"Yes?"

"Can you tell me anything about…about Jack Phillips? Do you happen to know where he lives?"

"He's dead."

"W-What?" She stiffened. The redhead looked interested.

"I heard it on the news—about a year ago, I believe. He was found dead in an alley in town, behind one of the bars."

Her eyes grew. "He was…murdered?"

"From what the papers said, he was involved in some sort of drug burn with one of the local dealers."

"Jack Phillips…he was…on *drugs*?"

"Papers said he was trying to muscle in on the local action and crossed the wrong guy." He pulled the slim bundle out of his sack, slipped between the blonde and her friend and stuck the mail in the metal box next to the front door of the Reynolds house. Before stepping away, he inhaled her sweet lavender scent and took in a much closer view of her delicious cleavage. It was tough doing it without making it obvious, but he managed. "I could tell Jack Phillips was not a good man."

"Really?"

"I only saw your mom a couple of times. She always looked sad. Every time I saw him, he always seemed angry. He seemed like he wanted to kill or hurt someone. I hope your mom's doing better now. I remember her being a very nice, friendly lady." Then he tipped his helmet and slipped away.

"Sir?" she called after him.

He turned around.

"Have you seen her lately? My mom?"

"Sorry. Glen Oak's not on my route."

As he went down the street, he tried once again to figure out what that beauty was doing with the redhead.

He decided that it didn't matter.

The only thing he cared about was seeing her again. And now he knew she was headed to see her mother. And he knew where her mother lived.

He grinned. All he had to do was stage something. He was an expert at staging; he'd been doing it for years. He could follow her while she was shopping and fix it so something in a window display would fall. Then he could suddenly appear and sweep her out of its path. This would impress her, and she might agree to go on a date with him.

This same thing had worked dozens of times. No reason why it shouldn't work this time.

The only obstacle would be the redhead. If he turned out to be an obstacle, something totally different would have to be staged.

Keenan didn't like anyone getting in his way when he was doing his thing.

***

Tiffany watched the little postman as he turned sharply at each house, shuffled up to the front door and shoved envelopes inside the mailbox. Every once in a while he glanced in their direction as he snatched mail from his pouch.

She could tell he liked her. He seemed friendly, too.

In spite of that, she couldn't ignore the feeling that something about the man just didn't feel right…

But that wasn't the most important thing going through her mind. What the postman had told them was unbelievable. She found that she couldn't concentrate on anything but the conversation in her head.

"He's dead. I heard it on the news—about a year ago, I believe. He was found dead in an alley in town, behind one of the bars."

"He was...murdered?"

"From what the papers said, he was involved in some sort of drug burn with one of the local dealers. Papers said he was trying to muscle in on the local action and crossed the wrong guy."

Jack Phillips was dead. The man Momma had brought into their lives after Dad died so tragically in that stupid hunting accident… The same pervert who'd come to her room so quietly during the night to play his "cuddle game" with her…

The bastard was dead.

And Tiffany knew exactly where his spirit had gone…

"Tifferoo?"

"He's dead, Chip. Dead."

"Yeah, I was standing right there beside you when the dorky mail delivery guy told us."

She gazed at the street in front of them, staring at it but not seeing it…not seeing anything, really, except for the image of the tall, broad-shouldered man with the small, slimy green eyes staring lecherously across the dinner table at her as he slurped soup and licked his lips, his smirk turning her blood cold.

How many times had she lain in bed at night, listening in utter terror for his quiet footsteps? How many times had she promised herself that she'd come back home one day and kill the monster?

How could she not have imagined that such a lowlife would not make other enemies? How could she not have imagined that one of them would turn out to be even worse than he was?

"My God, Chip... All these years I've hated him for tearing me away from my mother and forcing me to move away. Now he's dead."

"I heard, Tiffers. As I just said, I was standing right there."

"He's been dead for *two years*!"

"I managed to catch that one, too."

The street in front of her had vanished. So had Chip. All she could see was the irony of life, and realized in that one instant just how fragile and unpredictable life and its chain of events actually were.

If I'd just waited...

If I hadn't gotten on that bus when I did...

If I'd only stayed there another month, maybe six months...

Everything would have been different. I could have stayed and finished growing up. I might have even gone to college, pursued a career in something decent and found a job other than something that got me killed...

I'd still be alive. I'd still be with Momma...

"What's wrong, Tifferoo?"

"He was murdered even before I was."

"You'd have to check one of those fancy Internet cafes to find out exactly when it happened. Why? Does it matter?"

"I think so…I really do…"

"You sound almost sad and nostalgic about all this."

"Do I?"

"Listen to you. I know you can. You hear yourself, don'tcha? Your ears are stuck to the sides of your head. They're plugged in, aren't they?"

"I guess I wasn't expecting something like this to happen."

"What *did* you expect? For Mumsy and your perverted stepdad to live happily ever after, even after her little baby girl suddenly left home without a word?"

He had a point. There was no way her mother hadn't known what was going on, even though she'd never let on. "If I'd just waited to get on that bus…"

"Then what?"

She snapped out of her haze and searched his face. Surely he could understand what she was trying to say. "Don't you see? If only I'd waited… If I'd just stuck it out another couple of months, he would have died. Momma wouldn't have gone through all that by herself. Momma and I would have been together. We would have been happy again. We wouldn't have had to worry about him at all anymore."

"Why should you care? The asshole's dead. Isn't that enough?"

"He forced me to leave my mother! My *home*!" The anger surged right back in a violent wave. "He ruined my last couple of years before adulthood. If I hadn't gone to Hollywood, I wouldn't have been bullied into going to that stupid pool party. I wouldn't have been given that drink. I'd still be alive, Chip. I'd *still be alive*!"

"You can't go back, Tifferoo."

"I know." The anger went away much quicker this time, leaving her somewhat drained.

"Even if you could, what would you have done?"

It took her a moment to realize what he was getting at. "Nothing."

"Then why bother putting yourself through this?"

"I don't know."

"Isn't it enough that your mom no longer has to worry about him anymore?"

"I don't know."

"Tifferoo—"

"I'm sure she's been told I'm dead. I'm sure someone from this town saw a news item somewhere and told her."

"I guess I didn't think of that. Maybe one of your Hokeywood friends got the word to her."

"I changed my name to LeBouf the moment I got off the bus, and I really didn't make any friends while I was there."

His tiny green eyes blinked. "How could a babe like you not make friends? Got a mirror handy?" He raised his hand; a tiny mirror appeared in his palm. "Here. Take a gander. You're amazing."

Chip was being sweet, but he really didn't know what he was talking about. He'd never been in Hollywood and wouldn't understand its culture or mentality. "You really need to be in Hollywood a few weeks to know what I'm talking about. Trust me—I didn't make any friends."

"Then maybe she *hasn't* found out yet…"

He had a point, but she didn't want to get her hopes up. Now that Jack Phillips was dead, a lot of other things were possible. For one thing, Momma had moved. Tiffany didn't know if she was living by herself or had met someone else. Momma was a very attractive woman. She was still fairly young and had many good years left.

But did she know Tiffany was dead?

And if Chip was right, and she *didn't* know, what was their next step?

"We won't know what's going on unless I walk up to the house and knock on the door. What if she *does* know? She'll be standing there, looking at me. She'll have a heart attack. *Then* what do we do?"

"Try and get the paramedics here before—"

"Not funny, Chip…" She was in no mood for his humor.

"I guess that makes things a tad gnarly, then."

"In other words, I *can't* go and knock on her door."

"I kinda think you have to."

She thought about that for a few moments. She didn't want to admit Chip was right. But it was painfully obvious. She couldn't come all this way and not find out if her mother knew she was dead. And she couldn't come all this way without at least trying to see her and how she was doing. "I know."

"We just don't know the right way to do this. Not yet, anyway."

"No. We don't."

Chip tore off another clump of grass from the small front yard and gazed at it a few moments before popping it in his mouth. He nibbled on it and swallowed. "But at least we've got *some* idea."

"Whaddya mean?"

"Your powers."

"What about them?"

"They've been growing."

"So?"

"All righty, then."

"All righty, then, *what*?"

"Your powers. They've been growing."

"You've already said that."

"Maybe, but I haven't said something else."

"What's that?"

"Since they're growing, why not use them?"

CHAPTER 4

Keenan V. Durant reached the Kendra residence approximately twenty minutes after his exchange with the stunning blonde.

The house was a two-and-a-half-story brick home on North Waverly Avenue. It boasted a small, carefully maintained front lawn and trimmed bushes running in a neat line in front of the building.

Once he'd finished his business here, Keenan would cross the street and resume delivering mail to the homes on that side, until he'd reached the end of the block. Two more blocks and that would be it for the day. He'd grown to like this route; it took him just two hours to deliver the mail to all six square blocks and gave him a lot of free time when he returned home to his small apartment on West Glen Avenue, across the street from the Post Office.

He went up the three large concrete steps leading to Kendra's front porch and stuck the mail in its designated box. From the living room window, he could see the glare of the TV, telling him the old man was inside. Good. This wouldn't take long at all.

He went back down the steps and circled the walk that led to the back. This home was owned by John and Alice Kendra, a couple in their mid-forties. John worked as Sales Manager at the local Walmart. Alice did hair and nails at a beauty salon in town owned by a woman named Faye Dunning. The Kendra's had two boys, both in their mid-twenties. Neither lived at home; they'd both graduated from college and now led lives of their own, in Joliet.

Alice's father, Otis Turner, owned the house and lived there with his daughter and son-in-law. Otis was 75, had a bad heart and spent most of his time sitting in the living room, watching his soaps. Otis had made his mark in real estate decades earlier, during the Reagan Administration. Otis owned several prime pieces of property in town and two apartment houses in the neighborhood. He'd retired twenty years ago and lived with John and Alice in the house he owned and had bequeathed to them in his will.

Otis also owned a prime piece of property in town that had been chosen for the construction of a strip mall. Being the sole owner of the two-acre parcel, Otis was the only one standing in the way of the project and had said that once he went to the Great Beyond, the parcel would be left to his younger brother, William, who didn't want a strip mall to be built on the parcel, either.

Otis wanted the property to stay the way it was. It served as a playground for the daycare center across the street and also provided an athletic course for the elderly at the opposite end of the property, which offered a peaceful view of the lake. Otis hated the idea of a strip mall being built where so many toddlers and oldsters alike could enjoy themselves in the peace and quiet of the area.

Keenan had just been told that Otis' brother William had recently considered changing his mind about the whole thing. William had suffered a near-death experience just a few days earlier. Some texting idiot in her late twenties had nearly run him over in town while he was crossing the street to get back into his car. Just before the near-fatal incident, William had been told that the price of his brother's parcel had more than doubled during the last six months. At 71, William valued his skin much more dearly these days, and since he'd been told the parcel would put a million bucks directly into his checking account, he decided to sit back and watch how things turned out. William had also been told that Otis had recently been offered a substantial amount of money and was also reconsidering. However, William was advised not to confront his brother about it, since the revamped arrangement remained in its initial stages.

Otis was sitting in his ancient recliner when Keenan, using his very special and unusual talent, snuck into the house. Otis' chessboard covered the TV tray in front of him. His cup of tea sat on the end table on his left. It was commonly known that Otis enjoyed playing chess with himself and drinking Chamomile tea while watching his soaps.

Keenan quietly slipped into the room, snuck up behind Otis and deposited three drops of the special concoction from the tiny vial into the tea. He remained standing behind the recliner until Otis took a break from his chess game, picked up his cup, and had a sip of the Chamomile tea. After Otis had put down the cup rather awkwardly and collapsed in the recliner, Keenan slipped back outside.

Keenan delivered mail to more than a dozen houses on his way home before deciding to take a break. Instead of retreating to the fast-food place across the street for a cup of his favorite mint-flavored cappuccino, he sat on the park bench next to the curb to rest his feet. While watching passing traffic, he took his cell out of his pants pocket to make his scheduled call to the Regent's Bank in town, where his superior was anxiously waiting to hear of his progress.

As usual, he was placed on hold. While he waited, he fantasized once again about the delicious blonde lady he'd met in front of the Reynolds house. He found that he was totally mesmerized by the mere thought of her and realized that he could think of nothing else but the thick curtain of curly golden hair, the enormous blue eyes, the gorgeous smile and the luscious figure.

He decided in that same instant that he didn't want to wait too long to see her again. He'd already found out that she was a Sedarski. He also knew where her mother lived. Setting up something that would enable him to meet her again would pose no problem at all.

***

M. Murray Robertson II, President of the Regent's Bank of Peoria, sat at his desk, listening patiently to the man on the other end of the line, who'd been trying for the last fifteen minutes to persuade him to invest in a massive condominium project just outside Springfield. As the client droned on in excruciating detail about the amazing benefits a modest investment of three hundred and fifty K would realize in such a venture, Robertson eyed the lit screen on the disposable cell sitting on the blotter in front of him. It said simply, "*Postman*"...

This was all Robertson needed to perk him right up. If things had gone as planned, that idiot Otis Turner was finally out of the picture and the strip mall project could go on as planned. Robertson's friend and colleague, Marko Vaughn, would be particularly pleased. One of the town's biggest and most influential investors, Vaughn had been sweating over that chunk of prime property for several years and had grown weary of doubling his offers to entice Otis into selling.

This would definitely be a step in the right direction for the League. Once Mr. Waite was told about their progress, the pressure would ease off—at least for a little while. Pressure on League members had increased the moment Waite had taken over for Mr. Balbor. It hadn't eased up one iota—which was to be expected, given Waite's well-known reputation for being a vicious hardass—not to mention his obsession for absolute power. Waite had taken over just months ago, but they were all feeling the change—especially the League's Florida Chapter, known as The Diocese.

In any event, Otis Turner's beloved two-acre parcel would soon be cleared and leveled, and the strip mall—plus a few other incidentals that section of town desperately needed—would be built.

But it all depended on the Postman...

Robertson trusted the Postman. The man was strange, but at least he delivered. More than two hundred and fifty contracts in the last ten years. And, according to his latest inquiry with a trusted contact at the Peoria Police Department just a week ago, the cops were still looking at an impressive pile of unsolved cases. The Postman was a true master, and knew how to successfully stage an accident. Otherwise, nearly seventy-five percent of those contracts would have been considered homicides.

Great work for a harmless-looking nobody people waved at and quickly forgot as he shuffled down the street, delivering their mail. But, as Robertson and the dozen members of the Royal League of Peoria all knew, the Postman had more than a smile and a wave going for him. The man had the solid reputation for not being seen at the most appropriate moment. When you possessed this marketable and extremely unusual talent, you could get away with anything.

After nearly twenty minutes, Robertson decided that he was tired of listening to this ridiculous rant about the Springfield condominium investment. Robertson was worth more than a billion dollars, but there was no way he was going to hand over three hundred and fifty K to someone he barely knew for an investment he hadn't spent considerable time researching. That wasn't how a wealthy man operated.

Robertson was about to click off when the man abruptly stopped talking and hung up. Apparently he'd sensed Robertson's reluctance by his silence and decided that he'd been wasting his breath.

Relieved, Robertson picked up the cell and pressed the green button. "Yes?"

"Mr. Robertson?"

Normally he was less than thrilled to hear the man's nasal, high-pitched voice but strongly felt this call would be worth the minor irritation. "Speaking..."

"I've got good news, sir."

This was exactly what he'd wanted to hear. "Talk to me."

"The O.T. project is finished."

Robertson sat back and sighed. Marko was going to be thrilled to hear this. However, the details had to be discussed immediately. "Totally?"

"Yes, sir."

"Any problems?"

"None, sir."

"You weren't seen?"

"I was seen by everyone, sir. It's my job. But no one saw me go in or come out of the house."

Robertson grinned. The Postman had delivered the goods once again, and in pristine condition. Happy days were on the horizon…

"That really *is* good news. Your fee, as always, will be deposited directly into your safe deposit box."

"Thank you, sir. Will there be anything else?"

"We might have need for your services again in the next few days. It involves a minor matter. Actually, it's more of an irritation than anything. One of my colleagues seems to be facing a minor lawsuit. Some young idiot female slammed into him while he was pulling out of his parking space at the French Cuisine on Main Street, and now she's suing him for damages, pain and suffering, and the cost of her cell phone—which, incidentally, she'd been using to text with when she hit him."

"That *is* an irritation, sir."

"He doesn't need the aggravation right now. He's scheduled to leave the country in a few weeks to conduct some crucial banking business in Switzerland. Naturally he doesn't want this matter hanging over his head, and he doesn't want his trip postponed. His BMW is in the shop as we speak. It appears to have suffered major damage to the rear panel. He's been given an estimate of eight thousand dollars to repair the damage. He's insured, of course, but this female has hired an attorney to see if she can squeeze money out of him instead of going to Small Claims. She obviously knows who he is and how much he's worth and wants to see how much she can get out of him. She was driving a ten-year-old VW when she slammed into the BMW, and we've got this feeling she might use her attorney to add serious injury to the case. Needless to say, all this is making my friend irritable."

"I understand, sir."

"When he told me what happened, we both decided you could handle this one for us."

"Thank you, sir. Just let me know the details, and I'll take care of it."

"I'll call you as soon as we have everything worked out." Robertson clicked off.

Relieved, Robertson took one of his special hand-rolled, hundred-dollar Italian cigars out of the polished walnut case on his desk. Smoking in the building was, of course, prohibited, but since he owned the bank, they couldn't very well complain, could they? Especially since he'd spent more than fifty K on a special ventilation system that dissipated the smoke the moment it entered the twin air-vents in the ceiling, taking it straight up to the roof, then right back out into the open air.

He removed the SIM card from the disposable cell, dropped both pieces into the trashcan, pulled his personal cell out of the inner pocket of his $3,000 custom-fitted Baroni jacket, and pressed Number 3 on speed dial to talk to Marko Vaughn. Then he settled back in his custom-built, imported leather chair, carefully lit the cigar, pushed a light-gray wavy smoke ring up toward the ceiling fan and waited for his friend's voice to come on the line.

CHAPTER 5

Tiffany and Chip found her mom's new street and residence not long after their talk with the postman. The place was located in a development of attractive duplexes and condominiums on NE Glen Oak Avenue, just a few miles east of the intersection of North Indiana and Main Street.

Once the taxi dropped them off, Tiffany stood nervously behind the huge rose bush at the corner, taking in everything—the building itself, the flowers arranged carefully in front of the shuttered living room window, the short white picket fence spanning the concrete walk leading to the front steps. She could tell her mother lived there. The neat arrangement of flowers. The picket fence. Even the white laced curtains in the living room window. Everything looked so much like her.

Momma lives in that building.

It's less than a hundred feet away. She lives there—I know she does.

A blanket of overwhelming sadness slipped over her. It was much worse than what she'd experienced when she'd gotten on the Greyhound bus just five years earlier and realized that she might not ever see her mother again. This was worse than when she and Chip were standing in the middle of a city dump outside Raven, Ohio, and she discovered she was dead. It was even worse than when she'd put the spell on Lou Gates, the only man she'd ever truly loved, and on her very best friend Ashley Parker later on, to erase her forever from their memories.

She told herself she shouldn't feel this way. She'd come home, hadn't she? It had been a long, unbearable journey, but she'd managed, and now she was standing just a stone's throw away from where her mother lived. It didn't feel like home, but since so many other things had changed, such feelings didn't really matter.

But the fact remained: she'd come home, and shouldn't feel sad at all. If she worked this just right, she'd be seeing her mother again. This in itself should have told her she ought to be happy. And excited.

It only took her a moment to realize she was wrong. She really *should* be sad. She'd come home, but she was also dead. And even though she stood just yards away from the dwelling where the beautiful woman who had brought her into this world just twenty-three years earlier now lived, there was no way she could walk up to the front door and press the buzzer.

She'd become a spirit. She couldn't possibly show herself. She couldn't risk her mother's health by appearing to her when the woman might already know she was dead. Besides, her mother had already been through a tremendous ordeal. She was probably still on the mend from that and didn't need to face a surprise visit from her dead daughter.

"Problemo, Tifferoo?" Chip was standing behind her, sucking on a rose petal he'd pulled from the bush.

"What do *you* think? And do you always have to be nibbling on something?"

"Actually, I think we've come all this way, so the least you can do is go see her. And yeah, I have a fast metabolism. Besides, nibbling always helps me think."

"How?"

"How what?"

"How do you suppose I go see her?"

"I thought we'd already discussed that."

"You mentioned that my powers have been growing. It really didn't help."

"You're a shapeshifter, Tifferoo. Get it?"

"And what'll *that* accomplish?"

"Think about it."

"You want me to walk up to the door as someone else and press the buzzer?"

"See there? You figured it out all by yourself."

"Then what?"

"Tell her you're a friend or something. Be creative. You're passing through, and you wanted to pay your respects before—"

"Before what?"

"Before you leave town. There. Now you've got it in a nutshell. Must I explain everything?"

"You're forgetting one major problem with this."

"What's that?"

"I'll still be me."

"She won't know that."

"*I* will..."

"So what?"

"Did you *ever* have a mother, Chip?"

A shrug. "It's been quite a few centuries since Mumsy trained me to wipe my own butt, but yeah, I had one. Why do you ask?"

"Think about this. I'm dead, but I'm appearing as someone else so I can talk to my mother without giving her a heart attack."

He closed his eyes, raised his head and twitched his ears. "All righty rooty...someone else…mother…heart attack…"

"Are you thinking about it?"

"I'm trying to…"

"What's stopping you?"

"You keep interrupting me."

"Try harder."

He frowned. "You just interrupted me again."

She sighed and waited.

About twenty seconds later, he said, "I think I've got it."

"All right, then. Tell me."

"Tell you what?"

More anger flared up. She found it increasingly difficult to keep from reaching out, grabbing him by the pointed ears and shaking him. *I'm not a demon,* she reminded herself. *I'm not going to do anything bad to him. He's just being himself and doesn't know any better. Besides, he's my friend. He's quite a handful sometimes, but that doesn't change the fact that we're partners.*

And she knew exactly how to handle him.

She pointed to his head. "If you don't want me going in there and scooping out what I need—"

"All right, all right... I think I know what you're driving at."

“Then tell me how I can walk up to that door, ring the buzzer and stand there without melting into a puddle of warm mush while my mother looks me in the eye, smiles, and asks me who I am and why I just rang her buzzer.”

“You can do it, Tifferoo. You’re a strong lady—much stronger than you think. You went up against *Braithwaite*, for God’s sakes. That takes some serious ‘nads.”

“I don’t have ‘*nads*. At least, I didn’t when I was alive…”

“Just a figure of speech.”

“And just what does going up against Breath Mint have to do with this?”

He crossed his eyes. “I’m trying to tell you that you’re a lot stronger than you think. If you can go up against a super demon like *Braithwaite*—“

“I’m not *going up against* my mother. I’ll be *talking* to her, but I’m dead and won’t be able to tell her anything she needs to know. I won’t be able to hug or kiss her…or tell her how much I missed her…or talk about Dad, or anything else. For one thing, I don’t think my mind will cooperate, and then there are my emotions. I *am* a female, after all—“

“I get it. But you *will* be able to hug and kiss her, Tiffers. Don’t you remember? We’re dead, but we’ve still got substance. We need substance to blend in, get things done. I told you that the day we came back up and landed in that dump in Ohio.”

“I’ll still melt. I know I will.”

“You’re tough, Tifferoo. You sent the wolf guy back down—“

“I did it with your help. I couldn’t have done it alone.”

“Neither could I. And don’t forget, you were a novice at the time—“

The sound of a garage door hummed open. A moment later, an engine roared to life.

A silver Honda backed down the paved drive. Shaking, Tiffany crouched down closer to the rose bush as the shiny car backed out into the street and eased away.

A brief glimpse of long, curly red hair in the side mirror told Tiffany that her mother was driving the car.

***

Chip peered out from behind the rose bush. “Tifferoo? Did you just see your mom?”

Tiffany hadn’t moved. Chills had taken over as the silver car approached the end of the street, where it stopped at the stop sign, waited until two cars went past and then turned right.

Yes, that was Momma. The brief glimpse of thick red hair was all it took to convince her. It was Momma, and she’d just driven away. As Tiffany stared at the place where her mom’s car had just been, the chills gradually turned into a tingling.

Moments later, the tingling disappeared. The sadness returned, this time with a vengeance, and it took all the willpower she could find within herself to keep from falling apart. Warm tears gathered in her eyes. It took considerable effort to keep them from gushing down her cheeks.

“Tifferoo?”

She recognized Chip's voice, but she just didn't want to talk to him right now.

She wiped her eyes. She wanted to be somewhere else right now—somewhere far away from here. On the other hand, she wanted to see her mother. She knew she had to but realized it was *such* a terrible idea. She couldn't do this—it would be too much for both of them. Facing her mother would destroy her. The tears would gush out no matter how hard she tried to keep them inside. And no matter what sort of disguise she used, she knew full well that her mother would look into her eyes and see her right off. "*You have beautiful eyes, Baby*," she'd told Tiffany all her young life. "*They're not like anyone else's. They have a special light flowing inside them that I've never seen anywhere else. They're a special gift. I'm not really sure where you got it, but it's there, and when you look at someone, you'll be able to see right into their soul.*"

Momma would definitely know. Even if Tiffany chose to reveal herself as a homeless man in his seventies, Momma would look into the man's eyes and see her baby girl hiding inside.

"Tifferoo? What's the game plan?"

"I…don't know…"

"Did you want to go inside and look around?"

She spun around. "W-Why would we want to do *that*?"

He cringed at her sudden flare-up. "I don't know. Maybe to just go inside and, well…take a look?"

"At what?"

He smiled sheepishly. "Knickknacks? Mementoes? Stuff she kept from when you were growing up? In other words, proof that she's really living there."

"You want to go inside my mother's house and *snoop*?"

"Not actually *snoop*, as much as—"

"As much as what?"

He scratched his thick red mop and shook his head. "I'm not scoring any points here, am I?"

She couldn't believe him. She was going through her very worst moment and he was treating this as some sort of silly game. "*Points*? You want *points*? This isn't a *game*, Chip!"

"I didn't mean it the way it sounded…"

"Then how *did* you mean it?"

He didn't reply. His face suddenly pale, he backed up until his back came into contact with the rose bush. As he continued backing up, he slowly blended into it.

A moment later, he disappeared.

Tiffany went over and stared at it. He'd become so much of the rose bush that she could no longer see any sign of him. "What do you think you're doing?"

Silence.

"Chip?"

More silence. For all intents and purposes, Chip had actually *become* the rose bush.

"*Please* don't make me drift inside your head and figure out what you're doing…"

Silence.

She knew right then that she'd gone too far. *Mellow*, she urged herself. She knew she was no demon, but she'd obviously frightened Chip. "C'mon, Chip. This is me, now. We've been through a lot together."

More silence.

"*Please* tell me what you're doing in there."

"I'm trying to stay out of trouble—what else?"

"Why?"

"Why not?"

"Chip!"

"Tifferoo, you're a delicious babe and all, with a gorgeous face and a mouth-watering pair of—"

"Stop the nonsense and *talk to me*!"

"I'm just trying to say that even though you're a gorgeous babe, you can be, well…well—"

"Well what?"

"I'm not allowed to say the d-word when I'm talking about—"

"You think I'm acting like a *demon*?"

Silence.

"Chip?"

"Well…yeah…"

He was right. She *was* acting demonlike. Otherwise, why else would Chip blend into a rose bush in the middle of a conversation?

"Chip, please come out of there."

"You're all right now?"

"I'm all right now."

"You're sure?"

"I'm sure."

"You won't…that is, you won't do anything to me that might wilt my petals, or—"

"*Please* stop being a moron and turn back into Chip, all right?"

"In that order?"

"Chip!"

He materialized as himself and stepped away from the rose bush. Then he reached behind him and, grunting, pulled two rather large thorns out of his butt. "I hope you realize how much it hurts, pulling a thorn out of your butt, even when you're dead…"

"I'm sorry. I'm kind of…well, I'm not myself right now."

"I know. You're sort of like a Tifferoo on steroids."

"I'm just trying to figure out what to do."

He opened his mouth and immediately closed it.

"Go ahead and say it."

"You're sure?"

"I'm sure."

"I still think we ought to go inside and look around."

"You really think we should go in there and look through my mother's things?"

"At least we'll know for sure if it's really her living there. And if someone else is living with her."

"It was her. I recognized her hair."

"I still think we should make sure."

Despite her reservations, she knew he was right. This was the address the mail carrier had given them, but they really didn't know the whole story of what was happening with her mom these days. It would be stupid to approach this blindly. They had to know if Momma was living alone. What if she'd taken in a renter? What if one of Momma's sisters was staying with her? Momma had two younger sisters. Dad had a brother and a sister. Tiffany had been away for five years. That was a long time to be away and not keep up with the family's activities. Momma could have someone staying with her. And if someone else was there, she and Chip had to find out. Tiffany couldn't attempt any sort of meaningful reunion with her mother if someone else came into the picture to complicate things.

"All right. Let's go and see if we can—"

The sound of a vehicle came to a sudden stop just a few yards behind them.

They both turned.

The window on the driver's side rolled down. "Tiffany?" It was Momma. "Baby? Is that *you*?"

CHAPTER 6

Tiffany couldn't move. The chills and the tingling came back, both at the same time, and she discovered that all she could do was stand there and watch numbly as her mother pulled up the drive, put the Honda in park, opened the door and got out.

Time suddenly stopped. Momma just stood there, gazing at Tiffany, her mouth open. Momma's light-blue eyes glinted in the afternoon sun; Tiffany could tell the woman was trembling. Had she been told Tiffany was dead? Tiffany didn't think so. Momma wasn't the most stable person on earth. If she'd heard that her daughter had died, she would have already fainted.

Once the moment of total shock had passed, Momma took a cautious step toward her. "Tiffany? Baby? Is it…is it really *you*?"

"M-Momma?" Tiffany's voice sounded weak, like the final gasp of a dying woman. The chills and the tingling continued sweeping violently through her.

Momma took another cautious step toward her. Her arms slowly came up. "Come here, Baby!"

Time began moving again. Cold reality slapped her in the face, and in spite of the shock of seeing her mother for the first time in five years, Tiffany realized that her mind had actually begun working again.

Momma doesn't know I'm dead...

She honestly doesn't know...

This is so totally...so unbelievably—

"*Baby*!"

"*Momma*!" Sobbing, Tiffany ran into her mother's arms and clung tightly to her.

***

Five minutes later, after the hugging and the crying had finally subsided, Tiffany and Chip picked up the two small bags of groceries Momma had just bought and followed Momma into the house.

As Momma put the groceries away, Tiffany wiped away her tears and thought about the last five years. When she felt the tears gathering again, she forced them back and concentrated on other things, such as the cute kitchen Momma had obviously decorated herself, everything in light-blues and gold, her favorite colors, plus the stick-ons and magnetized knickknacks covering the stainless refrigerator door. A tiny wooden dairy cow with legs that jiggled when the door moved. A white card with the local mechanic's logo on the front. Another card with a dentist's name and number printed in bold letters on it. The local hair stylist. A thank-you from the ASPCA for her $20 donation. Something from St. Jude. A couple of scribbled personal messages.

"Go sit, both of you." Momma gestured to the table in the dining area in front of the window overlooking the fenced backyard.

Once Momma had finished putting the groceries away, she fixed coffee and joined Tiffany and Chip at the table.

Tiffany just could not believe she was back home with her mother. It seemed as if a hundred years had passed since she'd left. But when she'd rushed into her mother's arms just minutes ago, it felt like it had only been a few days.

If only it *had* been a few days...

But it hadn't. It had been five years since Tiffany had left home. Once in Hollywood, she spent the next four and a half years living in run-down apartments and efficiencies to make a go of it. All the while she'd lived there, she'd constantly fought off persistent men with power, listened to their lies and promises, closed her ears to insults and indecent propositions, and spent countless evenings sitting by herself, staring at phones that never rang. She was pawed at, groped, and forced to do things she didn't want to do. She was urged to be friendly with people who treated her badly, to attend parties she didn't want to attend. In the end, she said good-bye to Hollywood—and to life itself—when she was forced to attend a pool party thrown by Johnny Rock, the fabulously wealthy agent known for handling the most elite international celebrities. She was given a drink she didn't want by a popular TV celebrity who'd been following her around the pool the moment he'd seen her dressed in the skimpy two-piece her agent had instructed her to wear. The drink contained a date-rape drug that promptly sent her into cardiac arrest, killing her in minutes.

Just months ago, she'd come back from a very dark world she never wanted to see again. It was an abysmal place filled with horrible creatures and the smell of death and decay clinging heavily to the hot, sulphurous-thick air. If it hadn't been for a couple of those filthy creatures sending her and Chip back temporarily to the mortal world for an important mission, then to Florida for yet another crucial errand, she would still be down there in the foul darkness, avoiding those disgusting creatures.

What could she tell Momma about any of this? Could she tell her mother she was dead? That the body Momma had just hugged was merely temporary substance? That her loving young daughter had come back from the depths of Hell and had been fighting demons ever since? That, for some strange, unfathomable reason no one could explain, she now possessed powers the world's greatest magicians would gladly sacrifice their lives for?

Should she tell Momma she could read minds? Communicate mentally with people? Make subconscious suggestions that would enable people to forget about her, even if they loved and worshipped her? Should she tell Momma she could change her appearance? Her breast size? Her sex? Should she tell her that she had the power to cover her feet with beautiful, custom-designed, expensive-looking shoes?

She could tell Momma none of these things. Like it or not, she had to be careful about everything she told her. It wasn't because she was afraid Momma wouldn't believe her, or think her daughter had gone insane. She was afraid of putting Momma in danger.

Momma was smiling, saying nothing. Tiffany could tell her mother was studying her—taking careful inventory, as all mothers did when reunited with their children after a long absence.

Chip was also watching her. Although Tiffany was surprised that he'd been behaving himself, she knew better than lower her guard. Her zany friend tended to be unpredictable—and downright embarrassing—at the wrong time.

To find out what was going on inside the trickster's head, she directed her probe toward the thick red patch. But before she could penetrate his mind, she heard his inner voice. He was watching Momma as his words floated into her head. *"She doesn't know you're dead, Tifferoo."*

"I know," she sent back to him. *"Isn't that incredible?"*

"You said you changed your name. You never called her once you went to Hokeywood? Never sent her a line or two?"

"I called her a couple of times when I first got there but didn't talk to her when he—when Jack Phillips—answered the phone. I sent her a couple of postcards a few months later, but after that, things started going downhill pretty fast, and I never had the chance to—"

"Why didn't you keep in touch, Baby?" Momma asked.

Despite her smile, Momma's eyes glistened. It made Tiffany feel guilty and terrible all over again.

She noticed only then that her mother had aged a little more than she should have. It probably had a lot to do with Phillips. Momma had never been the same after Dad died, but her relationship with Phillips quite possibly put the added lines around

Momma's eyes, the slight wattle beneath her chin, and the look of vulnerability Tiffany had never noticed before. In spite of all that, she was happy to see that the brightness in Momma's eyes hadn't dimmed at all.

It's because of me. I've come back, and she's happy again.

"I'm sorry, Momma. I wanted to, I really and truly did, but…I guess I didn't want…I don't know…it was just that—"

"It was Jack, wasn't it?"

Tiffany looked down at the gold tablecloth.

"What…did he do, Baby?"

"Momma, I don't think we should—"

"It's all right if you don't want to tell me. He's dead now. I don't know if you know that, but—"

"The mailman told me. That's how we found your new place."

"But I have to know." Momma's eyes grew. Tiffany could clearly feel the urgency coming from her mother. "Did he…did Jack…did he…*touch* you? Did he…did he do *anything* that I should feel—"

"No, Momma." She didn't want to bring it all back. The bastard hadn't done all he'd wanted to do, but what he had done was enough to make her pack her few belongings and leave. But Momma didn't need to know the details. The man was dead, and Momma was now free. "He wanted to, but he never did. He did scare me, though."

Momma's eyes stayed on her. "He must have scared you badly enough to get you to leave home like that."

"He did, Momma, but it was more than that. I missed Dad so much..." Even after all these years, it still hurt to say it. "I was pretty vulnerable back then. I was a senior in high school and going through some stuff there, too. But even if Jack hadn't…even if he'd been a good man, I still wouldn't have accepted him. I loved Dad too much. I just couldn't accept facing the rest of my life without him. And when you brought another man into the house…" She shrugged.

"I miss him too, too, Baby. Believe me, there's not a day goes by that I don't think of your father and wish...well, just wish that stupid accident hadn't really happened."

"I know, Momma."

Momma went silent. Tiffany could tell by her mother's half-smile that she'd gone back to happier days, when they were all together. She stared out the window, at the flowers in the back yard. In a soft voice, she said, "I really hope there's an afterlife, Baby. And I hope there's a Heaven. If there is, I'm pretty sure your father's there."

"He is, Momma. He was a good man."

Momma sniffed and dabbed at her eyes gently with a napkin. She turned to Chip and smiled. "I'm sorry. We've been so busy chattering away about ourselves. We didn't mean to ignore you."

"It's all right," he said, grinning. "I get ignored a *lot*."

"You're obviously a good friend of my daughter's?"

"Yepperino." His stupid grin did not diminish. "I'm Tifferoo's best friend, you could say."

Momma blinked. "Tiffer*oo*?"

Tiffany sighed. "He's got a hundred or so nicknames for me, Momma. I'm surprised he can remember them all. *Please* don't ask him any of the others."

Chip was still grinning. "Actually, I've only got seventy-eight of them. A lot of them slip right off the tongue, though. Want me to—"

"*No*." Tiffany glared.

"It'll just take a couple of—"

"*Stop it*," she sent over.

He shut up and smiled sheepishly at Momma.

Momma smiled at Chip. "And what should I call you?"

"Everyone calls me Chip, Mrs.—"

"Please call me Sandra."

"All righty-rooty…Sandra…"

"Chip?"

"There ya go." He winked.

"Is that short for something? Or just a childhood nickname?"

"Actually, it's short for Cypripedium—"

"He's a real jokester, Momma…" Tiffany sent him another quick glare.

Momma laughed. "I can tell."

Chip beamed. "It's one of my many talents."

Momma turned to Tiffany. She was no longer smiling. "You didn't have to stay away, Baby. I was alone just six months after you left. If Jack hadn't been murdered, I would have left him. I knew he wasn't a nice man. I just…I think I…" She sighed deeply. "I don't know *what* I thought."

"You were lonely, Momma. We both were. We'd lost Dad. You wanted to have a family again."

Momma turned back to the window. She looked very sad. "Jack treated me very well in those early days. I had no idea he was…I honestly didn't know his horrible secrets. If I'd had *any* idea that he'd snuck into your room, baby…" She blotted her nose with her napkin and lowered her head.

"How'd you know, Momma? He never did it unless you were away, visiting Aunt Ellen or—"

"A mother knows, dear."

"It's okay. I'm here now. He's gone. Everything's gonna be just fine." Tiffany placed her hand gently over Momma's wrist.

Momma stiffened at her touch. "You're so *cold*, dear…" She placed her free hand on top of Tiffany's. "And so *pale*... I thought everyone in Hollywood stayed out in the sun to develop a dark tan."

"I…left Hollywood, Momma."

Momma gawked at her. "Whatever for? I thought you were doing so *well*…"

"Something came up. Besides, the place was getting to me. The long hours, the casting calls. Showing up at a place for a job and having someone tell me the whole project had been scrubbed. Fewer and fewer jobs were coming in, so I decided to call it quits."

"When was this?"

Tiffany snuck a glance at Chip. "Just a few months ago."

Momma turned to Chip. "Were you working in Hollywood, too?"

Chip grinned. "I guess you could say Tifferoosky and I—"

"Watch it..."

Chip massaged his left temple. "You could say we kind of, well, decided to split the scene together."

Momma stared at him. "Are you all right?"

He grinned. "Just a slight twinge I get every so often. An old football injury." He winked.

Momma didn't say anything. Tiffany could tell her mother was trying to figure out if he was sincere. After about thirty seconds, Momma asked, "Are you and my daughter…well, are you…together?"

He beamed. "Through thick and through thin."

"You mean…?"

"We're just friends, Momma."

Chip's smile beamed. "Actually, Tifferoo and I…well, we go way back—"

"You'd better be careful..." She sent him a glare that made him cringe in his seat.

"We've…worked together…on a few occasions," he finished.

"What did you do in Hollywood?" Momma asked.

"To put it mildly, I did my time with the Lesbian crowd—"

"That's *Thespian,*" Tiffany said quickly.

"Oops…" Chip reddened.

Momma held back a grin.

"*You'd better watch it*," she shot into his head, and he winced and massaged his forehead.

"I'm trying, Tifferoo..."

"Try harder!"

"Are you sure you're all right?" Momma looked concerned.

"Fine, Ma'am. Just that same nagging twinge again."

"Would you like an Aspirin?"

"He's fine, Momma."

He was still massaging his forehead. "Actually, I've been getting them a lot more often since—"

"*I said—*"

"Since we got off the bus."

Momma had a sip of her coffee. "Were you an actor? Or in some other aspect of the industry?"

Chip glanced at Tiffany before speaking. "I was more into scripts."

"You were a scriptwriter?"

"I kind of stuck around to inject some of my wry wit into them. A consultant, you could say."

"Have I ever seen any of your work?"

Chip smiled pleasantly. "Would you care to repeat the question?"

As soon as Momma asked again, Tiffany shot, "*Home Improvement*," into his head.

"*Home Improvement*."

Momma thought about that for a few moments. "Wasn't that on in the nineties? That came on more than twenty years ago…"

Chip grinned sheepishly. "I'm a lot older than I look."

Momma looked skeptical. "You must be."

"He was a quick study," Tiffany said flatly.

"Thanks, Tifferoo."

"Don't mention it...and I really mean that."

"I saw you in several commercials, Baby. One was a skin cream, the other an underarm spray. I also think I saw you modeling lingerie. You looked gorgeous as ever. I was *so* proud. I have them on tape and look at them whenever I'm...well, whenever I'm depressed and want to look at you and tell myself that you're still alive and just as beautiful as ever."

Still alive...

Tiffany had to force herself from crumbling. Luckily, she was able to keep the trembling under control.

"You're doing just fine, Tifferoo." Chip winked.

His words helped. "Thanks, Momma, but those were just about all the jobs I could get at the time."

Momma shook her head. "No wonder Hollywood has become such a joke. If someone looking like you couldn't find work—"

"A lot of women look like me out there, Momma. Beauty is the industry, and beautiful young girls are a dime a dozen. But it's also a very tough, ruthless profession. When a girl gets just a few years older, she rushes to the plastic surgeon and spends thousands of dollars so she can look the same in her forties. She keeps on doing it—especially if she doesn't want to get acting jobs as someone's mother, or grandmother."

Momma went silent.

"Momma? Are you okay?"

"It's been almost five years, Baby. I didn't know if you were alive or dead."

Alive or dead...

If only she knew...

"I know, Momma. I'm really sorry."

Momma took a breath and began smiling again. "Well, you're here now, so I'm happy again. In fact, I don't think I've been this happy in a long, long time." She got up, bent, kissed Tiffany on the top of her head and went over to the coffeepot. "Would you like some coffee, Chip?"

"No, but if you've got orange juice, I'll take mine in a big glass. A beer stein would work better. Some herbal tea with rose petals would also hit the spot...and if you've got some flowers you're about to toss in the trash—or some stale eggshells..."

Momma stared at Chip for the longest time. Tiffany could tell she was waiting for him to tell her he was joking.

"He's quite a kidder, Momma."

"He truly is."

Chip grinned proudly.

CHAPTER 7

That evening, Keenan V. Durant sat at his kitchen table, slurping pea soup from a big brown bowl.

It had been an eventful day. He'd been able to complete another important high-paying job for Mr. Robertson and the Royal League. And after talking with Mr. Robertson, he was given another one that would earn him another five thousand. This wasn't bad. Since he always completed each job within forty-eight hours after acceptance, five thousand dollars was a considerable sum.

He'd come a long way in the last hundred and fifty years, since the Civil War days, when he was a young man, bringing home money, food, and black powder taken from dying Confederate soldiers lying in the fields of Pennsylvania. Many needed fresh bandages, medicine and food as they lay on the ground, dying from bullet wounds and dysentery. However, Keenan—known as Seth Hawkins back then—had more urgent things to tend to. He was fifteen at the time, and completely loyal to his family and what his mother and father had instructed him to do to keep food on the table. Like his kin, he hated Confederate soldiers and had been told by his family and friends that the country would die a horrible death if the Union lost the war. To help his family, he simply walked up to the dying rebels, grabbed what supplies he could find, and quietly slipped away.

Even back then he discovered that he could come and go without being noticed. He'd always been small and slight, walking softly. As a result, he'd been overlooked and ignored all his young life. He'd routinely snuck into the enemy's headquarters and taken whatever he could find and carry, returning home to divvy out his swag among the family and relatives. He went out scavenging hundreds of times in the four years of the War, and even though he'd died in that freak accident in 1865, where the black powder he'd stolen had exploded in his face as he tried separating it into containers in his father's woodshed, he'd never been seen or detained by anyone.

Once freed of his mortal body, he'd gone down to the Dark Place to mingle amongst the myriad of lost souls in the Valley of Decay. He was then ordered by one of the subs to enter the Castle of Demons to sweep up the place and keep the roaches and rats away from the banquet table. Even after death, he was noticed only if one of the demons stumbled onto him in his work. His nickname most of his mortal life, the "one who is not seen," had literally followed him to the grave. In death, it was translated from the Latin by the super demon Asmodeus. From that day forward, he was referred to as, "*Qui non viderunt.*"

It wasn't long before Balberith ordered him to come back up and use his powers of camouflage and deceit to continue doing work for the demons. Finding it necessary to choose a mortal name, he decided on a phonetic version of the Latin when he returned to the mortal world. "*Qui non viderunt*" transformed nicely into Keenan V. Durant, and when he'd come to Peoria ten years ago at the request of Balberith, the Royal League gave him no resistance. The Peoria chapter wanted someone who could quietly eliminate minor irritations, and once he'd settled into his cover job as mail carrier for the Postal Service and began his undercover work, the Royal League of Demons realized Balberith had made an excellent choice.

Keenan began giving them what they wanted just two weeks after he'd started working at the Post Office. His first job was simple and direct. A local politician had been causing problems with the League by locking horns with Marko Vaughn, the town's largest real estate investor.

Just twenty-four hours after Keenan was given the job, the politician in question tripped while crossing the street and was promptly run over by a school bus.

It had been a gravy train ever since. He'd heard that Balberith's successor, Braithwaite, was nasty. But he'd also heard that the new super demon appreciated results. He hoped Braithwaite had heard about him. He realized the super demon was presently extremely busy handling things in Orlando, Florida, and might not know what was happening elsewhere.

But it didn't matter. Keenan would continue doing a great job, and when and if Braithwaite did drop by to check things out, he'd approve of the work Keenan had been doing.

Keenan finished his soup. It would be a relaxing evening. He'd already taken his latest parcel containing five thousand dollars, all in hundred-dollar-bills, and burying it in the ground beneath one of the bricks serving as his patio in his small back yard. So far, the bricks protecting the many envelopes covered an area of ten by twenty-five feet. Doing a rough calculation, Keenan figured that in six months, after buying more bricks, the area would have to be expanded another twenty square feet or so.

The mortal world had become his oyster, and as long as he didn't do anything stupid or suspicious, he'd be able to continue doing what he'd been doing as long as he wanted. For now, he had to keep a low profile. This was why he lived in a small apartment. And kept to himself. And purchased only the bare necessities. And didn't buy anything that would bring unwanted attention to himself.

He was a mail carrier. This was why he drove a Smart Car when he could easily afford a Ferrari, or Maserati.

After he washed the dishes, he'd retire to his study, relax in his recliner and enjoy his souvenir collection. With each job, he enjoyed taking something from his latest victim, bringing it home and placing it on the shelf of the walnut bookcase covering one complete wall of his study. His latest souvenir, a can opener he'd grabbed from the kitchen counter of Otis Turner's home, sat on the bottom shelf, next to the hairbrush he'd lifted from the luscious brunette he'd eliminated last month, who'd been causing her boyfriend, a local defense attorney working for the League, much aggravation for his wife and family.

Just as he began running hot water to wash the dishes, his cell rang.

He turned off the tap, dried his hands and went to pick it up.

It was Mr. Robertson. "I've got the details for your next job."

Grinning, Keenan picked up his pad and pencil from the pegboard and sat down at the kitchen table. "Just tell me what you want done, sir…"

CHAPTER 8

"How long are you and Chip going to stay with me, Baby?"

Smiling, Momma sat facing Tiffany at the dining room table. She had a sip of port wine.

Chip sat on Tiffany's right, staring dumbly at his plate of chicken and green bean casserole. Tiffany hoped he wouldn't say or do anything to make Momma suspicious. Chip's spiritual form was that of a flower; he'd assumed mortal form but couldn't digest regular food. Glancing at his plate, Tiffany saw that some of the chicken and a good bit of the casserole had disappeared. Since she hadn't seen him put anything on his fork, this made her suspicious.

"Baby?" Momma was waiting.

"A week or so, I guess."

Momma put down her glass. "Really?"

"We can't impose on you, Momma."

Confusion wrinkled Momma's face. "Tiffany, you're my baby. You can't possibly impose. I haven't seen you in five years, and now you're telling me you'll only be here with me for a mere *week*?"

Chip picked up his giant glass of orange juice and had a big swallow.

Momma watched him in fascination. "Are you sure you wouldn't like a little port instead?"

"No, thanks, Ma'am." He grinned and put down his glass. Then he picked up the pitcher of ice water Momma had placed on the table in front of him and gulped down nearly a quarter of it. "I'm just fine and dandy."

Momma shook her head. "I honestly don't know where you're putting all that liquid, young man. You know where the bathroom is, I take it?"

"Yepperino. But don't worry—I'm housebroken. My mother made sure she taught me neat stuff like that" He scooped some casserole onto his fork. Momma turned back to her plate and stabbed a slice of chicken with her fork. Chip put his hand over his fork and pulled it away. The casserole had disappeared. He put the empty fork into his mouth.

"Do you like the casserole?" Momma asked.

"Yes, Ma'am." He swallowed audibly and reached for the orange juice again. "It's very tasty."

Momma turned to Tiffany. "You never did say what you've been doing since you left Hollywood, dear…"

"No, Momma. I didn't."

This was the moment she'd been dreading. She'd been thinking about it ever since they first followed Momma inside. But even so, she still hadn't come up with a suitable story. She couldn't possibly tell Momma what they'd been doing. Tiffany had left Hollywood as a spirit—case closed. But she had to come up with *some*thing.

"I noticed that you don't have any luggage." Momma was looking at both of them. "How'd you get into town?"

Tiffany hadn't thought about that one. It was an innocent question, but the wrong answer would put Momma into a panic. If Tiffany didn't say the right thing, Momma might start grilling both of them. Tiffany knew she couldn't stand up to her mother for very long. And she certainly couldn't trust Chip to take charge. It was bad enough having him at the dinner table, making his food disappear without actually eating any of it.

"*Problemo, Tifferoo*?" Chip's thoughts raced over as he slipped his empty fork into his mouth again.

"I don't know what to tell her. I don't want her to worry, so I don't want to say the wrong thing—"

"The only thing you could say that would make her worry is that we're both dead, Tifferoosky."

He was right. But it didn't give her any ideas.

"You must have *some* luggage, dear. I can't see the two of you coming all this way—"

"We left it at the hotel," Chip said.

"Yes, Momma." She was surprised she hadn't thought of that. "We got off the bus at the Marriott, booked two rooms, then—"

"That's all the way across town, dear. How'd you get here? A cab?"

"Righterino."

"And you said the postman gave you my new address?"

"Yes, Momma. We went to the old address. He was delivering mail there and told us where you were. He also told us about Jack."

Momma was silent for a few moments. "I really want you to stay here as long as you're in town. I can drive you back to the hotel—"

"That won't be necessary, Momma…"

"That place is expensive, dear. There's no sense renting two rooms if you're going to be staying here with me."

"*We'll handle it, Tifferoo.*" Chip was chugging down more water as his thoughts drifted over.

"All right, Momma. If you insist…"

"We can drive there in the morning. It'll have to be before eleven. Otherwise, they'll charge you for another day."

"Yes, Momma…"

"By the way, you never said what you've been doing since you left Hollywood."

Tiffany picked up her glass of port and held it in front of her face. She was playing for time. Her thoughts were spinning, and as she slowly brought the glass closer to her lips, Chip said, "We work in nightclubs."

Tiffany nearly spilled her drink.

Momma turned to Tiffany. "Baby? Nightclubs? Really?"

Tiffany flushed and gave Momma a weak smile. Her thoughts raced.

"Just what exactly do you do?"

"We have our own act," he threw in, grinning.

"Really? What sort of act?"

"Illusions. We…well, we do tricks no one else can do."

Tiffany wanted to strangle him. "*Chip*—"

"Baby? I didn't know you knew how to do—"

"She learned," Chip said.

"Seriously?"

"It was kind of a spur-of-the-moment thingy," he added. "We both knew Hollywood wasn't gonna bestow us both with riches and accolades, so we decided to learn another trade. I'd learned a bunch of tricks while I was growing up, so at least we had sort of a head-start. Tifferoosky caught on like a champ, and since she's so easy on the eyes, we've never had a problem attracting audiences. We hit the nightclub circuit not too long after that and—"

"Tiffany learned all this from you?"

"Just little ol' me, myself, and my razor-sharp mind. All for one and one for all—or however that saying goes." He winked.

Momma gazed at him. "Really? You're an illusionist?"

"I was doing tricks before you were even—"

"*Watch it!*" Tiffany cautioned.

"Before I was even what, Chip?"

He grinned sheepishly. "I was gonna say, before you were even aware that Tifferoo had left home."

"What sort of illusions can you do?" Momma asked.

"Watch. And be prepared to be enthralled." He picked up his orange juice glass, tilted it and gulped it. All the while he was drinking, he said, "I'll bet you never saw anyone talk while they were chugging down orange juice, did you?"

Momma stiffened in her chair. "That's *incredible*! I've *never* seen *anything* like that!"

Grinning, Chip put the glass back down. "I'll bet you've never seen this before, either…"

"You'd better not do that head-spinning thing in front of my mother!"

Chip sighed. "*How about the tongue thingy?*"

"Just make sure it doesn't touch the floor."

"I'm sitting down, Precious..."

"I still don't trust you."

"*I might just surprise you this time.*" He grinned at Momma. "Here goes." He opened his mouth. His tongue slithered out and dropped down to the napkin in his lap. As it rolled back up, he noticed that something had stuck to it. It was a sliver of chicken. He flicked it off and let his tongue continue rolling back up, until it disappeared in his mouth.

Momma was shaking her head and laughing. "Amazing! Truly amazing!"

Chip giggled. "It's all done with mirrors, but we really can't give away where we keep ours, can we?"

Still laughing, Momma turned to Tiffany. "And what do *you* do, Baby?"

Tiffany reddened. She had no idea what she could show Momma without giving herself away.

Before she had time to panic, Chip once again came to her rescue.

"Hand her the salt shaker. Place her napkin over it and pick up the pepper shaker, then place your napkin over it. Close your eyes for a few seconds and make it look like you're concentrating. Then open your eyes. A second or two later, you both pull the napkins away, and voila! *You're holding the salt, while she's got the pepper. It's simple for us, but for mortals—"*

"I get it. And thanks." Tiffany smiled at her mom. "I think I've got something I can show you, Momma." Tiffany picked up the salt shaker and

handed it to her mom. "Hold this and cover it with your napkin."

Excited, Momma did as Tiffany suggested.

Tiffany grabbed the pepper shaker, picked up her napkin and covered it as well.

"Now what do I do, dear?"

"You've got the salt, right, Momma?"

"Yes…"

"And I've got the pepper?"

Momma nodded.

"When I say, "now," pull off the napkin. Got it?"

"Got it."

"All right, then." She turned to Chip. "Drum roll, Chip."

Chip turned his fork and knife into two drumsticks and did a clumsy drum roll on the table.

Momma gasped. "How did he—"

"Quiet for a second, Momma…"

"Oops…sorry…"

Tiffany lowered her head and closed her eyes. She waited about five seconds, raised her head and opened her eyes. "Now, Momma."

"What? Oh. Okay…" Momma pulled off the napkin and gasped. She was holding the pepper. When she was finally able to focus again, she saw that Tiffany was holding the salt. "My God…how did you…how can you…this is *incredible*!"

It took Momma several moments to regain her train of thought. She replaced the pepper shaker and stared at it—as well as the salt shaker—for the longest time, as if expecting them to change back.

"Good, ain't we?" Chip picked up his water glass.

"You two really are amazing!"

"Thanks, Momma."

"Are you expensive?"

"What's that, Momma?"

"I'm just curious about how much you charge."

Tiffany shifted uneasily in her chair. "W-Why, Momma?"

"I'm wondering if I can afford to pay you."

"Pay us? For what?"

"Well, for the last three years, I've been working at St. Jude Hospital down the street, in their Bookkeeping Department."

"That's right. You majored in Accounting before you met Dad."

"Well, since I've been on my own the last few years, I've had to take my skills out of mothballs."

"That's good, Momma. You were always good with figures. Do you like working there?"

Momma smiled. "The people are just wonderful. Yes, I really do like it. Anyway, getting back to your skills… Do you think that while you're in town, you can pay us a visit and give the children a show?"

Tiffany forced herself to keep from glaring at Chip. Even so, her next thought automatically shot directly into his head. "*See what you've done?*"

Chip grinned sheepishly. "*What's wrong with that? I like kids—especially when they're sick.*"

"*And why is that*?"

"When kids are sick, they're easier to deal with."

Tiffany glared.

"Got something against kids, Tifferoosky? You helped one out earlier this afternoon. You brought her dead dog back."

"As I told you before, I'm really not sure—"

"Well, Baby?"

"No problem, Momma."

"Good. I have a very good friend who manages the social events for the hospital. I'll call her in the morning, if that's okay with you."

"That's fine, Momma."

"But first, we'll take a drive to the hotel and get your things."

"Whatever you say, Momma."

Smiling, Momma got up. "This is going to be *such* a pleasant visit! I'm *so* glad you came back, Baby…" She grabbed the casserole dish and froze, gazing at it.

"What's wrong, Momma?"

She continued staring.

"Momma? Is there something—"

"I may be mistaken, but it doesn't look like we've eaten very much of this at all…"

DAY TWO - "FINDING A DEMON"

CHAPTER 9

The next morning, after coffee and a sausage patty, one three-minute egg and a piece of dry toast, Keenan V. Durant set out early to check out the house where his next victim lived.

Tanya Caldwell was eighteen, lived with her parents on North Indiana and worked at the local Waffle House as a waitress. She had long black hair and chestnut eyes. She was tall, about five-eight, and very slender, weighing about a hundred and ten pounds. She had a younger brother named William, several female friends, and a boyfriend named Burt Weller she saw regularly at the Mall across the street from where she worked. She belonged to Facebook, had a Twitter account, and spent several hours a day on her iPad, iPhone and laptop. She'd also been involved in two other minor fender benders in the last two years as the result of her obsessive texting.

However, the accident involving Ronald Alsworth was soon to be her undoing. The stupid bitch had hired an attorney for the case—a friend and colleague of her boyfriend—and was hoping to squeeze a significant amount of money from Alsworth to purchase a new car. She was claiming personal bodily injury—a dislocated shoulder and twisted ankle—and hadn't been to work at all since the accident.

Keenan parked his little lime-green Smart Car about half a block down the street from the Caldwell residence. Then, grabbing his binoculars, he focused on the front windows.

After seeing nothing of significance for nearly ten minutes, he decided it would be best to change his vantage point. He drove around the block and parked along the curb, which led to the back yard of the Caldwell residence. For the next twenty minutes, he trained the binoculars on the bedroom and French doors.

Again, he saw nothing out of the ordinary.

Like it or not, he was going to have to go inside.

He put the binoculars away, got out and crossed the street. There was little traffic. School was still a few days away, so there were no buses to watch out for. With so many retired and unemployed people in this area, the rush hour wasn't bad at this time. Luckily, he didn't have to worry about that, either. And he still had a full hour before heading off to the Post Office.

He snuck onto the rear of the property. Hunkering behind an overgrown bush, he watched the house for the next few minutes, his highly-developed sense of hearing picking up odd sounds coming from the center section of the house, where the kitchen would be.

The clinking of silverware.

The sound of something hard dropping on the floor.

A cough.

Someone muttering.

The flushing of a commode.

This told him at least three people were in the house.

Undaunted, he crept over to the other end of the building and crouched beneath the small bathroom window, listening.

Gargling.

A loud fart.

Some was obviously getting ready for work.

He slipped over to the screen door. The mother faced the oven as she fixed breakfast. He waited until she'd turned. Then, as she went over to the cupboard, he carefully opened the screen door and slipped silently inside. Using the powers he'd developed as an inferior, he turned invisible while crossing the kitchen.

In no time, he was making his way down the hall.

Tanya Caldwell sat on her bed, slipping on her designer tennies. "I'm getting ready for breakfast now," she said to the iPhone lying on the mattress beside her. "Now I'm putting on my shoes." She was wearing jeans and a lavender tee shirt, and her thick black hair had been recently washed. It hung heavily down her back, glistening almost blue in the overhead lighting. On the mattress beside her iPhone, a shoulder sling lay in a muddled heap. Once her shoes were laced, she grabbed the sling and slipped it over her head. "Now I'm putting on my sling," she announced to her phone.

Still invisible, Keenan went over to the corner hutch next to the full-length mirror as she adjusted the sling to support her left arm. Then she got up, went over to the mirror and stood in front of it, studying herself. She turned, walked about five steps and turned back around. Then, tilting her pelvis, she began limping with her right foot. She limped up to the mirror, turned around and limped away. Then she turned around again and came back. She spent another minute or so staring at herself in the mirror. "Not bad," she muttered. "Obviously injured, but still smoking hot."

She went back to the bed and picked up her phone. "I've got the limp and the sling looking really good." She waited. "Yeah, I think so." She waited again. "Prob'ly an hour or so." She laughed.

"Tanya!" yelled a woman down the hall. "William! Breakfast!"

"Coming!" Before leaving the room, she pulled off the sling and stuffed it in her oversized leather handbag. Then she turned and began walking normally again.

Still invisible, Keenan followed her down the hall.

***

"Whaddya plan on doin' today, honey?" Tall, dark-haired and slightly plump, Tanya Caldwell's mother placed a large plate stacked with pancakes, scrambled eggs and a dozen strips of crispy bacon in the center of the breakfast table. "And how many times have we told you? No phones at the table, please…"

Groaning, Tanya flicked off and pocketed her cell.

Her mom frowned. "Go 'head and groan. That phone is what got you in trouble in the first place. And it's happened more than once. In my day—"

"I know all about your day, Mom. No cell phones, no texting, nothing fun *at all*—"

"And we were *much* happier."

"I'll bet you were bored all the time, too."

"You'd be wrong. We had to use our brains a lot more than you kids do now. That's the difference."

"I've got friends, Mom—all kinds of friends. We like to keep in touch."

"Your friends don't have to know every single move you make every second."

Frowning, Tanya dropped down in her chair.

"Well? Whaddya plan on doing? I take it you're still not going in to work."

"I'm taking a few days off. I've got some things I need to do."

Her mom poured coffee into both cups on the table. "I just hope it doesn't have anything to do with that stupid lawsuit. You need to drop it and see what you can do about getting that car s fixed. As you just said, you've got all kinds of friends. I'll bet at least one of them can do body work. Anything you try doing to that man you slammed into will probably get you in serious trouble. There are all kinds of fraud, you know."

Keenan stood behind her as she fidgeted in her chair. Then he crept over to the other side of the room.

Tanya reached for the spatula. "I still think he backed up without looking, Mom."

"We all know you've got a heavy foot, Tan. I'll bet you were going just a little fast. Besides, you were texting, and we all know what happens when you text, don't we?"

"I wasn't texting when he pulled out and backed into me. I'd just finished and was watching where I was going. That fat cat's just trying to be a cheapskate about the whole thing. He can afford whatever I sue him for. Don't you know who he is?"

Her mom sat down. "Everyone in this town knows who he is. That's why your father and I don't want you doing what you plan on doing. Ronald Alsworth happens to be one of the richest men in this state. He practically owns most of Peoria, ya know."

"That guy owns half the supermarket chains in Illinois." Smelling strongly of Old Spice, Dad shuffled in dressed in his shirt and red striped tie. His thinning brown hair was brushed straight back. He draped his dark-blue jacket over the back of his chair, sat down and picked up his plate. He snatched up the spatula and selected three strips of bacon and a large serving of scrambled eggs. He replaced the spatula, picked up a bacon strip and began nibbling. "He's a billionaire, for God's sake." He reached for his coffee mug. "He could buy and sell this entire block a dozen times over."

"That's why you shouldn't mess with him, honey," Mom said. "You know how dangerous the filthy rich are. They can do some really nasty things and get away with them."

"Look at our beloved Capitol," Dad said. "If that place doesn't convince you to stay clear of corrupt individuals—"

"I'll be okay." Tanya clearly didn't want to hear what they were saying. "I know what I'm doing."

"They say he owns three of the most prominent judges in town," Dad said. "That alone tells me you should just forget all about going after him."

"Not if I can get him to buy me a new car and take care of my medical bills."

"Get 'im to buy ya a Charger!" Short and bone-thin, William came in, wearing faded Levis and a white tee shirt with the Cubs emblem displayed prominently in the center of his scrawny chest. "Those boys are really bad! And they fly like the wind! I'll even wash it for ya!" Jerking the brown hair out of his eyes, he sat down facing his sister, grabbed a stack of pancakes and dumped them on his plate.

"That's another thing," Mom said. "Aside from a slight sprain in your ankle, you were given a clean bill of health from the hospital." She glared at William. "And *please* use the spatula next time, buster!"

"How can you possibly make personal injury claims when you're obviously not injured?" Dad picked up his mug and had another slug of coffee.

Tanya poured a little maple syrup on her pancake and smiled. "I've got that covered, too."

Silence.

Dad shook his head. "I don't think I wanna know what else is going on here."

"Trust me, Dad. I'm learning a lot since I've been watching those court shows on TV."

Keenan silently backed away and became part of the kitchen hutch. He felt a belch coming on and used his hand to cover his mouth just in time. The belch, restricted to a slight blast through his nostrils, was inaudible, overwhelmed by the sound of the son munching loudly on a bacon strip.

"Chew with your mouth shut," Mom said. "How many times do we have to tell you?"

William shrugged and closed his mouth.

Dad finally said, "Care to elaborate?"

"Not really," Tanya said. "I'll let everyone know all the details after I get my money."

Mom got up and went to the hutch. She picked up a pile of paper napkins and stopped moving. She sniffed and looked around.

"What's wrong, Pats?" Dad asked.

She wrinkled her nose. "I just got a whiff of…*sausage*..."

"Sausage and bacon! *Mmmm*!" William nodded eagerly as he picked up a chunk of pancake and chowed down. He studied the plates in the center of the table. "Where are they, Mom? Still in the microwave?"

"I didn't cook any."

"Seems your sniffer's a tad off this morning, Pats," Dad said with a grin.

"I just hope there's nothing dead lying behind that hutch," Tanya said, frowning.

"Ga-*ross*!" William grimaced and shook his head.

"If we had mice," Dad said, "I think we prob'ly would have already seen evidence of 'em."

William nodded. "Mice turds."

Tanya shook her head.

William grinned at her. "They look like brown rice. One time, the guys scooped up some and went to that Chinese place on Main Street—"

Mom dropped her fork loudly onto her plate. "Enough of that kind of talk at the breakfast table, Mister! We're trying to eat!"

CHAPTER 10

Waking early, Tiffany covered her feet in a pair of tan tennis shoes with a tiny red star on each toe and miniature emeralds shaped in a wavy *T* over each ankle. She wondered for a moment if she should have put on the same footwear she had worn the day before. Would Momma notice? Probably not. This pair looked particularly cute, so she decided to keep them looking that way.

She went over to the door and pulled it open about an inch. Across the hall, Momma's bedroom door was closed. Relieved, she snuck out into the hall and tiptoed down the steps.

Chip was asleep on the living room couch. Momma's quilted afghan was pulled all the way up, covering him completely. She went over and nudged him.

He grunted and pushed the afghan down. Blinking, he noticed her and grinned. "We can't play around *here*, can we, Tifferoo? In your mom's house?"

"Don't be silly," she whispered. "We have to talk."

"*Moi*? Silly?"

"Will you please shut up and stop acting ridiculous?"

"I'm hurt. And shocked. And after all we've been through together, too…"

"Save the nonsense for later. We still have to talk."

"What time is it?"

"It's early."

"Whaddya wanna talk about? Can't it wait?"

"No."

He wiped some sleep from his eyes. "Sounds important. And unpleasant."

"You know what we have to talk about, so stop acting silly."

"I'll try, but I can't guarantee any results. Not *this* early..."

"I know this'll be difficult for you to grasp, but get up and try to function, okay?"

He sat up. The afghan slipped down. While Tiffany picked it up and folded it neatly, Chip yawned and ran both hands through his wild red thatch. "Let me guess. You wanna talk about changing the sleeping arrangements."

"In your dreams."

"Well, *duh…*"

"We have to talk about how we're going to handle my mother."

"Handle? You mean like—"

"Get your mind out of the gutter. She's taking us to the hotel this morning. She's expecting us to go inside and come back out with luggage."

His eyes glazed over.

"Luggage. You know. Suitcases? That sort of thing."

"I know all about luggage, Tifferoo."

"Then work with me here and stop zoning out."

"In that order?"

She bit her lip and forced herself to chill. "We have to show some sort of luggage to my mother—get it?"

He shrugged. "No problemo."

"Really?"

"After all we've been through together, how can you possibly doubt me at this stage?"

"I don't know. Your silliness always gets in the way. And then, of course, there's that zoning-out thing you do whenever I try to talk to you. In other words, yes, I still doubt you…"

"Look what I did earlier, at the dinner table."

He definitely had a point. But this was important. "Yes, but we've really got to be careful about this because—"

"Look what I did in Pittsburgh, when we splattered that demon in bird shit, stuck him on a plane and sent his ass back to Orlando."

That was definitely another point. "I know, but—"

"I didn't do badly in Orlando, either, did I? It took quite a bit of finesse on my part—which, incidentally, isn't exactly my forte—to dress up as a female prostitute and seduce that horny rich Arab geezer. And, if you remember, the outfit that asshole Daniel Grove gave me was a tad snug in the armpit area."

"I'm sure it was. And yes, you did a really fine job, but—"

"And don't forget Ohio, when we sent the wolf guy back down to the Dark Place. Admit it. If it hadn't been for my help—"

"Yes. Yes. I know." She knew full well that if it hadn't been for Chip, Gutril would have definitely beaten her. Chip had a bagful of quirks, yes, but she could trust him. They really had been through a lot together.

But this was Momma they were talking about, and despite everything they'd seen, everything they'd been through, he had to know that they should tread carefully. Momma had been through a lot in the last few years. Tiffany didn't want to cause her any more grief.

"I admit it," she told him. "I really do. And I thank you once again. But we still—"

"So are you trying to say that you shouldn't doubt me anymore?"

"This is my *mother* we're talking about."

He rubbed his temples. "Okay… Since you're forcing me down Memory Lane, let me remind you how I smoothed things over at the dinner table. And you're welcome about the chicken and the casserole. Flowers don't do well with beans. I could've thrown them back up, you know…"

"I know."

"That would've definitely changed the overall mood—don't you think?"

"It certainly would have."

"Instead, I acted like a true gentleman and put the food right back where it belonged."

"I know."

"So I accept your apology."

She stared up at the ceiling.

"Is that an apology, Princess? To me, it looks like you're pointing that gorgeous face at the ceiling. But I could be mistaken, correctamundo? This might be your subtle way of expressing your admiration. In certain cultures, staring upward is actually a sign of great reverence and devotion."

Tiffany wanted to slap him silly but knew it was much too late for that.

"Well?"

"Yes. It's an apology. Are you satisfied?"

"Reasonably…"

"But we still don't know what we'll do when we get to the hospital."

"Listen, Tiffers…as I've been trying to tell you, you really need to trust me. Just take my lead and let me do this. I don't mean to brag, but—"

"You two are up early." Momma was standing in the archway in her light-blue terrycloth housecoat and fuzzy pink slippers, her face puffy with sleep, smiling at both of them.

***

After breakfast, Momma backed the Honda down the drive.

Tiffany sat beside Momma, with Chip in the back. He'd been fairly quiet since breakfast. Tiffany had seen him scoop a couple of eggshells out of the trash while Momma wasn't looking. She wanted to smile at his reply to Momma after her remark about stopping at the store on the way home and stocking up on a couple of gallons of orange juice. Chip had grinned and said, "It's really good for the petals." And when he'd seen Momma's quizzical look, he reached up and ran a hand through his thick red mop.

Once they were on their way, Tiffany asked, "Don't you have to go in to work today, Momma?"

"I called in." Momma smiled. "When I told them my baby daughter showed up on my doorstep after five long years, they totally understood."

"Can you just take off like that?"

"I seldom take time off, dear. As a matter of fact, they still owe me a week from last year. As I've already said, they're very nice people. Very understanding."

Minutes later, they were heading southwest. The Marriott was only about fifteen minutes away, and Tiffany was still worried about what they'd do once they went into the hotel.

"*Don't worry about it, Tifferoo*," Chip sent over from the back seat.

"*I can't help it,*" she replied. "*I don't want to have to steal someone's luggage just so Momma doesn't get suspicious.*"

"*It's a fancy place, isn't it?*"

"*What's that have to do with anything?*"

"*Don't those fancy places have gift shops?*"

She practically smiled. "*I hadn't thought of that.*"

"*Besides, with your powers growing so much, you could grab a paper bag from a trash can and turn it into a piece of expensive-looking luggage.*"

"*You think so?*"

"*Tifferoo...look what you do with your shoe fetish.*"

"*I don't have a shoe fetish—*"

"*What do you call it, then?*"

"*I just like to—*"

"Are those different shoes, dear?" Momma asked suddenly.

Tiffany stiffened in her seat. She wondered for a moment if Momma had picked up on her mental conversation with Chip. She thought it best just to downplay this and see what happened. "W-Why do you ask, Momma?"

"I don't remember them being tan."

"Don't you like them?"

"I love them, dear. You always did have excellent taste."

"Thanks, Momma."

"Tifferoosky just loves her shoes," Chip said flatly.

"She always did." Momma chuckled. "When she was a little girl, every time we went to the Mall we had to stop at every single shoe store we passed so this young lady could try on at least a dozen different pairs."

"You're exaggerating, Momma…"

Momma laughed. "You honestly don't remember, do you, dear?"

"I don't remember trying on *that* many shoes…"

"We could shop for me, your father, and whatever we needed for the house inside an hour. Then we'd spend the next two or three hours in the shoe stores, watching you try on every single pair that struck your fancy. It used to drive your father *crazy*!" She laughed. "And also the sales ladies!"

"Did it really drive Dad crazy?" Tiffany remembered shopping with Momma and Dad as a child. She also remembered trying on different shoes, but nothing about Dad going crazy. "I don't remember him saying anything…"

"He didn't, Baby."

"Why not?"

Momma beamed. "You were his little princess. He loved it when you were having fun. He didn't want to take anything away from you."

Tiffany sat back and rode out the wave of warmth she always felt whenever she thought of her father. *I really shouldn't cry. I want to, but we have entirely too many other things to think about right now…*

"Did she ever pick out a pair she actually wanted?" Chip asked.

"Eventually," Momma said, "but as I said, it usually took *hours*… And then it was always a toss between two or three pairs she seemed to love equally."

"*Why am I not surprised*?" he sent over.

"Oh, stop. So I used to be obsessed with shoes..."

"*Used to be*?"

"So why do they look so different?" Momma asked.

"How do you mean?"

"I could've sworn they were white yesterday."

"We *are* illusionists, ya know," Chip said.

Momma glanced at him in her rearview. "What does that have to do with—"

He raised a brow. "With illusionists, you can never be sure what you're actually seeing."

She watched him for a few moments. Then she glanced at Tiffany, who nodded.

"*You did it again*," she sent him.

"*I'm funny that way,*" he said, grinning.

"You're funny in more ways than one."
"I'm what you'd call a multitask clown."
"Well, you're half right..."
"Oucherino."

CHAPTER 11

After breakfast, Tanya Caldwell got ready to leave the house.

Before opening the front door, she pulled her props out of her bag. She wanted to make sure she looked legit if anyone was watching. She had to assume Mr. Megabucks Alsworth had hired someone to keep an eye on her to make sure she was really injured, and not just trying to pull something. She already had the fake medical papers and X-rays Burt had bought from one of his buddies working at the hospital, so she was okay in that respect.

But she still wanted to play it safe. Entirely too much money was riding on this.

Once the sling was properly placed over her shoulder and the fake bandage Velcroed around her right ankle, she carefully opened the front door, stepped out onto the front stoop and limped slowly down the front steps, making sure she hesitated on each step so she appeared to be regaining her balance before moving on. She held her iPhone close to her face and concentrated on looking really convincing as she limped down the walk.

"I'm leaving the house right now," she told Burt.

"How do you look?" he asked.

She smiled. "Pathetic."

"See anyone around?"

"I don't see anyone, but that probably doesn't mean anything."

"Well, Alsworth has the juice to hire snoops. I just found out that he owns a detective agency on Main, across the street from the Police Department. There could be six private dicks and a couple of insurance investigators swarmin' around out there, for all we know."

She casually looked around. Occasional traffic passed, going both ways. Two people were pulling out of their driveways, and the woman across the street was taking inventory of her flower garden. "I still don't see anyone."

"They could be using binoculars. Or a scope. This is big money we're talking, Tan."

"I know."

"Just be careful."

"I will."

"And make sure you don't move your lips much when you talk to me. These assholes have been trained to read lips, ya know."

"Never thought of that."

"You need to."

"Talk later."

***

Still invisible, Keenan V. Durant kept about ten feet behind her. He could tell that the girl was really into this, making sure she looked like she'd been in a serious accident. Too bad she had no idea that some very rich men had paid him a lot of money to deal with her.

He maintained his distance and made doubly sure he didn't belch his breakfast sausage again, or slip on the pavement and spook her. Since they were only a few houses down from Glen Oak, it wouldn't be long before she'd have to cross the street. Glen Oak was pretty busy at this time in the morning. North Indiana led to Main. Main served as a major artery, so there would be plenty of opportunity to shove her into heavy traffic. This bit of business shouldn't take long at all. It was still early enough for him to get back to his car and begin his mail route.

The girl kept up her slow, limpy pace. She really looked convincing. And she was cute, too. Too bad she had to die. But she was trying to gouge one of the League members. These were rich, important men; they controlled not only the town, but also a large part of the state. Along with Springfield, which supported a much larger League, there were too many members to run afoul of. This girl had no idea what she was doing. She was small-time and wanted only to soak a rich man out of a few thousand bucks. If she actually knew how far up Ronald Alsworth really was, she would have just settled in Small Claims like a good little girl. But she was definitely a product of her generation—narcissistic, selfish, spoiled, arrogant and self-absorbed—and didn't care about anything other than her looks, her social network, and how much she was owed.

She limped on by, chatting away on her cell, not even watching where she was going. Walking up to her and pushing her into traffic would be as easy as snatching up a kitten and tossing it from a balcony. No fuss, no muss…

The great thing about it was that it would earn him five big ones.

Not bad for an hour of his time.

***

Momma was about half a block from North Indiana when Tiffany spotted a slender young girl with long black hair limping down the street, approaching the intersection. Her left arm was in a sling, her right ankle was covered with a thick bandage, and she was talking on her cell.

A moment later, she saw the mailman she and Chip had talked to the day before. At first, Tiffany hadn't noticed him. She'd originally thought the girl was alone. However, as they went past and approached Main, she saw the man.

Then she noticed that he looked different.

He seemed almost translucent—as if someone had placed a dirty shower curtain in front of him.

What was going on? Had the early morning sun cast its glare on the windshield, obscuring Tiffany's view of him?

Or was this something else entirely?

Just as they went past the intersection, Momma slowed and stopped at the traffic clog in front of them. Tiffany turned in her seat. The young girl had approached the end of the block. Behind her, the mailman, still blurred and out of focus, also stopped. The girl continued talking on her cell while watching the traffic. She seemed more concerned with her phone call than the traffic and wasn't paying attention to the furniture truck rapidly approaching. As the girl stepped down from the curb, the mailman moved up closer to her and held his arms straight out. From Tiffany's vantage point, it looked like he was about to push her into traffic.

What on earth was going on?

"Hold on, Momma." Tiffany pushed open her door.

"What's wrong, dear?"

"I'll tell you later."

"Tifferoo?"

"No time to talk!"

Before Momma or Chip could say anything else, Tiffany had slipped out and pushed the door shut.

In seconds she was running down the street.

***

Keenan V. Durant maintained his distance of ten feet behind the Caldwell girl as she limped over to the end of the block.

Main Street traffic rushed past. The girl stood dangerously close to the curb, chatting away on her phone, barely glancing at the heavy stream zipping past. She didn't even lower the cell from her face as she stepped down onto the macadam. A big rig headed in their direction, moving fairly fast behind three cars. As the first car passed, the girl stepped down with her good foot. When the second vehicle passed, she appeared to be waiting for the rig to pass as well. There was nothing directly behind the truck. However, another small group was coming up fast about a quarter of a mile farther down.

Keenan guessed that this new group would be passing in less than ten seconds. If the girl continued with her charade, she wouldn't have enough time to cross. He decided to push her just as soon as the rig went by. Once she was down, she'd have to fight the sling and wouldn't have enough time to get back up.

She'd be dead in seconds.

People would say she tripped. Others might say she panicked and fell while she was turning around to climb back up onto the curb. In either case she'd be dead, and unable to cause anyone further trouble.

The third car passed.

She remained talking on her cell while waiting for the rig to pass.

Keenan stepped closer and put both his hands out in front of him. Just as he was about to give her shoulder blades a mighty shove, someone farther down the walk, on his right, began yelling.

***

"*Excuse me!*" Tiffany ran down the walk just as the girl was about to move directly into the path of several fast-moving vehicles.

The moment the girl heard Tiffany's voice, she froze and turned in Tiffany's direction. Then, noticing the traffic, she quickly climbed back onto the curb.

Tiffany walked the last ten feet or so before stopping just a few feet from the girl. At a much closer distance, the mailman became a little clearer but still appeared to be enveloped in a hazy cloud. Tiffany could tell that he was watching her as he cautiously backed up and stopped a safe distance away.

Tiffany ignored him. The girl obviously could not see him. Tiffany suspected no one else could see him, either. This told her something very strange was happening.

He was a demon. He had to be. And judging by what she'd just seen, she was certain that he wanted to kill this girl.

Tiffany had to get her away from him. She also had to make sure she did it without making him realize she knew he was there. Some strong inner sense told her it would be best if this demon didn't suspect who or what she actually was.

"Can I help you?" the girl asked.

Tiffany glanced at the girl's sling. "Are you all right?"

"I'm fine, Miss. I was just in an accident."

"I'm so sorry. How far are you going? My mother and I can take you—"

"No, it's all right. Thank you."

"But this traffic…" Tiffany glanced behind the girl and forced herself not to look directly at the mailman. He continued backing up, watching her with each step.

Now she knew for certain. He definitely was a demon. No mere mortal could make himself invisible.

"You're liable to get really hurt—especially if you stumble. Please let us take you where you want to go."

"I don't wanna be a bother—"

"It's no bother at all."

The girl thought it over. "All right." She smiled and pocketed her cell. "This is very nice of you."

"It's no trouble."

The girl limped over to Tiffany.

Tiffany took the girl's arm. "You can't possibly outrun this traffic. C'mon. We're parked just down the street. That silver Honda."

The girl stopped moving. "You said…your *mother's* driving?"

"Yes." Tiffany smiled. She could tell the girl was suspicious. "I'm Tiffany. Tiffany Sedarski. I used to live here."

"I'm Tanya Caldwell. Nice to meet you, Tiffany. You know, you kind of look, well, familiar."

They started walking. Tiffany kept her gait slow to stay with Tanya's limp. She was beginning to get the impression that the girl wasn't injured nearly as much as she let on. She still held onto the girl's arm but couldn't sense any significant pain emanating from her.

As she limped along, the girl kept glancing at Tiffany. "I think I may have seen you on TV or something. Were you ever a model? An actress, maybe?"

"A few years ago, but I left Hollywood several months ago."

"Really? How come?"

"A number of reasons. Do you have far to go?"

"Just a couple of blocks. I really appreciate this."

"It's no problem. In your condition, you shouldn't be trying to cross such a busy highway. The traffic's awful this morning."

"I know. Rush hour can be a real drag."

"And where you were standing, I didn't see a light."

The girl smiled sheepishly. “I guess I picked the wrong place to cross.”

“Good thing we came along.”

The girl stopped limping. For long moments she just stood there, gazing wide-eyed at Tiffany. “You know, I believe you actually saved my life.”

Tiffany smiled. “As I just said, I’m glad we came along when we did. But please do me a favor and be more careful, okay?”

The girl smiled. “Okay.”

They reached Momma’s Honda. Tiffany opened the back door. As she waited for Tanya to get in, Tiffany turned and risked a casual glance behind her.

The mailman was gone.

CHAPTER 12

"Where do you live, Tanya?" Momma asked as she pulled away from the curb to rejoin the flow.

"North Indiana, Ma'am. About half a block north of the intersection."

"Are you still in school?"

"I finish this year."

"*What's going on, Tifferoo?*" Chip sent over from the back seat.

"I don't know for sure. I just have a strange feeling about all this."

"Whaddya mean by strange?"

"I think I saw a demon back there."

"Here we go again..."

"Tanya, that's Chip," Tiffany said.

"Chip?" Tanya smiled. "Cute name."

"Thanks." He winked. "My momma liked it, too."

"Would you mind telling us how you got hurt?" Momma asked.

Tanya fidgeted in her seat. Tiffany could tell something was definitely going on that might explain what just happened. "I was passing the French Cuisine in town the other day when someone parked out in front of the building suddenly backed out of their spot, and I ran right into him."

"Were you texting at the time?" Tiffany asked. She could tell this girl was clearly attached to her cell by the way she stood at the curb, heavily engaged in conversation and totally oblivious of the passing traffic.

Tanya looked down.

"Tanya?"

She sighed. "It was only for a moment. I just glanced at my iPhone and when I looked up, there was this shiny black BMW pulling out. I really didn't have enough time to—"

"You were at fault, then," Tiffany said.

"I really think he should've been looking before he backed out."

"He probably was," Momma said.

Tanya didn't reply.

"How fast were you going when you hit him?" Tiffany asked.

"Not very."

"How fast is that?" Chip asked.

Tanya sent him a quick glare and then looked down again. "Maybe twenty-five."

"And just how badly were you hurt?" Momma asked.

Tiffany could tell Tanya was getting irritated by the questions. She fidgeted in her seat, then pointed as Momma approached the next intersection. "You can drop me off here."

"Are you sure?" Momma asked. "The only thing there is—"

"It's all right. I don't have far to walk."

"As you wish." Momma slowed down and stopped at the light.

"I really appreciate the ride, Ma'am. Thank you." Tanya pushed the door open and got out awkwardly.

Just as she began limping away, Tiffany turned to Momma. “I’ll be right back.” She slipped out, slammed the door behind her and hurried down the sidewalk. “Tanya?”

Tanya stopped abruptly and turned. She tried hiding her angry expression but wasn’t very successful. “Y-Yes?”

“I think I know what you’re doing,” Tiffany said.

“P-Pardon me?”

“It’s dishonest. You know that. And it’s fraud. You’re liable to get into serious trouble if you pursue this.”

Tanya blinked. “I don’t know what you’re—“

“Yes you do. I honestly don’t think you’re hurt as much as you’re letting on. This tells me you’re trying to—“

“He’s a rich man. He can afford this. My car’s gone. I paid three thousand dollars for it, and it’s gonna take at least that much to have it fixed.”

“That still doesn’t make it—“

“I know what I’m doing, Tiffany. I appreciate what you’re saying, but rich people are real creeps. They own everything and they always wanna own more. My father works for one of them. He works nearly sixty hours a week, and now it looks like his company might be moving to Mexico. My dad said that the rich jerks running the company have done a study and found out that they can save more than a million dollars a year if they use Mexican workers. Doesn’t that suck?”

“Yes, but—“

“I’m just trying to make a little difference.”

"I know."

"So at least you can understand, right? I'm not really a bad person. A lot of people like me. I have all kinds of friends."

Tiffany felt sorry for the girl but knew she wouldn't be able to convince her to drop whatever she was planning—not by any conventional means, anyway. But she had no choice. The mailman was obviously a demon. If he was, he was probably working for the Diocese. If so, the "rich creep" Tanya had targeted was undoubtedly a member. Tiffany needed to stop this before something horrible happened to Tanya.

"Well, thanks again for the ride." Tanya gave her a quick smile. Then she turned and began limping away.

"Tanya?"

The girl stopped and turned back around awkwardly.

Tiffany projected her thoughts into Tanya's head. *"You need to stop this right now. You're a very nice young lady, and you're better than this. If you persist, you'll get into serious trouble. I'm not going to let you do that. Instead, you're going to toss that sling and start walking normally, and when you're asked what you're going to do about the case, you're going to tell them you're going to drop it and accept whatever settlement is already in the works. You'll respect yourself again and won't have to worry about going to prison, or someone coming after you. Do you understand?"*

Tanya's large chestnut eyes appeared blank. Then she nodded.

"Good. Now walk away and live the rest of your life happily, without trying to hurt or cheat anyone. Make a phone call and tell whoever you have to that you're no longer going to pursue a lawsuit. And please stop texting while you're driving. It's very dangerous, and it's totally unnecessary."

In conclusion, Tiffany added, *"You won't remember anything about me or what I've just told you. All you'll remember is that you were given a ride by some people you never saw before."*

Blinking, Tanya looked around as if she had no idea where she was. Noticing Tiffany, she smiled weakly and said, "Thanks again for the ride."

Tiffany smiled back. Then she turned around, went down the walk and got back into the Honda.

"What was that all about, Baby?" Momma asked.

"I just told her she might not want to consider filing a lawsuit for her accident."

Momma was watching Tanya walk down the sidewalk. "Well, whatever you said obviously worked, dear. That girl just tossed her sling on the grass and took the bandage off her ankle, and now she's walking without as much as a limp."

"*Tifferoo the ball-buster strikes again*," Chip sent over.

Tiffany just smiled.

***

"What the hell do you mean, you were interrupted?" M. Murray Robertson III barked into the phone. "Are you trying to tell me you didn't complete the job you were to be so generously compensated for?"

Sagging in his seat, Keenan V. Durant loosened his collar. He didn't want to look in the rearview and see his reflection because he didn't want to look at failure right now. He'd never considered himself a failure—not until now. Up until now, he'd completed his long list of contracts as planned. Everything had been delivered on time. Not once had anything gone wrong.

He'd never encountered anything like this before and still could not believe what had happened. He had absolutely nothing to say in his defense—nothing that could explain any of this. In all his many years of performing successful contract hits, he'd never before had an issue, nor had he ever expected to have one. When he used his spirit form to turn his mortal essence invisible, nothing could possibly go wrong. There were never witnesses to worry about, never anyone to stand in his way. Not once had he ever been forced to postpone or cancel a contract because someone had stepped into the picture at the wrong time.

Nothing had ever gone wrong in his many years of successfully completing more than two hundred and fifty contract hits.

However, finally, something had.

And now here he was, sitting behind the wheel in the Smart Car, struggling to think of something—*anything*—he could say that would convince his employer he was not totally at fault in this case. He needed *some* sort of a defense. Mr. Robertson was an extremely powerful man; he could easily make one simple phone call that would start the ball rolling to send Keenan back down to the Dark Place.

"Are you still there?" Mr. Robertson was waiting. Keenan could tell by the sound of his voice that his employer wasn't about to wait much longer.

"I'm…still here, sir…"

"Well, what's your explanation? This job was to be wrapped up in an hour. My colleague is scheduled to fly to Europe very shortly. He doesn't want this irritation hanging over his head!"

"I understand, sir."

"I'm glad you understand. That makes this even easier. So you understand. What, then, are you going to do about it?"

"This will be taken care of by this evening, sir."

"This *evening*?"

"Yes, sir. I have my mail route to think about—"

"Your mail route doesn't concern us. You were given an important job. You botched it up."

"No disrespect, but I didn't botch it up, sir. As I said before, I was interrupted."

"And because of this…interruption…you were unable to complete this job?"

"Yes, sir."

A pause. "What exactly was the nature of this so-called interruption?"

Keenan took a breath and collected his thoughts. At least the man was patient and understanding enough to want to hear what happened… "Someone else stepped into the picture, sir."

"How so?"

"I was about to complete the job. In fact, I was two seconds away from turning her into—"

"I'm not interested in what *almost* happened. Tell me what *did* happen."

"Someone distracted the girl. It was extremely sudden and unexpected."

"Go on…"

"This person…she just stepped into the picture and walked away with the Caldwell girl."

"Just who *is* this person you're talking about?"

"Her name is Sedarski, sir. At least, that's what her mother's name is. She's the daughter, and—"

"This Sedarski woman... You're telling me she just whisked Caldwell away? Just seconds before you were able to complete the job?"

"Yes, sir."

"Did you hear any of the conversation?"

"I was right there, sir. They didn't see me, of course, but I heard every single word."

"Tell me what they said."

"It actually sounded very innocent. The Sedarski girl—young lady, sorry—walked right over and told Caldwell that it was much too dangerous to cross traffic in her condition, and that she and her mother could take her wherever she wanted to go."

"Where was Sedarski when this interruption happened?"

"She and her mother had just passed by in a silver Honda."

"And they obviously stopped."

"Yes, sir."

"And then she just got out of the car and walked right up to the girl?"

"Actually, she ran."

"Ran?"

"Yes, sir."

"Why?"

"I don't know, sir. As I said, the Honda was going by. Then it stopped about halfway down the block. There was a traffic jam, and then—"

"All right, the car stopped. Then what?"

"The Sedarski woman got out and started yelling at Caldwell. Then, as I just said, she ran up and started talking to the girl, and then they went back to the Honda and got in."

"What else?"

"That was it, sir."

"And you say they were talking about safely crossing the street?"

"Yes, sir."

"And then Sedarski offered Caldwell a lift?"

"Yes, sir."

"You're right. It does sound innocent. I'm a little concerned why Sedarski was yelling, but that really doesn't matter. Whatever she did botched up the works."

"Yes, sir."

"Anything about this Sedarski woman we should be concerned about?"

"I don't think so, sir…"

"Why'd you call her a "girl"?"

"She's young, sir."

"How young?"

"Early twenties."

A pause. "Could she possibly be a high school chum of Caldwell's?"

"I don't think so. They didn't seem to know one another."

"Describe Sedarski."

"Blue-eyed. Slim figure. Lots of curly blond hair. She's…a real, er, knockout, sir."

Silence.

A moment later, Mr. Robertson said, "You have until eight o'clock tonight to finish this job."

"That should be more than—"

"If Caldwell is not eliminated by eight o'clock, I'll be forced to find someone else."

"I understand, sir…but that really won't be—"

"Call me when the job is finished." Then he hung up.

Keenan V. Durant stuck the cell back into his shirt pocket and waited for his nerves to settle down. Then he started up the car and eased away from the curb.

CHAPTER 13

They reached the Peoria Marriott Pere Marquette a little after ten. Double parking, as well as a flurry of activity on the sidewalk in front, caused some congestion. A few spaces in front of the building on the next block provided sufficient parking.

Momma parked in one of the three available spaces. She was about to get out when Tiffany said, "It's all right, Momma. We'll only be a couple of minutes."

"It's no trouble, dear. I don't mind stretching my legs."

"We'll be back in five minutes—I promise."

"But—"

"Please stay here, Momma..."

Momma sat back in her seat and rubbed her temples.

"What's wrong, Momma?"

"I...suddenly feel light-headed. I guess I needed more than two pieces of buttered toast and coffee for breakfast."

"Just wait here and relax, all right? We'll be right back."

Momma nodded and leaned back against the head rest.

"That was cruel, Tifferoo," Chip said as they went down the walk leading to the building's entrance. "Doing a job on your own mother?"

“Oh, stop. Do you really want her watching how we magically turn two discarded boxes into luggage?”

“Discarded boxes? And just where are we gonna find those?”

“The kitchen, silly.”

“What kind of discarded boxes?”

“Does it matter?”

“What kind of discarded boxes would we be looking for in a hotel kitchen?”

“As I just said, it doesn’t matter—not if we’re gonna change them into something else…”

“But how do you know they’ll even *have* discarded boxes?”

“They will, believe me.”

“How can you be so sure?”

“I spent a little time in hotels when I was alive. Hotels always seem to have stuff like that—“

“That’s right. You made some of those naughty movies when you were in Hokeywood.”

She swatted him sharply on the shoulder.

“*Ow*! That *hurt*!” Grimacing, he grabbed his shoulder.

“How many times must I tell you? I didn’t make *any* of those…well, those…you know what I mean.”

“All righty. I believe you…and *ow!”* He gingerly rubbed his shoulder.

“As I was saying, I know a little about hotels. They get food deliveries, office supplies, furnishings… Trust me, they’ll have boxes lying around. And don’t forget—you were the one who suggested this in the first place.”

Chip massaged his shoulder and continued looking clueless.

"Don't act stupid, now. You were in a fancy hotel not too long ago. Don't you remember? Disney Village?"

"Actually, all I remember was squeezing into that stupid dress that chafed the hell out of my pits. That, and the look on that horny old goober's face when I showed him my equipment."

"I really wish you'd quit harping on that. I should think your pits had healed long ago."

"It was very traumatic, anyway."

"You can be quite a whiner, you know."

"You asked."

"Believe me, I'm already regretting it."

The ornate lobby was reasonably busy, but far from packed. Several small groups flocked the center of the huge, highly-lit area, reading local maps, checking out the brochures and having quiet discussions. Tiffany and Chip crossed the room and began looking at the signs that led to different areas of the hotel.

Wanting to speed things up for Momma's sake, Tiffany walked up to the man at the desk.

"May I help you?" he asked, smiling pleasantly. His golden name plate said *ART*. Tiffany's first reaction was that the man looked vaguely familiar. He was about her age, nice-looking, clean-shaven, tall and slender. His dark hair was slicked back. He had bushy black brows and black-framed glasses. He glanced at Chip and immediately turned his attention back to Tiffany.

"Where's your kitchen?" she asked.

He didn't reply at first. He kept staring at her, squinting as if trying to focus.

"Is something wrong?" she asked.

He smiled. "Excuse me…but aren't you Tiffany Sedarski?"

"Yes I am. Do I know you?"

"I'm not sure you remember me, but I used to sit behind you in English class in eleventh grade. I'm Art Hollister. I—"

"I remember. How are you, Art?"

"Fine. Just fine. I never thought I'd ever see you again in person. Last I heard, you'd gone to Hollywood and were making commercials."

Tiffany shrugged. "I did make several, but I left Hollywood a few months ago."

"Really? I thought you were doing fine. I think I might have even seen you in a lipstick commercial."

"I did two of them, but those jobs were few and far between."

"That's a real shame. You looked sensational in them." He reddened. "Not that you don't look sensational anyway…"

Tiffany smiled. "Thanks, but commercials like that are really meticulously put together. I wore a ton of makeup, and they're very good with lighting. They also have an airbrush artist to take any imperfections out of the final prints."

Art shook his head. "I didn't see any."

She could tell Chip was looking silly again. She ignored him. "Those guys are good."

He remained smiling. "Maybe…but I still don't see any."

Tiffany reddened.

"*You two want a room?*" Chip sent over.

"*Oh, stop.*"

"I guess you know I had a *huge* crush on you back in high school," Art said softly.

"No, I didn't know."

"Are you, well…I mean…is there a husband? Boyfriend?" He didn't glance at Chip.

"What am I?" Chip shot over. *"Chopped liver?"*

"I'm not attached or anything," she said, "but my friend and I aren't going to be staying long in town."

"Really? That's a shame." Art looked sad.

She thought it best to move on. "Could you please tell us where we can find the kitchen?"

"The *kitchen*?" He acted like he'd never heard of such a request.

"Yeah," Chip threw in. "It's the big shiny room where they usually keep the food. There's probably a freezer in there, an oven, a bunch of sharp knives hanging from the wall, and—"

"*Stop it*!" she sent over.

He shut up instantly.

Art gazed at Chip. She could tell he was trying to decide if Chip was being a smartass.

"Actually, we need two empty boxes," she said. "And since we were passing by the hotel—"

"What kind of boxes? Any particular size?"

"Any size'll do, actually."

"I think I might have two in my office. We just got a shipment of FAX paper in this morning. Can you wait a second?"

"Sure."

"Be right back." He hurried over to the door marked *OFFICE.*

Chip giggled.

"What's so funny?" she asked.

"Art, huh?"

"Don't even go there."

Chip giggled again. "A *huge* crush? Art and Tifferoosky? Sounds kind of catchy—"

"You can stop your nonsense right now."

"Tiffany Sedarski Hollister." He looked serious. "That just rolls right off the—"

"*Please* don't make me turn you back into that stupid flower. You'll look really silly, sitting in a big pot in front of the window…"

***

Art returned two minutes later carrying two white office supply boxes folded flat under his arm. He slid them onto the desk. "Will these do?"

"They're just fine," Tiffany said. "Thanks, Art. We really appreciate this."

"I don't suppose I'll get to see you again before you leave town?"

Tiffany sent him a sparkling smile. "One never knows."

He lit up. "Well then, in case I don't, it was really great to see you again, Tiffany."

"Nice seeing you, too, Art. And thanks again for the boxes."

Just as they left the lobby, Tiffany said, "Let's change them now, before we start walking back to the car."

"Want me to do it?"

"Sure."

Chip closed his eyes and in seconds, the two boxes turned into two dark-blue pieces of empty luggage covered with pink polka dots and caricatures of farm animals covering most of the center in a wild collage.

He handed over one to Tiffany as they went outside. "Okay with you?"

She stared at both of them, then at him. "*Polka* dots? *Farm* animals? Seriously?"

He grinned. "I thought I'd be spontaneous. Artistic. Inspired."

She didn't reply.

"We *are* illusionists, you know…"

Tiffany still didn't speak.

"Your momma would probably enjoy a collage of farm animals and—"

Frowning, Tiffany pointed to the luggage.

He blinked. "Lemme guess. You want me to change my works of art into something more mundane and slightly boring?"

"No, I want you to get rid of the polka dots and the farm animals."

"What about my inspiration? My spontaneity? My lust for my artistic expression?"

"Quit being a butthole and just do it."

Sighing, he took both of them, placed them on the sidewalk and turned them both olive-green, with no images or polka dots.

She looked them over quickly. "Much better."

Chip looked like he was about to be sick. "But…they're so…*blah*!"

"In this case, *blah* is good." She picked up one.

"Just make sure your Momma doesn't handle them. I can make them look like suitcases but I can't change their weight."

"I think I could've figured that one out on my own, thanks."

They got back in Momma's Honda and placed their luggage on the back seat, beside Chip.

"Any trouble at the desk?" Momma asked.

"No trouble at all, Momma."

"Tifferoo could've gone on a date if she wanted to," Chip said, giggling. "Flowers, candy, a luscious evening gown—even a nifty corsage and perhaps a rented limousine with pipe-in music—"

"*I'm going to kill you,*" she sent over.

"Really, Baby?"

"Just some guy who remembered me from high school, Momma. It was no big deal."

As Momma pulled out, Tiffany shot him a look. "*Slowly and painfully,*" she added.

***

Keenan V. Durant got the call from M. Murray Robertson III shortly after one, about fifteen minutes after he'd finished his route for the day.

Keenan practically dropped the phone when he saw the name on the display. The only thing he could think of was that his employer had changed his mind and decided to use someone else to take care of the Caldwell girl. If this happened, he'd be sent back down to the Dark Place and would stay there forever. The Legion of Demons didn't tolerate failure.

It took all his inner courage to press the phone against his left ear and hold it steady, without dropping it. "Y-Yes, sir?"

"This must be your lucky day," Mr. Robertson said flatly.

Had he heard the man correctly? Had Mr. Robertson just said the word "lucky?" Or was Keenan's imagination working overtime? "Sir? Would you care to repeat—"

"The Caldwell girl. It seems that she's changed her mind about the whole business."

Once again, Keenan wondered if he'd heard the man correctly. "Changed her *mind*?"

"For some reason I can't understand, the girl decided against using her attorney to bilk money from my colleague for that stupid fender-bender. Do *you* know anything about this?"

"N-No, sir…"

"You're *sure* you had nothing to do with this?"

Keenan realized that this could be the perfect opportunity to regain his position—as well as his respect—with his employer, as well as with the League. But since he had absolutely no idea what was going on, any false claims he made would arouse suspicion—especially if Mr. Robertson or any of the other members became inquisitive. "I haven't seen her since the Sedarski woman snatched her away from me, sir."

"Haven't talked to her on your cell?"

"I wouldn't have any reason to, sir…"

"I guess you wouldn't." A pause. "Well, something obviously convinced her to change her mind… And since it happened so suddenly, I figured she might have been frightened off."

This sounded very strange. "What exactly happened, sir?"

"I got a call from Ron Alsworth not ten minutes ago. He said the girl's attorney contacted his attorney and said she'd changed her mind and no longer wanted to go ahead with a criminal case."

"So I guess that means she decided to stick to Small Claims?"

"That's the kicker. Judging by what I was told, the girl doesn't want to take this *anywhere*."

"Really?"

"As I just said, she was either scared off or developed a couple of legitimate brain cells since you came so close to turning her into a highway statistic this morning."

"This is very odd…"

"I'll say."

"So you'll still want me to go through with the contract?"

"There's no need for that now, is there?"

"But sir…a contract is a contract—"

"Normally, yes. But in this case, you're finished with her—agreed?"

"But—"

"No need to eliminate someone who's no longer a threat, is there?"

"No, sir..."

"Eliminating someone needlessly would not only be foolish, it would also arouse unwanted attention. We surely don't want that, do we?"

"Of course not…"

"I'll let you know when we'll need your services again."

"Yes, sir—"

The man had already hung up.

Keenan pocketed his phone. A frown took over his features as he shuffled down the street, where the Smart Car awaited him at the end of the block.

The more he thought about it, the more he was convinced that the Sedarski woman was responsible for this. Nothing else made any sense. She was the one who'd interrupted the hit. She was the one who'd taken the Caldwell girl out of the line of fire. She was also the one who'd escorted Caldwell to her mother's car and took her away.

Who knew what she'd told the girl as she and her mother drove away?

She was responsible, and would pay dearly.

She had just cost him five thousand dollars for one hour's work.

And because of her, he nearly lost his flawless reputation with the Royal League.

CHAPTER 14

Tiffany and Chip sat at the dining room table, enjoying coffee and orange juice, while Momma brought over her cell phone from the counter and opened her address book.

"Who are you calling, Momma?" Tiffany asked.

"My very good friend Abby. As I've already said, she handles most of the entertainment functions at the hospital. She's been there quite a while and really knows how to put a shindig together. She was also the lady most responsible for helping me land my job with them in the first place."

"She sounds like a nice lady, Momma."

"She is, dear. You'll love her."

"I can't wait to show off." Chip nibbled on some coffee grounds he'd taken out of the trash when Momma wasn't looking.

"*Just cool it*," Tiffany sent over. "*And* please *wipe your chin. You've got coffee grounds on it*."

"*Now what fun would* that *be?"* he sent back. But he did as she'd suggested.

"We don't want to attract attention to ourselves, do we? I've already spotted one demon in this town. We can't afford to let him get suspicious."

"Are you sure that nerdy mailman's a demon?"

"Yes."

"Just because he made himself invisible?"

Since Momma was busy with her address book, Tiffany sent him over a quick glare. *"How many mortals do you think can make themselves invisible?"*

"Good point, but that still doesn't mean we can't show off for the kids."

"As long as we stick to basics, we'll be fine."

"Basics?"

"Things that don't look too fantastic."

"Name one thing I do that's too fantastic."

"Your head-spinning thing."

"I don't consider that—"

"Any mortal would consider it fantastic—and suspicious."

"I guess that raises a valid point..."

"And your tongue thing—especially when you let it drop all the way to the floor while you're crossing your eyes."

"Those are two *things."*

"I just don't want you assuming that only one of those is off-limits."

"Bummer. I really like my head-spinning thingy. It amazes people."

"It also scares them. As I just said, mortals can't do things like that. You don't have spinal disks to worry about. Mortals do. Any mortal trying that would snap his neck into a million pieces. We'll be playing to children here. Don't forget that. And whatever you do, please *don't fart when you've finished. It's gross, for one thing. And as I just said, our audience will be children."*

"Tiffers, you're really no fun at a party."

Tiffany sent him another quick glare. *"Need I remind you that the last time I went to a party, some horny idiot gave me a drink that killed me?"*

"Oops...I guess I forgot—"

"Abby?" Momma sat back and smiled. "This is Sandra. I'm calling to let you know—"

A pause.

"She's doing just fine, thanks."

Another pause.

"Yes. She really is just as beautiful as those photos I showed you."

"Oh, Momma..." Tiffany reddened.

Another pause.

"Five years, actually."

Another pause.

"I know, and yes, she's just as sweet as ever—and after several years in *Hollywood*. Anyway, I'm calling to tell you that she came back with a friend she worked with out there, and both of them have become professional illusionists."

Another pause.

Momma laughed. "Yes, I know. Isn't that strange? She went to Hollywood to become an actress and now she's an illusionist..."

A pause.

"Very. Both of them are. I guarantee they'll have you enthralled. Listen...I was wondering if you'd like to have them come over in the next couple of days to entertain the children."

Momma went silent for a few moments. Then she sighed. "No, of course not." She placed her free hand over the phone. "You won't charge the hospital a fee, will you, dear?"

"Of course not, Momma."

"No, Abby. Tiffany said they'll do it for free."

A pause.

Once again, she cupped her hand over the phone. "She said she'd love to have us come over tomorrow at around four. Will that be all right?"

"That's fine, Momma."

"We'll be there, Abby."

***

Keenan V. Durant sat in the Smart Car across the street from the Sedarski condo on NE Glen Oak Avenue.

The mother's silver Honda was parked in front of the garage. However, there was no sign of activity anywhere outside. The drapes were drawn in all the windows, making it impossible to see what was going on inside.

He checked his watch. It was 4:10. Hard to decide what to do when he had no idea what the Sedarski girl was up to. He was still trying to figure out why she'd walked over to the Caldwell girl at the most inopportune time and scooped her away. The way everything happened was entirely too suspicious to dismiss.

Had she seen him? There was no way. No one could see him when he was invisible. No mortal, that is…

Yet, some nagging inner sense told him *something* strange had happened…

He wondered if the redheaded guy had been with her. Keenan hadn't been able to see anyone else in the Honda, but that didn't mean anything.

The redhead could have been sitting in the back seat on the driver's side.

He decided to start with what few facts he knew and work from there. As far as he could figure, the Sedarski girl had been away for some time. Otherwise, she would have known about the mother's husband being dead. This could be a simple homecoming, and the redhead was just a friend the daughter had brought along with her.

In any event, he had to do something about this. He couldn't tolerate anyone coming to town and messing up the natural order of things. It had taken him years to build up his reputation with the League. He knew how easy it would be to ruin it.

There was no way Keenan V. Durant would let someone come to town and upset his livelihood. She'd already cost him five big ones; he wasn't going to let her get away with that. Who knew what Mr. Robertson or the League thought about this? If they lost confidence in him, they'd simply send fewer jobs his way. And once he no longer had mortal support, he'd be sent back down.

There was only one thing he could do about this. He had to get the girl out of the picture. And if the mother got in the way, he'd have to do something about her, too. The redhead would pose no problem; he seemed harmless.

Keenan got out of the compact and crossed the street. Turning invisible, he snuck up to the front walk and moved closer to the bushes. Then he cut across the narrow piece of lawn separating the properties, until he reached the rear of the building.

Hearing nothing, he tiptoed over to the back door and listened.

***

While Momma was rinsing out the cups in the kitchen sink, Tiffany slipped into the living room, closed her eyes and changed into a red tee shirt, tan Capri's and a pair of light-blue open-toed sandals with two-inch heels and silver sequins running along the length of the outside. Then she went over to the couch and sat down.

"Nice, Tifferoo." Chip nodded approvingly. "Very stylish."

"Aren't you going to change? Momma will think you're a slob if you stay in the same outfit."

"Righterino. Coming right up." Chip waved an arm over himself, which simply changed the colors of his outfit. "*Voila*!"

Tiffany just shook her head.

"What's wrong? Not enough flair? Not enough elegance or style?"

"None of the above, actually."

He arched a brow. "Last time I used my imagination and artistic flair, you yelled at me."

"That was different."

"Howzat?"

"That was luggage. This is clothing we're talking about."

He stared at her in silence.

"You have no idea what I'm talking about, do you?" she asked.

"Not a clue."

"Just change your outfit, okay?"

While he watched her, farm animals suddenly covered his top.

She shook her head. "What is it with you and farm animals?"

"I like the way they treat flowers." He shrugged. "Well? Do I get rid of them again?"

"If you're so set on farm animals, go right ahead. I really don't care."

"Thanks, Tifferoo."

"Just turn the cow around, all right? I'd rather see her face, rather than her butt and that thing in the middle."

"That's an udder, Tifferoo."

"I know what an udder is, thanks. I just don't want to be looking at it when I talk to you."

"No problemo." The cow's hind end suddenly became her face. She was smiling. "Better?"

"The smile's a little silly, but I guess it's all right…"

He sat down in the chair facing the couch. "What do we plan on doing at the hospital, by the way? I may be a little off-base, but I'm pretty sure we won't be able to do anything scary or gross to entertain sick kids…"

"Thanks very much for pointing that out."

"I'm not as uncouth as you think…sometimes."

"I know all about your sporadic bursts of couthness, thanks. And by the way, no, I have no idea what we can possibly do to entertain sick children."

"We've got to think this out before your momma takes us there tomorrow."

"Really? How about that?"

"My, we sure are cranky…"

"I'm just nervous. I don't want Momma to get suspicious, and I sure don't want to do anything to jeopardize her job—or her standing in the community."

"I hear ya." He ruffled his hair and looked pensive for a second. "Maybe we could get away with doing some of your boyfriend's routines he did in Pittsburgh."

"You mean Jimmy Russo?"

"Yepperino. Him."

"Maybe—and he's not my boyfriend."

"You don't remember the way he looked at you?"

"Of course I remember."

"You don't think he—"

"It's not important anymore, is it? Especially since he can't even remember me."

"I was only trying to—"

"I know what you were only trying to do. Let's get back to our act."

"All righty…"

"Anyway, I was thinking of his bouncing-ball trick. The one he did out in the street."

"Sorry, but I was knocked out at the time. When you're knocked out, you don't get to see too much going on around you."

"He pulled these little rubber balls out of his pocket and made them bounce away from him. There must've been dozens of them. Then he made a tiny flame appear over them as they bounced down the street."

"Flaming bouncing balls?"

"It made quite a hit. It was also very distracting."

"I was thinking more of those birds he set loose on the demon guy."

"I guess we could do birds… Doves, maybe… Kids like doves because they're pretty and gentle, and aren't scary."

Chip frowned. "One drawback about that..."

"What's that?"

"I don't think we'll be able to keep them from dumping shit on the kids' heads…"

"Well, duh…"

"It would be entertaining, though."

"You're sick."

"And you're a slow learner, Princess."

Momma came into the living room. "I hope I'm not interrupting anything. I just came in to tell you dinner will be ready in…" Then she stopped and stared curiously at them.

"Something wrong, Momma?"

"When did you two change clothes? I didn't hear you go upstairs."

Chip chuckled. "Did you forget already? We're illusionists."

"What does that have to do with—"

Grinning, Chip waved his hand, and the cow on his shirt uttered a soft, "*moo...*"

"My God!" Momma shook her head. "You two really *are* fantastic!"

"It's nothing…" Chip's tiny green eyes twinkled. "When you're a genius, anything's possible…"

"You're sick," Tiffany said. "And *so* boring..."

"Well, as I just started to say, dinner will be ready in about an hour. I'm gonna make coffee. You may join me if you like. Would you like some?"

"Sure, Momma. Chip?"

"Any orange juice?"

Momma laughed. "Now why didn't I think of that?" Then she went back into the kitchen.

Tiffany got up and followed her into the kitchen.

And froze.

The mailman, as translucent as he was earlier that morning, was standing in front of the refrigerator, watching Momma walk over to the coffeemaker.

"You coming in, dear?" Momma turned and went over to the refrigerator. The hazy figure of the mailman stepped quietly aside just as she reached for the handle to open the door. Momma obviously didn't see him or sense his presence. "It should be ready in just a couple of minutes."

"One moment, Momma… I need to remind Chip of something." Forcing herself to stay in control, Tiffany turned around and went back into the living room. She walked right over to where Chip was sitting.

"What's wrong?" he asked softly.

She took several deep breaths before she was able to respond. Then she immediately sent her thoughts plummeting into the thick red thatch, making him slam the back of his head against the back of the armchair.

"There's a demon in the kitchen with Momma, and we've got to do something about it right now!"

He sat forward and gently massaged the back of his head. *"Are you sure?"*

"Of course I'm sure!"

"What's it doing with her?"

"Nothing...yet. She can't see him."

"*Invisible?*"

She felt her composure crumbling. "*Yes! Invisible!*"

Chip tilted his head. "*That same demon you saw with the Tanya chick? The wimpy mailman?*"

She nodded.

Chip got up. His eyes were on the archway. "*Any ideas?*"

"*Yes! We've got to get him out of the house!*"

CHAPTER 15

Standing invisible in the Sedarski woman's kitchen, Keenan V. Durant watched the daughter come in and suddenly stop just a foot or so beyond the doorway.

"You coming in, dear?" The mother made her way for the refrigerator. "It should be ready in just a couple of minutes."

"One moment, Momma… I need to remind Chip of something."

The daughter turned around and went back into the living room.

The mother opened the refrigerator door. Keenan sidestepped to stay out of her way. She pulled out a large carton of orange juice, closed the door and went over to the tiny table in front of the window in the dining area. Moments later, the daughter and her red-headed friend came in. Both were acting kind of quiet. He wondered if they were having some sort of spat.

What they were doing didn't matter. The only thing that did matter was that he was going to act very quickly. If he had to start things rolling with the mother, that's how this would have to be played out.

The mother poured orange juice into a large glass. She set the carton down and then went back to the counter to get the coffee ready.

This put her in a vulnerable position. By gently tapping her elbow, he could make her spill her cup. This would be no different from the hundreds of other accidents he'd caused during the last ten years. She'd consider his "tap" nothing more serious than a muscle twitch and would spill the hot brew all over herself. And when the daughter rushed over to help, he'd direct his shoe into her path.

If he worked this just right, the three of them would be the victims of a horribly weird accident.

He considered himself a master at staging weird accidents. He'd caused some doozies since he'd come back up from the Dark Place. As the result of his subtle interference, people had tripped over their own two feet, turned an ankle at the wrong time, pressed the gas pedal instead of the brake, electrocuted themselves when breakers were mysteriously switched back on, misjudged the number of rungs on a ladder, and placed their home protection revolvers too close to their alarm clocks. Some had developed a sudden spasm as they approached a helicopter or stepped between moving vehicles at the wrong time. Others had tripped and fallen down steps, stalled on the railroad track in the path of a speeding train, found themselves trapped in a falling elevator, got a loose shoe lace caught in an ascending escalator and taken the wrong dosage of pain medications.

Keenan V. Durant was the master of the freak accident. He'd worked his magic in nearly half of the fifty states over the last century. He had few peers. Unlike other demons, whose arsenals included mind transfer, manipulation, shape-shifting and distraction, Keenan V. Durant's single ability, the art of invisibility, had enabled him to accomplish whatever he wished. And since the Royal League of Peoria had been consistently using his services over the last decade, he was convinced that his one and only ability would be all he'd ever require.

In this case, a coffee spill would be perfect. The mother would slip and fall, taking her cup and the coffeemaker with her on the way to the floor. The same thing would happen to the other two when they went down after her. The domino effect would not kill them, but as long as he got the daughter out of the picture, he'd be satisfied.

Thirty years ago he'd made an Alabama horse farrier slip and fall on a few carefully rearranged hoof shavings. Once the big, heavily-muscled gorilla went down, Keenan calmly walked over and forced the man's anvil to topple off the table. Luckily, it was a fairly small size, and reasonably easy to tip over. Even so, it killed the man instantly when it mashed onto the back of his head.

In this case, knocking over the coffeemaker would make things even more complicated. It would cause a wet, slippery mess on the floor and add to the chaos. When the redhead came over, he'd trip and fall onto the daughter and the mother. Once the threesome began squirming, a simple kick to the daughter's temple would complete the deed. It would look like a legitimate accident, and no one would be the wiser.

Confident of his plan, Keenan V. Durant was good to go.

Just as the mother turned away from the coffeemaker with her fresh hot cup, Keenan silently moved toward her. All he had to do was reach out and lightly tap the mother's elbow.

But just then, the daughter came right over.

"Momma, can I borrow the car keys? Chip and I have to do a quick errand. I'm sorry, but it just can't wait."

***

"What are you talking about, dear?" Momma asked. "I'm ready to prepare dinner…"

"I know, Momma. And I promise this won't mess up dinner. But this is sort of an emergency. We'll be back long before dinner."

"What is it, dear? Maybe I can help. We can have dinner, then—"

"It's my fault, Ma'am," Chip said. "I think I might have left something in my room at the hotel."

"But—"

"It won't be a problem, Momma." Tiffany forced herself to keep her gaze on her mother. It was extremely difficult to ignore the hazy figure of the man standing next to the refrigerator. Tiffany had to situate herself directly in front of Momma so she wouldn't see him and inadvertently give herself away. "We'll be back within the hour. Then we can have dinner…"

"I just don't think you'll be able to drive to the hotel, find what you want, and return in time—"

"I promise we won't be late for dinner, Momma. We wouldn't leave if we didn't have to."

"Baby, can't you just call them and—"

"It's kind of a sensitive issue," Chip said softly.

"Really?"

Tiffany was pleased that he wasn't resorting to his usual silliness. It showed a side of him she hadn't actually seen before.

"All right, then." Momma turned back to Tiffany. "I'll hold off on dinner until you get back." She went over to the nook and picked up her keys. The demon backed away so she wouldn't accidentally bump into him. Momma handed her the keys. "Be careful, dear. People are driving crazy nowadays."

Tiffany smiled. "Momma, I lived in California for five years. It doesn't get much worse than how they do things out there."

"Be careful, anyway."

"Yes, Momma." Tiffany went over to the back door. The mailman was standing just off to the side as she opened the door. It took all the willpower she could muster to refrain from elbowing him in the face and kicking him in the groin before she went outside. She knew she couldn't do anything like that in front of her mother. If Momma even suspected an invisible demon was standing in the room with them, she'd freak out.

She just hoped she was right about this—that the demon was targeting her, and not Momma. If Tiffany was wrong, she and Chip would have to come right back and figure out some other way of luring the demon out of Momma's house.

Tiffany turned on her way down the walk and risked a glance at Chip. Just as Chip grabbed the door to close it, the mailman slipped quickly in front of him and hurried in her direction. *Good. He's targeting me—not Momma.* She turned back around and made her way toward the front, where Momma's car was parked.

Just as she opened the driver's door, Chip opened the passenger door. The mailman stood off to the side, obviously confused. He couldn't possibly get in the front with the two of them.

Just as Chip was about to get in, Tiffany said, "You'd better sit in back."

Chip just looked at her.

"*He needs to get in, too*," she sent over. "*He's standing right beside you.*"

"I guess I need to make this sound legit."

"Please try."

He nodded knowingly. "Still a little pissed about this morning?"

"Shouldn't I be?"

"I thought we were buds."

"That doesn't mean you're entitled to paw all over me!"

"I can't help it, Tifferoo. I've got two paws." He held up his hands. "And you've got two—"

"I'd watch it if I were you!"

"That's my problem. I've been watching *both* of them."

She frowned. "I don't want you watching them while I'm driving. You'll distract me. I might get both of us killed."

"Ah…I guess you've got a point."

"You know I do."

"So you want me in the back?"

"Definitely."

He closed the front door, opened the rear door and stood there a moment. "You really know how to hurt a guy, Tifferoo."

"Only when you need it," she said as the mailman slid silently into the back.

"*You can get in now.*" Then she turned toward the front.

Chip slipped into the back and pulled the door shut.

CHAPTER 16

The plan had changed.

Keenan suddenly realized that he had just been given an even more effective method of getting rid of the Sedarski girl.

Right now she was looking right at him—well, almost—as she backed her mother's car out of the drive. Then she turned to face the front and pulled away, heading west, toward North Indiana and Main.

The redhead sat beside him, gazing out the side window but saying nothing. Keenan wondered if he should be suspicious but realized that the girl was still peeved at the redhead for groping her earlier.

Nothing odd about that, was there?

In fact, he couldn't see *any* sane man who *wouldn't* want to grope such a fine-looking lady…

But this was no time for distractions. The important thing was that he was close enough to her right now to do the deed without any complications. It wouldn't be much of a problem to reach out and snap her neck while she was occupied with her driving. The most sensible method was to wait until they'd stopped at an intersection, *then* do her in. Once she was out of the picture, he'd overpower the redhead as well. Then, still invisible, he'd simply get out of the car and walk away before the police showed.

He situated himself directly behind her and gazed at her reflection in the rearview. She certainly was beautiful. It was a shame he had to pull her plug. But this was necessary. She'd cost him five thousand bucks. He couldn't let her off the hook. He had his pride to think of.

When they were halfway down the block, he eased forward in his seat. Her hair smelled like lavender and flowers. He closed his eyes and thought about what sort of vision she'd be in bed. That hair strewn out from the pillow, like golden feathers... Those luscious breasts… Those big blue eyes staring up at him… Those lips—

Focus, he told himself. Reluctantly he sat back and forced himself to concentrate on his plan.

He decided to wait until the right moment, then touch her right shoulder very lightly. The moment she turned, he'd reach around the neck rest and twist her head sharply. She was probably around five-six and weighed around one-twenty. She didn't appear to be very strong; performing the deadly move should be easy. Her neck was so delicate and swanlike; he didn't anticipate any difficulty.

Just as they approached the intersection, he moved forward again and prepared himself for the business at hand. But before he could touch her shoulder, she glanced at the rearview. "Once we get to the hotel, I think I'm gonna park somewhere in the back."

"Any special reason why, Tifferoo?"

"Last time we were there, it was almost impossible to find a vacant spot out in front on Main Street. There are only so many spots in front of the building, and most of its valet parking. Since we're kind of short on time, I figure it'll be easier to get inside through the back."

"And it'll get us closer to our room."

"Besides, there should be more parking back there. And if the cleaning crew's out in the hall, we can ask them if anyone found your necklace."

"Hope so. That necklace is old. My grandmother's great-great-grandmother gave it to me. I hope no one stole it."

"We could offer a reward…"

"How much do you have on you, Tifferoo?"

"About a hundred dollars."

"I've got maybe fifty. That should be enough."

"Hope so…"

They stopped at the intersection.

Keenan sat back. Since they'd be parking behind the hotel, he might have an even better opportunity to nail them without an audience. As soon as she parked the car, he could do the deed and get away without anyone noticing. If he pushed the visors down and made sure the Honda was parked a fair distance away from the hotel, it could be hours before the bodies were discovered.

Fifteen minutes later, they went past the entrance of the Marriott and turned right. Using the Fulton Street entrance, she slowed down, cut toward the back and eased down the aisle, until they were fairly close to the rear entrance of the building.

It was a little close for comfort, but he could work with that. All the windows were drawn. If anyone was snooping, he couldn't see any signs.

A minute later, she pulled into a parking space fairly close to the building, stopped abruptly, put on the emergency brake and switched off the engine.

Keenan moved forward.

Just then, the blonde turned quickly in her seat.

"Hello, Mr. Postman," she said, looking directly into his eyes. "Fancy meeting *you* back there!"

***

"Y-You can…s-*see* me?" Startled, the mailman sat bolt upright in the back seat.

"Of course I can see you. I'd look pretty silly, talking to an empty seat, wouldn't I?"

The figure sitting beside Chip suddenly appeared more distinct.

"I can see him too, Tifferoo," Chip said.

The demon's sudden shock had undoubtedly destroyed his concentration, making him visible again.

This was going to be fun.

"What's wrong, Mr. Postman?" she asked. "Are you so flustered that you've lost your powers?"

He remained sitting bolt upright, his head pulled back. He gulped and sputtered, his jaw quivering as he struggled to speak. "I-I don't…this is…how can this…how can you possibly—"

"Would you like to know how I can see you when no one else can?" she asked.

He swallowed audibly and fidgeted. "Y-Yes…I don't…this is just so…so—"

"Let me put it this way, Mr. Postman. I can see you even when you're invisible, and I know what you are and what you tried to do to Tanya Caldwell."

The mailman paled and began trembling.

"And just in case you're wondering…yes, my friend and I know."

He swallowed audibly. "*Know*?"

"We both know you're a demon. And considering the limited powers you have, I'd say you're one of the lowest of inferiors. In your case, a bottom-feeder."

"H-How did…who are…what's…w-what's going *on*?"

"First of all, you need to tell me why you've targeted me."

He stiffened.

"You know exactly what I'm talking about. Why me? Is it because of Tanya? Because I stopped you from killing her?"

Swallowing audibly, he nodded awkwardly.

"I guess I kind of ruined your game, eh?"

"B-But how…why…who are—"

"The only thing you need to know right now is that you're caught. We know who and what you are, and we're not going to let you continue what you've been doing. In fact—"

The mailman twisted to his left and groped frantically for the door handle.

"Chip, do your thing. Now."

"No problemo." Chip instantly turned into his spiritual form, the Cypripedium Calceolus. Just as the mailman succeeded in turning the door handle, the flower drifted over, wrapped its leaves around him and squeezed. The petals brushed the mailman's right cheek. His eyes closed instantly. Then he went limp and fell back in the seat.

Moments later, the flower unraveled from the motionless torso, slithered back to the other side of the seat and turned back into Chip. "It smells kind of ripe in here, Tifferino. Methinks our local mail carrier has just let loose with a thick aroma of some fresh sausage—"

"Obviously." Tiffany opened her window. "Is he out cold?"

The mailman slumped in the seat and did not move. His eyes were closed; he'd obviously fallen into a deep sleep.

Chip checked the inferior's eyelids. "He's colder than a mackerel."

"Good work."

"What did you expect, Tifferoo? Mediocrity?"

"Of course not. When you're not clowning around, making funny noises or acting weird—"

"I get it. So…what's next on the agenda?" Chip regarded the sleeping inferior. "We can't very well cart him to the nearest toxic landfill and send him back down, can we?"

"Even if we knew where the nearest landfill is, it would take too long. Momma will worry if we're not back soon."

"Well, we sure can't do what we did with that bastard in Pittsburgh, can we?"

"No, we can't drive him to the airport and stick him on the next flight to Orlando." Tiffany began studying the unconscious inferior when the idea hit her. "I think I have a much better solution."

"What's that?"

"I could be very wrong, but something tells me his power of invisibility is all he's got."

"You could be right. Otherwise, he would have been able to get away. But we're really not sure, are we?"

She smiled. "What do you think would happen if he lost his power?"

Chip chuckled. "You're a babe, Tifferoo…but you're definitely mean and nasty when you wanna be."

"We're dealing with demons. You know how I feel about them."

"Righterino. If you zap this one, he won't be able to do his shtick anymore."

"Or do anything else to them."

"Great idea…but do you think you can actually take it from him?"

"It's worth a try, isn't it?"

Chip shook his head. "When he comes to—"

"He won't suspect anything."

Chip's tiny green eyes grew. "You're gonna clean out his head and do your thing…without him knowing it?"

"Exactly."

The pointed tips of Chip's ears twitched. "Tifferoo the Demon Buster is back at it!"

Tiffany turned to the unconscious Postman and focused on the broad forehead. "*Can you hear me?*"

A slight nod.

"*All right. Besides invisibility, what other powers do you have*?"

"None," he whispered.

"*None at all*?"

He shook his head.

"*Okay, then. When you leave here, you won't remember anything that happened in this car. You won't remember me, my friend, or my mother. You won't remember coming here. And when you wake up, you won't feel any different. However, one thing will be very different. You won't ever be able to become invisible again. In your own mind, everything will be the same, and you will think you're invisible even though you won't be anymore. But you won't know that because that is one of the things you won't be able to remember. As far as you're concerned, you'll still be the same person you were before, and you'll only remember that Tanya Caldwell walked away from you this morning. But you won't know why, and you won't pursue it...or her...or me...or my friend...or my mother...ever again. Nod if you understand.*"

The Postman nodded.

"*Good. Now go back to sleep and stay that way until you're instructed otherwise.*"

The Postman went limp.

Tiffany turned back around and started up the Honda.

Chip got out, opened the passenger door and slid in beside her. "Think it'll work?"

She eased out of the space and drove out of the rear lot and around the corner. "I think we'll definitely know either way."

"Where are we taking him?"

"Back to Glen Oak."

"And then?"

"He's probably parked somewhere in that area. I'll drop him off a block away from Momma's and tell him to get back to his car and drive back to his own place."

Chip shook his head. "I've never known anyone like you before, Tifferoo. Even when you strip a guy of his powers and dump him back with the wolves, you're really *nice* about it."

"Is that a bad thing?"

He shrugged. "That's just it. I'm not sure."

"At least I'm not a demon."

He chuckled. "Princess, if you were, you'd be the baddest ass of them all."

Tiffany laughed. "Always the charmer…"

CHAPTER 17

Momma was fixing pork sandwiches and cole slaw when Tiffany and Chip came back. Momma looked surprised. "You two weren't gone nearly as long as I thought you'd be. Usually, whenever you have to reclaim something at a hotel, it takes quite a while."

"I told you we'd be back soon, Momma."

Momma d glanced at the wall clock. "But you weren't gone much longer than half an hour…"

"Tifferoo knows how to get people to open up," Chip said.

Momma smiled. "Were you able to find your necklace?"

"Yepperino, Ma'am." He pushed down his shirt collar. A glittering silver necklace showed brightly just below his protruding collarbone and vanished the moment he let go of the collar. "It was right where I left it. On the sink in the bathroom. Right behind the Tums bottle. And beside the soap dish—"

"*Enough*," Tiffany warned.

"You're lucky," Momma said. "Some of those cleaning people aren't very honest."

"People are usually honest with me, Momma." Tiffany smiled as she sat down at the table.

"I can attest to that," Chip said, joining her. "As I just said, folks just open right up and tell Tifferoo everything they know."

"My daughter always had that talent." Momma brought over a large metal bowl filled with cole slaw. “All it takes is one look at those big beautiful blue eyes, and people automatically forget who they are and what they were doing.”

“Oh, Momma… *Please* stop…”

“See there?” Momma laughed. “Even after all these years, she still gets embarrassed whenever someone mentions her attributes.”

“I’ll bet Tifferoo was quite a heart-breaker in high school,” Chip said.

“Now *you* can stop.” Tiffany had had enough.

Chip grinned at her. “*Want me to tell your mom how you’ve become a demon ball-buster while we’re sitting here, having all kinds of ginormous fun and laughs?*”

“*Only if you don’t mind my telling her why a flower is sitting in the chair where you used to be ...*”

“*Touché*…” Chip slumped in his seat.

“Baby?” Momma looked worried as she brought over the plate with the pork sandwiches.

“Yes, Momma?”

“Are you all right?”

“Why do you ask?”

“All of a sudden, you seem upset.” Momma went back to the sink, picked up a jar of sliced pickles and a jar of mayonnaise and brought them over to the table. “And there’s a vein sticking out from the side of your neck I’ve never seen before.”

Tiffany smiled sheepishly. “I’m okay, Momma. I guess I’m just a little hungry.”

“*It takes a lot of energy to de-demonize a demon.*” Chip gave her a devilish wink.

Tiffany shot him one last quick glare as she reached for a bun.

Momma slid the cole slaw over to her. "Tell me something, Baby. Why were you and Chip acting so strange before you left?"

"Strange?" Tiffany sat up in her chair.

"You need to be more specific," Chip said with a grin.

Momma had a sip of coffee. "You both looked like you'd just seen a ghost."

Tiffany spread some mayo onto her bun, placed a couple of pickle chips onto it and tried her best to stay calm.

Chip picked up his glass of orange juice. "*Your momma's no dummy, Tifferoo.*"

She glanced at him. "*That's what I've been trying to tell you since we got here.*"

"I was just hungry, Momma." Tiffany closed her bun and had a nibble. Then she smiled. "This is delicious. I feel better already."

"Me, too," Chip said, dropping a spoonful of cole slaw on his plate.

"Good," Momma said. "Have some pork." She picked up the plate and held it toward him.

"Yes, ma'am." Chip grabbed a pork sandwich and dropped it on his plate. As soon as Momma put the plate down and began fixing one for herself, he positioned his glass of orange so she couldn't see his plate.

Tiffany ate more of her sandwich and glanced at his plate.

It was empty.

***

As Keenan V. Durant crossed the street, he had the strange feeling that something didn't feel right.

What was going on? Why did everything feel so *wrong*?

For one thing, he couldn't remember what he was doing in this neighborhood. His car was parked one street down from Glen Oak. The Caldwell girl lived a block or so north, on North Indiana. From where he was parked, the Caldwell house sat just five minutes away.

But that didn't explain why he was here…

It made no sense. The Caldwell job had been cancelled. Mr. Robertson had just called him a few hours ago, telling him the girl had changed her mind about the lawsuit. Apparently she'd decided not to pursue a pain-and-suffering case and didn't even want to attempt to file the incident with Small Claims. Mr. Robertson said that since she'd no longer become a nuisance, there would be no need to eliminate her.

It had cost Keenan five big ones, but those were the breaks. You didn't question the League, and you didn't go against their orders.

Another job was bound to come up. He'd been averaging twenty-five jobs a year for the last ten years—it wouldn't be very long before he was called again.

So why was he here?

Last he remembered, he'd just finished his mail route and was walking back to the compact. Then he must have started zoning out or daydreaming—as he'd done quite a few times in the past—and simply lost all track of time.

He studied his watch. 5:15. Damn. He'd finished his mail job *hours* ago. And his route ended a couple of miles west of here.

How the hell did he get here? And why was his car parked along the curb in front of an unfamiliar house on this unfamiliar street?

He stopped walking and rubbed his temples. He'd never had a memory problem before—what was happening to him?

Was it stress? Was he tired? Or was he just a little miffed at losing an easy job?

It wasn't your fault. Robertson changed the game plan.

Stuff like that happened. There was no reason to get worked up over it. Similar things had happened dozens of times during the last few years. It would serve no useful purpose to develop an ulcer over such a trivial thing.

Besides, demons didn't develop ulcers; they gave ulcers—as well as hundreds of other maladies—to mortals.

Sighing, he slipped behind the wheel of the Smart Car, pulled out and went up to the end of the block. Then he made a right and another right, came back down Glen Oak and passed a condo with a silver Honda sitting out in front of the garage. Something stabbed at his memory, but he couldn't quite get it together.

It didn't matter. If it wasn't right there, dead-on, it wasn't important.

Moments later, his cell buzzed.

It was Mr. Robertson. "It looks like we've got another job for you."

Keenan grinned. Things were looking up already. The Caldwell fiasco hadn't cost him much time at all. "Just let me know what you want me to do, sir."

"This is kind of a rush job. Will that be a problem?"

"Not at all. How quickly will you need it done?"

"Tomorrow morning will be perfect, as long as it's before lunch. But I need to stress that this one is extremely vital. It concerns a member of the Police Department and has to be done very discreetly."

"I'm your man, sir."

DAY THREE - "THE ILLUSIONISTS"

CHAPTER 18

The next morning, Keenan V. Durant got up early, enjoyed a small breakfast of toast, marmalade and herbal tea, and left his apartment by seven o'clock. Dressed in his postal uniform, he planned to complete his latest job before starting his mail route. Once this bit of business was taken care of, Keenan would drive directly to the Post Office on West Glen and State Street, grab his sack, sort his mail, bundle it all up and begin his daily routine.

Harry Conlin of the East Peoria Police Department had been a Police Sergeant for the last three years and a member of the local Police Force for the last fifteen. He was thirty-nine, had a wife and two teen daughters, and was well thought of in his community and among his peers. He boasted a wealth of friends and had just been assigned to lead a special task force unit to handle drugs coming in through a pipeline that had been traced from Chicago.

"Conlin's going to be a major problem," Mr. Robertson told Keenan the evening before. "The moment he was given his new assignment, Conlin publicly stated that he doesn't care where the pipeline leads or who it involves. He also said he was prepared to arrest and incarcerate anyone involved in the investigations. That's when the flags went up. You see, several of our League members regularly provide designer drugs and other recreational items at our monthly board meetings and quarterly conventions, and many of our multi-million-dollar deals involve certain necessary added incentives. We cannot tolerate any operation—undercover or otherwise—that could jeopardize these crucial deals. Conlin has said that he doesn't intend to lead this task force gently. He's interested only in results, and if he has to take these investigations all the way up to the top of the food chain, this is what he intends to do. This, of course, is totally unacceptable, since most of my friends and colleagues, as well as myself, are sitting at the top of the food chain."

"I can understand why you want him eliminated, sir."

"As I said, we cannot tolerate a police investigation at this point in time. Once Conlin is taken out of the picture, a suitable replacement will take over that section of the Police Department. This replacement owes us several favors. He already knows that these favors will be considered paid in full once he's in place and operating according to our standards."

"Once Conlin is eliminated, what happens to the task force?"

"It will remain in place, of course. However, it will no longer affect us. The new man will be running it somewhat differently. It will appear that he'll be operating just as Conlin had, but the end result will focus on totally different scenarios. Many findings as well as key evidence will be nudged aside or simply made to disappear. To make this sort of thing less conspicuous, other issues will pop up at the most convenient times. This is not by any means anything new. Our Government has been operating this way since the drafting of the Constitution. When Asmodeus was here long before Balberith, he set several of these procedures in place. They've been working splendidly for more than two hundred years—why change them if they still prove efficient?"

"I understand, sir."

"Right now, we need to focus on Conlin. He'll be at the Police Station until nine. I've been told that he's going to spend his lunch hour at the Children's Hospital at St. Francis, on Glen Oak Avenue. He must be taken care of before he can get to the hospital."

"Why the Children's Hospital, sir?"

"His younger daughter has been a patient there for the last week or so. She seems to be suffering from some mysterious malady. We at the League fully understand what's been going on, but we've all sworn an oath to keep this one to ourselves. Conlin goes there several times a week to see her."

"I understand, sir."

"Take care of him. And make it look like an accident. A huge amount of money is riding on this."

"Yes, sir."

"If this goes down as we'd like it to, there will be an additional bonus of five thousand dollars that will be deposited directly into your safe deposit box."

***

After their morning briefing in the Squad Room, Police Sergeant Harry Conlin went down the long, well-lit hall that led to the rear entrance. He was thinking of his daughter Mandy, who'd taken sick over a week ago and had been staying at Children's Hospital ever since. She'd come down with a fever, but that seemed to have subsided over the last couple of days. Even so, she didn't seem to be getting better, and he and wife Felicia were worried. Test after test revealed nothing; the last MRI also showed nothing out of the ordinary. But that didn't matter because something very bad was happening to their precious daughter. The child lacked the strength to get out of bed, and the staff at the hospital had been working around the clock to devote their best efforts to see that she was given the best care.

His cell buzzed. It was Felicia, and she sounded just as tired as she had been since Mandy had taken ill. "Hi, Babe," he said, trying his best to sound cheerful. "Where are ya?"

"I'm about to drive to the hospital," she said. "I'll probably be there most of the day."

"What's going on?"

"Abby Turner called to tell me there would be some special entertainment at the hospital today."

"Entertainment?"

"Apparently two illusionists are in town and have agreed to entertain the kids. Abby said they're very good. I'm hoping they'll be able to raise Mandy's spirits."

"Know any of the details?"

“Abby hasn’t said too much about them. She did say, however, that one of them is the daughter of one of the ladies working in the Business Office. I also heard that this woman’s daughter was a Hollywood actress.”

“And now she’s an illusionist?”

“That’s the rumor. I don’t care where they’re from or what they’ve done before…as long as they can help the children.”

“When will they be there?”

“Abby said between four and five.”

“Hmmm… Well, it’s gonna be a pretty hectic day, but maybe I’ll be able to sneak back this afternoon to catch their act.”

“Mandy’ll love it if we’re both there with her.”

“I know. Take care, Babe.”

“Love you.”

“Back atcha.” Conlin pocketed the cell and forced himself to focus on the morning’s events as he approached his cruiser.

This morning he’d begin his new tactical team’s surveillance of a suspicious shipment of utility vans that had found their way to the loading dock of one of the Sandwich Hut franchises in East Peoria, on Main and Washington.

The Sandwich Hut chain was owned by Samson L. Huitt, one of Peoria’s wealthiest residents. Huitt was a self-made billionaire and had been a major contributor to various charitable organizations, including Children’s Hospital. However, Huitt had also been involved in a political scandal a couple of years back and had squeaked by through the skin of his teeth. Talk coming from the office of the Chief of Police said Huitt had bought his way out of the scandal and also that he'd bought some high-caliber legal protection through the services of one of Peoria's most prestigious judges.

The scandal involved Sandwich Hut's District Manager, who'd been a principal player in a drug bust several years earlier. The man's name was Pablo Harrison, a Mexican-American with a somewhat questionable background. Rumors traced Harrison to a direct tie to the Garza cartel bringing drugs in from Puerto Rico. However, only days after the investigation began, Harrison's financial records—as well as other crucial personal records—mysteriously disappeared and were never seen again.

This told Conlin that the pipeline went way up, and that investigating it was going to piss off several important, well-connected people.

But it didn't matter. Conlin was being paid to do a job and was determined to do it the best way he knew. A crook was a crook; it didn't matter how rich he was or who he got into bed with.

Once assembled, Conlin's tactical team was given a list of possibles to begin its watch. Sandwich Hut was, of course, among the top five on the list. And since there were only two shops in the East Peoria area to focus on, spotting the vans posed no trouble.

Just why a group of more than twelve vehicles was sitting in the back lot was anyone's guess. Conlin's tactical team had been instructed to keep a vigilant watch on suspicious activity and had immediately set up a base to monitor the area. The vans had materialized the night before and hadn't been moved since. Two members of the team had set up in their own observation van and had been watching them the moment they were spotted.

Just as Conlin was about to open the driver's door of his cruiser, his cell buzzed again. It was his partner, Sergeant Joe Weeks, who was in charge of the surveillance team and had pulled an all-nighter behind the UV monitors.

"What's up?" Conlin asked.

"Not much," Weeks said. "Just checkin' in. What's your twenty?"

"I'm just leaving the Station. I should be there in about twenty minutes. No activity at all?"

"None that we can see. We've got eyes on both sides of the lot as well as facin' the vans. Dexter stuck a camera on the back of the building. He squeezed it in next to the line hooked up to the a/c unit. It's about thirty yards away from the loading dock and hidden by the meters, but we can still see what's goin' on if someone sneaks outside and approaches the vans."

"I'm just about to get into my car. Later."

Conlin opened the door to his cruiser and got in. Just as he fired up the ignition, he spotted something across the street. A short, light-boned guy in a postal uniform was standing beside a lime-green Smart Car just off Columbia Street.

The little guy was waving at him.

***

The big cop left the Police Station shortly before nine and went down the long aisle of parked cars that took him to his cruiser.

Ten minutes earlier, Keenan had parked just off of Columbia. From that point on he sat in his car, watching the heavy traffic as well as the activity in the rear parking lot of the James Ranney Public Safety Building, where the Police Department was located.

He'd parked in the perfect spot. The heavy traffic whizzing by made it extremely dangerous to open the door of his car. Anyone stumbling or tripping while approaching or getting out of their vehicle would not have time to get out of harm's way.

The moment Conlin got in his cruiser, Keenan slipped out of the Smart Car and stood between the front of the vehicle and the compact parked in front of him. Seconds later, Conlin's cruiser eased out of the lot, in Keenan's direction. Keenan began waving and hoped he looked pitiful enough to get the cop to stop and ask what was wrong.

Just as the cruiser was about to pull out, Keenan leaned against the side of his car and let his head drop.

The cruiser stopped abruptly. The door opened. Conlin stepped out. "You all right, sir?"

Keenan opened his mouth, but nothing came out. He lowered his head again.

Dodging traffic, Conlin sprinted across the street. Mindful of the passing traffic, the big cop stayed close, studying him for possible injuries. "What's goin' on, sir? You all right? You hurt?"

Keenan took a deep breath and coughed. He placed his hand on his chest and grimaced. "Chest…pain…hard to breathe…" He coughed again. "Can't get…my breath…"

"I think I'd better get you to a hospital." Conlin grabbed him by the arm. Looking both ways, he waited for a break in traffic. When an opportunity presented itself, he helped Keenan across the street, where the cruiser was parked. He then directed him to the passenger's side of the vehicle and, letting him lean against the side of the cruiser, opened the door. He grabbed Keenan around the waist and gently lowered him onto the seat.

Just as Conlin was about to close the door, Keenan whispered, "My little dog…he's in the back seat…poor little guy…can't leave him… Please…*please* get him…he'll panic…he gets so scared…I just can't…I can't leave him by himself—"

"Sure. No problem. But once I bring him back, I've got to notify the hospital. I can get ya there in five minutes."

"Please, Officer…*please*…my dog…"

"Yes, sir. I'll make sure I bring him right back to ya." Conlin turned and got ready to cross the street again.

Turning invisible, Keenan slipped out of the back seat and carefully approached the unsuspecting police officer.

Another thick, fast-moving stream headed their way.

Keenan moved in closer. Just as he was about to push the cop into traffic, he stared at the man's broad back and concentrated on where he should place his hands. The man was close to a foot taller than Keenan and at least a hundred pounds heavier. Conlin would have to be slightly off-balance for the fall.

The left side, most likely. That would make Conlin stumble and perhaps roll out in traffic. The maneuver would also provide Keenan with the biggest advantage.

Keenan took two quick steps to the left. At that same moment, he experienced a brief flash of his zoning-out episode the day before.

What was going on? Why was he suddenly unable to concentrate?

First things first. Push Conlin out into traffic, then try and figure out why you zoned out the day before…

Remember...this simple task could earn you ten big ones...

He couldn't waste any time. The opportunity had presented itself and he had to do it *now*…

He took one last step forward and held out his hands.

In that same instant, the big cop glanced to his left. "What the *hell*…?" Then, using his proven reflexes and professionally trained coordination, he ducked out of the way just as Keenan V. Durant leaped out into traffic.

The sound of screeching brakes shattered the steady roar of the traffic as three fast-moving vehicles whizzed past, running him over.

Everything went dark. A giant jolt of excruciatingly hot pain shot violently through him, vanishing an instant later.

Keenan V. Durant's last sensation was that of falling, falling, falling...

CHAPTER 19

Momma, Tiffany, and Chip arrived at the Children's Hospital precisely at four o'clock that afternoon. A large woman met them at the entrance. She was about five-eight and big-boned, with thick, dark-red hair pulled back and tied in a bun. She looked about Momma's age or a couple of years older. She had light-blue eyes and a pretty smile. She wore a white uniform, and her nametag said *ABBY*. She walked right over to Momma, smiled beamingly and took Momma's hands. "Sandra, I'm *so* glad you could bring your daughter and her friend to see us!" she said in a loud, low-pitched voice.

"They were only too happy to come, Abby."

Abby hugged Momma. Then she pulled away, turned and smiled at Tiffany. "You must be Sandra's daughter. Hi, Tiffany. I'm Abby Turner." She held out her hand.

"Hello, Ms. Turner." Tiffany shook the woman's hand. It was large, strong and warm. "It's very nice to meet you."

"Please…call me Abby." She glanced at Chip. "You must be—"

"The name's Chip, Ma'am." Chip wiggled his ears and shook Abby's hand.

Abby watched Chip's ears in fascination. Her eyes grew.

Laughing, Momma said, "I told you they were amazing."

Abby turned back to Chip. "Hello, Chip. Is that a nickname? Or your full name?"

He shrugged a shoulder. "Everyone calls me Chip. In fact, I've been called Chip for the last century or two."

"*Watch it.*" Tiffany sent him a glare.

"*Just helping with the illusion thingy*," he replied.

"Just don't go overboard."

"Me? Go overboard? Shirley, you gist."

Tiffany sighed deeply and bit her lip.

Abby said, "All righty. Just to let you know what's going on… First of all, we're not gonna waste any time with formalities. I've arranged everything, so you don't have to worry about being paraded over to the Business Office to sign or discuss anything. On the other hand, we don't have much time to waste. Since this was put together very quickly, we're all kind of rushed. In other words, you won't be able to spend much more than an hour or so with the children. Many of them tire easily, and you'll need to be careful to make sure we don't stress them out. We've assembled as many as possible in the rec room down the hall, and they've been waiting for you. Is there anything you might need for your performance?"

"Like what?" Chip asked.

Abby shrugged. "Props? Anything you might require to help with your routine?"

"Props?" Chip tilted his head.

"She's talking about cards or something to juggle," Tiffany said. "Stuff like that. Right, Abby?"

"Well, I was thinking of…" Then she stopped.

A tiny light bulb suddenly appeared a few inches above Chip's thick red hair.

Abby's jaw dropped.

Tiffany smiled sheepishly. "It isn't often that Chip gets an idea. When he does, he likes everyone to know about it."

"You know me *so* well, Tifferoosky…"

Momma and Abby—as well as the four nurses and the half-dozen other hospital workers standing around them—gazed at the light bulb in fascination.

A moment later, the light faded and the bulb vanished.

"Speaking of props…" Chip held out his hand. A deck of cards materialized in his palm. "You mean like this?"

Abby gasped.

"Or how about this?" The cards vanished. Two shiny marbles appeared in his palm, clicking as they kept bumping into each other.

The workers around them applauded.

"*Don't show off so much so soon,*" Tiffany warned.

"*Just want them to see my hand—so to speak…*" He winked.

Abby's eyes had filled the sockets. "My God," she whispered. "I can't wait for the children to see you two in action!" Her eyes remained huge as she gestured toward the hall behind her. "Please. Follow me."

***

A wide, open doorway awaited them at the end of the long, well-lit corridor.

"How many children will be watching us?" Tiffany asked Abby as they went down the hall.

"Well, the hospital has a hundred and twenty-four beds. Many of the children aren't able to be moved, unfortunately. Then we have those who are contagious, so they have to be contained as well. However, we've managed to clear forty of them. These are children who have been brought in with illnesses that don't seem to be contagious. They are presently being treated, and some of them are actually getting marginally better. Others, unfortunately, are not, but they are presently stable."

"We're not talking diseases here, are we?"

"That's just it. We're not sure. Many of the tests done on these children have been inconclusive. Their symptoms are showing up as various forms of flu, but they don't seem to be responding to any of our standard treatments."

"That's odd."

"Extremely."

"And how long have these kids been here?"

"Some of them were brought in close to a year ago."

"A *year*? And they're still here?"

Abby frowned. "I'm afraid so."

"Are they getting *any* better?"

"That's just it. The ones who have been here that long got better after a few weeks, then relapsed."

"So now they're worse?"

Abby shook her head. "Not worse, but certainly not any better. It's baffling, to say the least. You can't imagine how many specialists have been brought in, many of them from Europe, for consultations."

"Well, I hope I can help them feel a *little* better—for a few hours, anyway."

"You're gonna be just fine, Baby," Momma whispered behind them.

Tiffany just nodded. The image of a room filled with sick children tugged at her heart.

The doorway opened into a large crowded room lined with beds.

All eyes were on Tiffany as she followed the nurses and attendants through the doorway.

"Where's your friend?" whispered Abby. Suddenly worried, she turned around and stared down the hall.

"*I'm already in the room, Tifferoo,*" Chip sent over.

"For a minute, I thought you'd deserted me."

"You know me better than that, Muffin. I've never been one to pass up the chance to show off."

"Silly me. What was I thinking?"

"He's not far," Tiffany told Abby, winking at them both as she went in. Then, taking a breath, she passed an island of medical equipment and, stepping carefully over a couple of heavy-duty extension cords, stood in the center of the room. She was a little nervous but told herself this would be okay. Her powers had been growing since she'd come back up from the Dark Place, and there was very little she could not do. And since she'd vowed long ago that she'd use these new powers only to help people, she knew she'd have no problem turning this day into something very special. As she watched the hopeful young eyes staring back at her in wonder and excitement, she told herself that this would be a day these children would remember for a long time to come.

Beds were set up in neat rows. The children lying in their beds had their heads propped up with extra pillows. The ones able to get out of their beds sat on pillows and blankets spread out in a semicircle on the linoleum floor. Many of them were just a few feet from her. They wore their hospital garb and sat looking up at her with hopeful, wide-open eyes. She smiled at every one of them and felt a sadness she hadn't experienced in a long time. Every child in this room was sick; she was going to do her very best to ease their suffering as much as possible. She knew she could do some good, even if it was only for a few minutes, and she promised herself she'd give them a performance they'd never forget. She wasn't a magician, but she remembered the things Jimmy Russo had done in his Pittsburgh act and realized just how little it would take to dazzle the audience—especially when you had the power of real magic at your fingertips. She had no idea what she could actually do, but when that tiny thread of doubt trickled into her head, she remembered the things she'd done since she'd come up from the Dark Place and knew right then that she would not disappoint anyone in this room.

"Hi," she said, smiling brightly. "I'm Tiffany!"

There was some applause. Several kids shouted out, "Hi, Tiffany!"

"I've come here with my friend Chip." She looked around. "Has anyone seen him?"

Silence. More than a dozen kids shook their heads. Every child anxiously scanned the room.

Still smiling, Tiffany lowered her voice. "I'm going to tell you a secret. Chip is actually in this room, but no one can see him. Does anyone know why?"

One little girl with curly red hair sat on the floor about six feet away, on Tiffany's left. She slowly raised her hand.

"Yes, sweetie? Why do you think you can't see him?"

"'Cause he's hiding!"

"Yeah!" shouted the dark-haired little boy sitting next to the little girl, nodding vigorously.

Tiffany nodded. "Maybe…or maybe he's working his magic so you can't *see* him..."

Silence.

"Does anyone see anything in this room that looks weird or out of place?"

The room grew totally silent as every child—along with Abby and Momma, who stood inside the doorway—scanned every bed, table, fixture and piece of furniture. The dozen or so health workers and nurses blocking the doorway also looked around for him.

"Give up?" Tiffany asked.

"That lamp!" One little boy was jumping up in bed and pointing to the brass floor lamp sitting over in the corner, a few feet inside the doorway.

"Are you sure?" Tiffany asked.

The little boy nodded. "Sure!"

"How can you be so sure?"

"Saw it move! Saw it move!"

"The lamp!" shouted another child.

"He's the lamp!" shouted another, pointing.

"I just saw it move, too!" shouted one of the health workers—a big guy with broad shoulders and a dark buzz cut.

"All right, then." Tiffany watched them in silence for about ten seconds. Then she turned to the lamp. "Chip, if that's really you, you can come out now!"

Total silence. Everyone gazed at the lamp.

Several seconds later, the lamp shade suddenly changed shape, then color, as it turned into Chip's thick red thatch. The upright brass post of the lamp broadened and, also changing color, transformed into his slender form. Just a few seconds later, Chip grinned and held out his arms. Then, wiggling his ears, he let his tongue drop halfway to the floor and immediately pulled it back into his mouth.

The room turned into screaming chaos.

Tiffany joined in the applause. Momma, Abby Turner and everyone in the group flocking the doorway applauded. Abby's mouth gaped open in awe. There were tears in Momma's eyes, but her smile was one of great pride. Tiffany watched the children's excited reactions and immediately felt more confident. She also experienced a strong sense of genuine warmth filling the room.

Once the chaos and the applause died down, Chip walked over and stood next to Tiffany.

"What do we do now?" she sent over, smiling at the kids. *"You know I'm new at this."*

"Want me to take the lead, Tifferoo?"

"Just as long as you don't go overboard..."

"You're no fun at a party."

"These are kids, Chip...and they're all sick. Please *don't scare them..."*

"Trust me, Lamb Chop."

"*I'll try.*" She turned. "Kids, this is Chip. Say hello, Chip."

Chip turned to the kids, smiled and said, "Hello, Chip!"

Instant laughter.

Once the laughter died down, Chip sent over, "*Ask me why I turned myself into a lamp.*"

"Why did you—"

"Out loud, Sweet Cakes. This is part of the routine. Think Abbot and Costello."

"Who?"

He shook his head and scratched his jaw. *"Children should be seen and not heard. They were a couple of really funny guys I bumped into when I was up here in the fifties. Now...go ahead and ask."*

"All right. Why on earth did you turn yourself into a lamp?"

He shrugged. "I decided that turning myself into a walking X-ray machine would scare everyone."

Laughter.

Tiffany turned to the children. "He's really silly, isn't he?"

Laughter.

"Silly!"

"Silly!"

Chip blinked. "Me? Silly?" Then he wiggled his ears and did a backward flip. The instant he landed, he grabbed his nose and twisted. The sound of an angry duck resonated loudly in the area.

The room erupted in more laughter.

Nearly a full minute later, the children finally quieted down.

Chip stared at Tiffany but didn't say anything.

"Something wrong?"

"Not really…"

"Then why are you staring at me like that?"

"I've just noticed…you're quite a babe."

"Gee, thanks."

"It wasn't a compliment."

"Funny. It sure sounded like one."

"It wasn't, though."

"What was it, then?"

"A kind of disappointed observation."

"Disappointed? Please explain."

"Well, as I just said, you're quite a babe…"

"I heard you. I was right here. I even watched you when you said it."

"Goody. You're paying attention."

"But why are you disappointed?"

"I was just wondering…what can you do?"

"Me?"

"Yepperino. You. As opposed to me. We *are* in front of a live audience, you know. You can't just stand there and look beautiful. You've got to be able to actually *do* something."

Tiffany thought that one over. "I really don't know. I don't usually go around, acting silly like you."

Snickers from several of the kids sitting on the floor facing them.

"You ought to try it. It's fun." He turned to the audience. "Ain't it fun to act silly, kids?"

"Yeah!"

Laughter.

"Yeah! Silly!"

Chip turned to Tiffany. "Can you make yourself invisible?"

"Well, gee, I honestly don't know. I really haven't thought too much about that."

"As I just said…we're in front of a live audience, and they want to see what we can do. They've already seen me do a few terrificoso feats of miraculous and death-defying skill…but I'm just warming up. I didn't want to enthrall them all at once."

"We certainly wouldn't want *that*, would we?"

The attendants in the hall laughed.

Chip shrugged. "So then…this leaves you to take over. In other words, let 'er rip!"

"All right." Tiffany lowered her head and went silent.

Chip waited.

"Invisible," whispered one child.

Chip frowned and turned to the audience. "Why is it that women take so long to do anything?" He held up his arm. A huge clock appeared on his wrist.

Laughter and applause.

Chip lowered his arm; the clock disappeared. "Tifferoo? You still in there?" He made a fist, raised his arm and made it look like he was tapping her on top of the head. The sound resembled a woodpecker worrying a tree.

Laughter.

She glared. "I'm trying to concentrate, but you keep distracting me. And please don't touch my head again."

"All righty-rooty. I'll be quiet."

"Good. Just don't touch my head."

Chip turned back to the audience, rolled his eyes and stood silently.

She looked at him after a few moments. "What was I supposed to do?"

Chip wiggled his ears and began pulling out his hair and dropping it in thick red clumps on the floor.

More laughter.

He bent, picked up the thick red knots and put them all back. "Invisible—remember?"

"Yes. Now I remember."

"Good. We're on a roll, then."

She nodded but didn't reply.

Chip waited another ten seconds. When she still hadn't done anything, he said, "Now would be a good time to do it."

"I can't."

"Why not?"

"You're staring at me."

"So are all these kids…"

"They're different."

"How are they different?"

"They're not silly."

Laughter.

Chip rubbed his temples. "Want me to turn my back?"

"Yes. Please."

He turned and stared up at the ceiling. "Just don't take forever, okay?"

"I won't."

"Promise?"

"You're distracting me again."

Chip shook his head and said nothing.

Tiffany winked at the audience and put her index finger up to her lips.

Chip sighed and stared at the floor. "But before you try doing this, Tifferoo, there's one important thing you need to know…"

Silence.

"Tifferoo?"

More silence.

Chip spun around.

Tiffany had disappeared.

CHAPTER 20

Shortly after four-thirty, M. Murray Robertson III received a call from Orlando, Florida, just as he returned to his office after a long, irritating two-hour budget meeting in the conference room of the Marriott Hotel. The call was from a Daniel Grove, who said he was calling on the behalf of his employer, a Mr. Brett Waite, who wanted to talk to him regarding an extremely urgent matter.

A cold tingling sensation oozed thickly down his spine as Robertson took his seat behind his massive oak desk. Brett Waite. That was the mortal name Braithwaite, the super demon that had replaced Mr. Balbor, had chosen for his hundred-year reign in the mortal world.

An "extremely urgent matter…"

This was not good. In fact, it was very, very bad.

He's calling me... The more he thought about it, the more frightening it sounded. *The new super demon is calling* me!

His hand nearly dropped the phone as he waited for his heart to settle down. His mouth felt stuffed with cotton, but he managed to get the words out. "Hello, uh, Mr. Grove, this is Murray Robertson speaking. I'm—"

"I'm putting the call through to Mr. Waite right now, Mr. Robertson," Daniel Grove said flatly.

Grove's cold, professional manner sliced through Robertson, convincing him this was definitely not going to be pleasant. Even so, he struggled to maintain his composure. "Is there something I can help you with? I mean, is there something you can tell me before Mr. Waite—"

"I'm putting him through now, Mr. Robertson."

Click!

The sound reverberated deafeningly in his ears.

"Robertson, this is Brett Waite." The voice was loud and brash, tearing into Robertson's ears even worse than the abrupt click. He fought even harder to keep a firm grip on the phone. "You've been told who I am, yes?"

"Y-Yes, sir…" Robertson hoped some pleasantries might help make this conversation more encouraging. "And please let me say how nice it is to hear from—"

"Let's not waste any time on any needless bullshit, all right? This is *business*—not social. Besides, I'm not the social sort. And one thing I don't want is to waste my valuable time trying to explain to a moron why I'm calling him when I should have left my office two hours ago. Do you have any idea what's going on in your neck of the woods?"

"Sir?"

"Let me put it bluntly. I just received word that an inferior who'd been working with you the last ten years is now back down in the Dark Place. Know anything about that?"

What the hell?

Robertson sat up. He suddenly realized that his palms were sweating. He very carefully wiped them, one at a time, on his trousers, while keeping the phone close to his ear. "N-No, sir…"

"I didn't think so. Any idea who I'm talking about?"

"No, sir…"

"How many inferiors do you and your colleagues have working for you in that area?"

"Just two, actually. In Peoria, I believe we have a total of ten, but I've personally only been working with one of them over the last—"

"What's this idiot's name?"

"He goes by Durant. Keenan V. Durant. He's been working as a mailman for the local Postal Service, and he's been doing exemplary wet work for us over the last decade."

"Well, someone over there with obviously more clout than he had didn't like him, and kicked his ass back down."

"Back *down*?"

A heavy sigh. "Down. As opposed to up. Get it? The idiot's no longer up there with you. Someone sent him back down without bothering even a teensy little bit about protocol."

"But sir…how could that be?"

"I'll tell you how that could be. Your inferior obviously met up with the wrong badass."

"Sir?"

"Let me put it another way. If you want to keep doing what you've been doing, you'll need to get yourself another inferior, and you'll need to get one who knows what the hell he's doing."

"Sir, I just don't understand any of this. How could anyone send a demon back down without—"

"Since I'm obviously talking to an idiot, I guess I'm gonna have to spell it out. Your inferior met up with another demon, and the one he met up with was obviously more powerful than he was."

"I didn't realize there *was* another demon up here, sir…"

"Then I guess that probably means your idiot sent himself down, doesn't it?"

Robertson didn't reply. Something inside him told him to keep quiet.

"Listen to my voice, Robertson, and try to absorb what I'm saying. Your mailman met up with someone more powerful. Apparently, this other demon didn't want him infringing on his territory. In this case, I'm reasonably certain the *he* we're talking about is a *she*, and if it's the *she* I think we're talking about, that two-horse town of yours has just acquired a major problem."

"A *she*, sir?"

"Yeah. *She*. You know. Tits? Ass? Pussy? Long hair? Pouty lips? The works. This bitch has been a major thorn on my colossal butt ever since I first laid eyes on her."

"How do you know the demon's a *she*, sir?"

"When your mailman first arrived down here, he was wandering around like a dickhead and got a little too close to the Castle. A couple of the subs spotted him and demanded to know what he was doing there. He started babbling about a bunch of things that made no sense, so they took him into the Castle and gave the problem to Asmodeus. Asmodeus took the inferior aside and did a simple mind probe. You'll never guess what Asmodeus saw."

"W-What…did he find, sir?"

"Everything was hazy and muddled, of course, but Asmodeus did manage to catch a fleeting glimpse of blond hair and blue eyes in the idiot's subconscious."

"Sir?"

"What part of that weren't you able to grasp?"

"The blond hair and blue eyes, sir."

"The blonde is the demon I just told you about. She's the one I tangled with here in Orlando not too damned long ago."

"I was never told about an inferior coming to—"

"Are you deaf as well as dumb? She's a *rogue*, you idiot. No one *knows* where she is or when she gets there. She goes where she wants. And she's not even an inferior!"

"What *is* she, then?"

"She's a pariah. An outcast. Why she even ventured into our neck of the woods remains a mystery. Some say she was pulled in through the Meddaworld by one of our horny subs. But that's no matter. She's become a huge problem and needs to be stopped and sent back down. She's a threat to all of us."

"What exactly does she do, sir?"

"Good."

"Pardon?"

"You *are* deaf, aren'tcha? I said *good*. The bitch does *good*. You know—good rather than bad? That sort of thing. She's a goody-two-shoes who struts around, working her shtick and making things miserable for the rest of us. And as I just said, she needs to be *stopped*."

"What's her name, sir? How can I find her?"

"Her name is Tiffany, and she travels with a stinkweed inferior calling himself Chip. You believe that? A *demon* calling himself *Chip*?"

"Is there anything else I should know, sir?"

"I'd think that should be quite enough. She pals around with a redheaded stinkweed who happens to be an inferior. He's a trickster, so he's small potatoes. The blonde is our real problem. Everywhere she goes, people start feeling good and things aren't nearly as fucked up as they were before she got there. It's absolutely revolting."

"I'll get someone to find her and bring her back down, sir."

Waite barked laughter. "If only it were that easy. If I'm right about what's happening, make no mistake about it, this bitch is extremely formidable."

"What's she look like, sir?"

"She's a looker—which makes this even more difficult. She seems harmless, but make no mistake, she's far from it. She's already sent two other subordinates down below."

"Two, sir?"

"Did I stutter? Yeah, dammit. Two. Just a couple of weeks ago, she stuck a very capable subordinate from Chicago on a plane and sent him back me in Orlando. To make matters even worse, this subordinate was covered with bird shit when we found him."

"*Bird* shit, sir?"

"That gooey white stuff that comes out of a bird's asshole."

"Sir, I didn't mean—"

"As you can already guess, that was a helluvan insult, and I'm really burned about that. This subordinate was useless when he got here, so I had to send him back down below. He'd been in Chicago for decades and had managed to completely defile the political arena and turn the entire city into a cesspool of corruption. He was even a key figure in the Dallas hit-job back in '63, so as you can probably tell, he was no pushover. This bitch, however, totally destroyed the bastard in just a couple of hours."

"Sir, I don't understand how someone who isn't even an inferior can—"

"Even before she managed that bit of business in Pittsburgh, she manipulated several colleagues of mine into abandoning a multi-billion-dollar deal that would have enabled me to build a terrorist training camp in Central Florida that would have made the one in Upstate New York look like someone's back yard."

"She does sound…well, dangerous, sir…"

"Needless to say, I want her *badly*. I'd love to have her here so I can send her back down personally, but I'd be satisfied if she was just sent back, period. I can always take a few days off and drop down there just to make sure she's where she's supposed to be."

"I'll do my best, sir. I've got someone in mind already."

"Is he capable?"

"Very, sir."

"Like I said, she's extremely formidable. And she shouldn't be up here, doing all this damnable good. It's unnatural. If she keeps this up, she's gonna make us all look like a bunch of dickheads."

CHAPTER 21

Once the commotion finally died down, Tiffany reappeared.

The applause filled the room once again.

Tiffany surveyed the scene. A feeling of nausea quickly took over. It looked like a hazy gray cloud had settled above many of the beds, and when she closed her eyes, the sourness that had overpowered her when she first entered the Dark Place just months earlier brushed her face, making her eyes water.

The sourness of the Dark Place.

These children had obviously been infected by a demon. She scanned the room again. The grayish mist had settled over every single bed.

"That was great, Tifferoosky!" Chip was grinning from ear to ear as he came over, applauding.

Tiffany didn't reply. She was trying to overcome the nausea.

"Tifferoo? You okay?"

"No."

"What's wrong? You disappeared like a champ. In fact, you did it even better than I—"

"A demon made these kids sick," she told him.

"Seriously?"

"I can tell."

"Think you can fix it?"

"I have to try."

After about a minute, the applause finally died down.

Tiffany forced the nausea away and smiled at the audience. "Is anyone feeling better after watching Chip and I do some of our tricks?"

A flurry of applause.

Once the commotion settled down, Tiffany said, "Would you like to feel even better?"

More applause. Some of the weaker patients struggled to sit up in their beds.

"All right, then. I'm now going to do something very unusual and very special!"

"More tricks!" shouted a boy from his bed.

"Disappear again!" shouted the boy next to him.

"This next thing I do will help many of you feel better. What I am going to do is give each of you a small piece of my heart."

The room turned deadly silent. The hospital staff didn't move. Everyone's eyes had focused on Tiffany. Momma's hands covered her mouth. Her eyes were enormous.

Tiffany held out her hands, palms up, and closed her eyes. *I have to get rid of the evil that has been making these innocent children sick. I don't know exactly how I can do this, but I'm going to use every bit of love I can find within me to do it. Hopefully, this will work.*

Just then, a small white flame materialized an inch or so above each palm.

The entire room gasped. Several children clapped briefly and immediately turned silent.

As Tiffany held her hands steady, she closed her eyes. *I am going to visit these children. This glow will be the gleaming essence of health and happiness coming from my heart. It probably won't completely cure the children, but it might make them feel better when it interferes with the sickness and disease that has weakened them. Once the child begins feeling better, the shroud from the Dark Place will fade and disappear.*

Tiffany opened her eyes and walked over to the first bed. She reached out with her left hand and placed it directly above the sick child's forehead. The moment she held the white glow over the child, the tiny flame grew momentarily, the gray mist disappeared, and the child began smiling. Tiffany moved immediately to the next bed, repeating the procedure. For the next fifteen minutes or so, she watched in silent approval as the gray mist disappeared, one by one.

The room had turned wild in laughter and applause. One by one, the sickest children sat up in bed and began clapping and squealing. When Tiffany was confident she'd destroyed all evidence of sickness from the room, she lowered her arms to her sides and walked back to the center of the room.

As she passed one of the beds, a little girl reached out and grasped Tiffany's wrist. She had big brown eyes and black pigtails, and was sitting up. She looked up and smiled. Tiffany could tell by her expression—and by the child's bright aura—that she was no longer in pain. "Thank you, Tiffany!"

"What's your name, honey?"

"Carrie."

"You're welcome, Carrie."

As Tiffany turned to walk away, Carrie said, "Tiffany?"

"Yes?"

"I feel *much* better now!"

"I'm *so* glad."

The little girl covered her heart with her left hand. "Will this piece of your heart stay with me?"

"As long as you wish it to…"

"Forever and ever, then!"

Tiffany gently patted the little girl's head and went back to where Chip was waiting for her.

The applause thundered in the room for the next several minutes.

Their routine ended with Chip turning into a large flower. Tiffany, who'd turned herself into a plain-looking bag lady, walked up to it. Then, touching the petals, one by one, she turned into a man, then a child, then finally the beauty she'd been before they'd started the skit.

During the tumultuous applause, Abby, Momma and members of the hospital staff rushed over. Abby and Momma hugged them both while the staff looked on, waiting eagerly to shake their hands. Meanwhile, the room exploded in applause and high-pitched screams.

As Tiffany and Chip were led back out into the hall, Abby and a female doctor, whose name was Nadine O'Hara, asked them if they possibly had time to visit a sick child in a different wing.

"We've subjected her with test after test," Doctor O'Hara said grimly, "but nothing seems to help. She's been here for more than a week now, and we still can't get a handle on her condition.

Needless to say, the parents are out of their minds with worry. Could you possibly spare a few minutes with her? Judging by what we've seen, your presence might help, and it certainly wouldn't hurt."

"We can spare as much time as you like," Tiffany said.

She and Chip followed them down the hall, to the awaiting elevators.

***

The little girl's name was Mandy Conlin. She was thirteen, had light-brown hair, large emerald green eyes and a pretty face, and lay in bed.

Several people were sitting in chairs on the other side of the bed when Tiffany and Chip went in. A man in a police uniform stood behind a chair in which a pretty blond woman sat holding the hand of a young brown-haired girl who strongly resembled Mandy. The man was tall and broad-shouldered, with chestnut hair and eyes. Three others stood off to the side—a couple in their thirties and another little girl with chestnut hair who looked vaguely familiar. But Tiffany's attention went directly to Mandy, who lay in the bed, her eyes nearly closed.

The gray mist hovering above the child's head appeared darker than what Tiffany had seen in the other room. This made her wonder if the child had been infected more recently than the others.

Before Tiffany approached the bed, Abby whispered, "Her family is right there, on the other side of the bed. Her father is the police officer. They've agreed to let you talk to Mandy." She patted Tiffany's hand gently. "Do what you can, Sweetie."

"I'll do my best." Tiffany went over to the bed. She smiled at the family, and they smiled back. Then, turning to Mandy, she bent over the side of the bed and whispered softly, "Mandy, I'm Tiffany. They tell me you're hurting, but no one knows why."

Mandy didn't respond.

Tiffany placed her left hand on Mandy's left hand and closed her eyes. She immediately felt a dark, cold presence and stiffened when she realized this child had indeed come into contact with the Dark Place.

"*You don't deserve this, Mandy.*"

The child stirred slightly.

"*I'm going to make this right, and I'm going to do it right now.*"

Tiffany forced her consciousness into the child's memory. She went back day after day, until she caught the image of a nurse entering the examination room. She could tell immediately that this person wasn't a regular nurse. The aura surrounding the lanky figure was a dark gray.

The woman went over to Mandy, patted her on the head and, scanning the room, dropped something very tiny down the back of the child's blouse. Then she smiled and quickly left the room.

The very next moment, the child's face paled, and she slumped in her seat.

Tiffany pulled her mind out of the little girl's memory palace, held her frail hand more tightly and focused on her conscious mind.

"*Whatever is hurting you will no longer hurt you, understand? Everything bad and dark is leaving you right now, and by the time I let go of your hand, you'll feel much better. Do you understand?*"

Mandy suddenly blinked and turned her head in Tiffany's direction.

Mandy's mother gasped and covered her mouth. Her father stiffened and gripped the back of the chair.

While holding Mandy's hand, Tiffany held out her free hand, palm-up. The tiny white flame instantly appeared. "*I think I might have a tiny chunk of my heart still lying around for you, Mandy…*"

Tiffany lowered her hand until it was just a few inches above Mandy's face. The flame immediately grew longer. The dark gray cloud hovering above her dimmed instantly.

Moments later, Mandy's eyes opened wider. Then they cleared up, and she stirred on the mattress. A minute later, she tried pushing herself into an upright position. Her father rushed over and helped. His eyes were wet as he helped his daughter. Then he turned to Tiffany and mouthed the words, "Thank you so very much..."

Smiling, Tiffany straightened and gently backed away. The moment she let go of Mandy's hand, she caught one last flash of gray. An instant later, it vanished completely.

The flame in Tiffany's hand shortened and immediately disappeared.

A moment later, something tiny and white appeared in its place in her palm.

"You're going to be fine from now on, Mandy. Have fun and be happy. And ask your parents to take you out of here." She winked. "Hospitals are for sick people."

Mandy's family and friends flocked around the bed. Everyone was crying and laughing.

Her right hand clenched tightly shut, Tiffany quietly left the room.

***

Another female doctor, this one with the nametag that said *Dr. Stennis* on her lab coat, stopped Tiffany just as she and Chip were about to walk down the corridor. "I…don't know what to say," the short, slight woman whispered. Her large deep-blue eyes bulged. "I've never *seen* anything like that before." She shrugged. "What…what did you just *do* in there?"

"I just told her she was going to feel better," Tiffany said. "It was really no biggie."

"No *biggie*?" Dr. Stennis took a deep breath. "The monitors…the moment you left the room, they—"

"It worked, didn't it? That's really all that matters. The little girl needed to get well. I just helped her do it a little faster."

"But *how*? I can't begin to tell you the number of procedures we've done with this child—with *all* these children—"

"I honestly don't know what I can tell you."

The woman stared at her in silence. Tiffany could see the fear—as well as the confusion—in her eyes. "Have you ever…done this…sort of thing…before?"

"Actually, no."

"Then how on earth—"

"As I just said, I don't know..."

The doctor gazed at Tiffany. Tiffany could see the suspicion in the woman's narrowed eyes. She entered the doctor's head and shuddered at the disturbing thoughts. *This woman could not possibly have done what I just saw her do,* Stennis was thinking. *This makes no sense—none whatsoever. No one can perform a simple parlor trick and heal a room filled with sick children. There must be some other logical explanation for what happened. There is nothing that will medically explain this phenomenon. I really need to make some calls and get the AMA in on this—*

"*You don't need to call anyone*," Tiffany quickly sent over. "*The important thing is that the children are no longer sick. You're a doctor—this is all you should care about. And since this hospital will be credited with healing these kids, your grants will continue and so will your reputation for being a top-notch hospital. Can you possibly understand what I'm telling you?*"

The doctor stood there numbly, not speaking. Then she nodded and began rubbing her temples.

"And if anyone questions you," Tiffany added, *"all you need to say is that the children's maladies all ran their course and that they're all well again."*

Abby cautiously approached them and gave Tiffany the strangest look. "Is this what you *really* are, Tiffany? An illusionist?"

"You saw our act," she said.

"We all saw it. We've never seen anything like it before. You did things the most famous magicians in the world would not be able to do." She shook her head. "But that's not what's troubling us. You just healed a little girl in there, and most of the others who watched your act are no longer showing any evidence that they were even sick."

"Why is that troubling you?" Tiffany asked. "Isn't it enough that the children are getting well now?"

"Well, yes, but—"

"And the hospital no longer has to spend hundreds of thousands of dollars on tests and medicines that might not help them at all?"

"Well—"

"All you need to know," Tiffany sent over to her, *"is that love heals, and where there's love, there's also magic."*

Abby gazed at Tiffany in awe. When she spoke again, her voice had become a whisper. "Tiffany…who are you? I mean really?"

Tiffany shrugged. "I'm your friend's daughter…and I don't like to see suffering—especially in children."

"Neither do we," another female doctor said, approaching them. "None of us likes suffering. None of us can tolerate a *child* suffering. This is why I chose the medicine profession—why *all* of us chose it." She shook her head. "But that doesn't mean we can actually *cure* everyone. We have the best doctors, the best facilities, the best technology money can buy." She shrugged. "What you did in there, with those children… What you did to the Conlin girl—"

"I just took away their pain," Tiffany said.

The woman threw out her arms. "But *how*?"

"You wouldn't believe me if I told you," she said.

"Please," she said. "Try us."

Tiffany gazed at the woman. "*The children are well. This is all you need to know, and all you have to remember whenever someone from the AMA, the Medical Board, or any other health official, asks you.*"

The woman said nothing else. Her glazed expression suggested that she'd received Tiffany's message.

Momma was heading quickly toward them. "Baby, you and Chip—you're both so fantastic!"

"It's all in the wrists," Chip quipped, holding up his hands.

"Thanks, Momma."

"You didn't tell me you could actually *heal*—"

"It was magic, Momma. Chip and I…well, we discovered magic a little while ago. This is real magic because it deals with the imagination. There are no tricks, and it only works if you truly believe. That's why it worked so well with children. For some reason, only children believe in true magic. That's really all I can tell you."

Two more doctors were headed their way. They both looked troubled.

Tiffany gave Chip a worried glance. "*I really need help here. I'm afraid I crossed the line, and now I don't know how to fix it, or make things right—*"

"*Don't fret, Babykins.*" He gave her his usual wink. *"I'll get us out of this.*"

One of the male doctors said, "We'd like a word with you in private, Ms. Sedarski…"

"Magic's how it really works," Chip said, moving closer.

The other male doctor looked skeptical. "Sir, this is a serious matter, and—"

"Suppose I told you that anyone can work magic," Chip said.

Silence. Everyone in the group stared at him.

Chip gazed directly at the skeptical doctor. "Suppose I told you that anyone can work magic as long as they were in the presence of someone who actually can."

"Sir, what does this have to do with—"

"Want a demonstration?"

The man didn't reply.

"Suppose I told you that you could work magic right now, in front of all of us."

He shook his head. "Sir…"

"How about you, Doc?" Chip was looking at the man standing beside him, who blinked but didn't reply.

"I'll make this one easy. Visualize one of your instruments and make it appear on the floor at your feet."

"Please," the doctor said. "I don't think you realize what—"

"Sir, this is ridiculous!"

"Baby?" Momma looked frightened.

"*What's the doc thinking of, Tifferoo*?" Chip thought, glancing at Tiffany.

"*His stethoscope.*"

"*All righty- rooty, then.*" Chip pointed to the floor at the man's feet. "Look what you've just done."

An instant later, a stethoscope appeared on the floor for a few moments before vanishing.

Everyone gasped.

"My *God*..."

"What just happened?"

"Sam? Did you just do what—"

The doctor's face reddened. "I have no idea how I did that!"

Two more doctors arrived and began asking questions.

During the commotion, Tiffany and Chip elbowed through the crowd and hurried outside. As they went down the walk, Tiffany bumped into a tall, gray-haired, gray-bearded man in a neat dark suit. "Excuse me," she said.

The man smiled. He had the clearest blue eyes she'd ever seen. "My fault entirely, young lady," he said, nodding. "Have a very nice day." He nodded again and resumed walking.

Tiffany caught a flash of warmth. When she turned around, the gray-haired man had already disappeared inside the building.

"Tifferoo? You okay?"

"Just preoccupied, I guess."

"I can see why. We caused quite a stir in there."

"I know. I was able to handle a couple of them, but if word gets out—"

"Yepperino. We've got to make tracks."

"And much sooner than we'd planned."

Tiffany moved closer to the trashcan and opened her palm.

A tiny white seed slightly larger than the eye of a needle rested in the center of her palm.

"Tifferoo? What's going on?"

"I don't know, but apparently this little thing has been making Mandy Conlin—and probably all the other kids—sick."

"And you think it's from the Dark Place?"

She nodded.

Chip suddenly looked grim. "Know what this means, don'tcha?"

She dropped the seed inside the can, amongst the paper cups and discarded bags. "It means there's another demon in town."

CHAPTER 22

Two doctors who had witnessed the strange stethoscope trick hurried down the hall. One of them, Doctor Emil Jones, already had his cell phone out and pressed tightly against his ear.

"This is not good," the other, Doctor Jonathan Petrie, said as he opened the office door.

"I know," Jones agreed. "Too many things are not happening right. You know the odds against curing one child's illness just by mental suggestion, or any other sort of delusional—"

"Astronomical." Petrie was shaking his head as he closed the door. "Make anything out of that other bit of nonsense?"

"You mean when we first walked over?"

Petrie nodded. "Scales told me his stethoscope just materialized on the floor the moment he thought of it."

Jones scowled. "Scales is usually pretty level-headed about most things."

Petrie shrugged. "I thought we all were."

"We sure were—until those two came over and completely turned everything upside-down."

"Upside-down?"

"You know what I mean."

"I'm afraid I do."

Jones said, "You can't possibly consider that magic act as anything ordinary or normal, can you?"

"Of course not. No one can actually disappear in front of a live audience—not without the usual distractions, of course. A box, perhaps. One of those fancy curtains the sexy assistant in the flimsy outfit brings out to keep the audience's attention away from the actual trick…"

Jones shook his head. "In this case, the magician was actually the sexy one."

"Noticed that too, eh?"

Jones frowned. "I'd have to be blind—or dead—*not* to…"

"Why do I keep getting the feeling those two aren't actual magicians?"

"We're talking about forty sick kids who don't seem to be sick anymore."

"I know exactly what we're talking about, dammit."

"Just so we're on the same page. Taking everything else into consideration, that stethoscope trick is the least of our concerns."

"Like it or not, it's part of the equation."

"How do you figure?"

"The magic angle everyone seems to be talking about."

"Dammit, Jonathan, there *is* no such thing!"

"How do you explain what just happened less than twenty minutes ago?"

"That's just it. I can't!"

"Years of college, pre-med, med school, private practice, and working side-by-side with the best experts in the field of Pediatric Medicine…"

Jones sighed and rubbed his temples. "Then something like this happens."

Petrie was frowning again. "I just can't wrap my head around this, Emil. In my logical, highly-educated mind, there is no way in hell that two people without any sort of medical background or experience can walk into a hospital, perform a few magic tricks, and heal all those kids like that."

"No way in hell is absolutely right." Emil Jones tapped his cell with his finger. He pressed some buttons, then rapped the phone a couple of times sharply on the desk top. "Damn phone's picking helluva time not to work!"

"Who're you calling?"

"The FBI. A couple of colleagues I knew at med school periodically consult with some people in their Fraud division."

"You think this is fraud?"

"I don't know *what* it is, dammit. All I know is that two people neither of us ever heard of showed up and did a few pretty clever magic tricks which seemed to heal forty kids, some of them with severe illnesses—and in less than an hour." He tapped his phone again.

Jonathan Petrie looked pensive. "Maybe they really *are* healers."

"You can't seriously believe that, can you?" Jones was pressing buttons again.

"I don't know *what* I believe, Emil."

"What *I* know is this: if they can do *this*, we're sort of unnecessary—don't you think?" Jones pocketed his cell and picked up the desk phone.

"That's one way of looking at it."

"Is there another?" Jones glared at the phone receiver.

Petrie tilted his bald head. "Equipment malfunction?"

"You can't be serious. We're talking about millions of dollars of—"

"I know."

"Now…what the hell's wrong with *this* damned thing?" Jones slammed the phone down.

Moments later, the door opened slowly. A tall, gray-haired man dressed in an immaculate dark suit appeared in the doorway. He sported an impeccably-trimmed gray beard and had such a friendly face, both Jones and Petrie suddenly felt less irritated than just moments ago.

"Can we help you?" Jones asked.

"I was told to come and see you two gentlemen," the visitor replied. He came in and approached Jones. "I have a grandchild staying here. She's been sick for several weeks now, and I just received a phone call from someone here saying that she's been miraculously healed." He extended his hand. "I just came here to thank you two gentlemen—and also the rest of your staff—for your excellent, blessed work." He walked over to Petrie and shook his hand as well. "My wife and I will never forget what you've done for our little Jeannie."

Jones said, "I'm…very glad this…worked out for you, sir."

The gray-haired man smiled, nodded, then turned and approached the door. Before leaving, he turned back to them. "You're doing a very great service here. All of us appreciate your efforts, and I intend to send the hospital a check to demonstrate my genuine appreciation for all you've done."

Petrie smiled. "*Thank* you, sir!"

The gray-haired man shook his head. "No. Thank *you*, sir. Both of you." He waved, opened the door and left the office.

Jones and Petrie stared at the door for nearly a minute.

Just then, they both snapped out of their haze at the same time and seemed to notice one another for the first time.

Petrie stared at his right hand and wondered why it felt so warm. He shook it and glanced at his colleague. "What were we doing?"

Jones stared at the phone on the desk. "I think I was making a call."

"To whom?"

"I honestly don't remember." Jones gazed at Petrie for several moments. "Were we just talking to someone?"

Petrie scanned the room. "I don't think so. Why?"

Jones stared at the floor. "I think I just zoned out for a few seconds."

"It's no wonder. It's been a hectic day."

"Yes." Jones rubbed his temples. "You're absolutely right. I think we should make a trip to the Recovery Room and see how everything's going with those kids."

Petrie nodded.

The two of them left the office.

CHAPTER 23

At 5:45, Custodian Daniel D. Lyon was ready to call it quits with the broom detail bullshit. But at least he didn't have to worry about the floor below. Some entertainment troupe, he was told, had come in to bring sunshine and cheer to the sick brats. They didn't go into much detail, but he could tell from up here that something heavy-duty was going down. It sounded like those stupid little morons had gone to the circus and were watching a bunch of clowns running around, acting all kinds of silly. Security even had the entire floor blocked off.

This was all well and good. Daniel liked it quiet. That was why he came here in the first place. Sick kids were generally quiet. And it sure did make his day when he was given the go-ahead to make them stay that way.

He was about to turn the corner when Karl "Horse Face" Timmons staggered by and told him in his gruff, old man's voice that Dan had missed a spot. "Ya need to keep a sharp eye on those corners, kid," Timmons barked. "I can see them damn dust bunnies from here!"

"Dust bunnies?" Daniel squinted. He couldn't see what the asshole was talking about. But it was really no wonder. Timmons was one of those morons that liked exaggerating. He especially liked doing it if involved making more work for a member of his crew.

"Can't see 'em?" Timmons pointed to what amounted to a dollop of gray fuzz the size of a quarter sitting in the corner. "Bigger'n shit."

"Yeah, whatever..." Daniel pushed the broom over. Once he'd trapped Timmons' ginormous "dust bunny," he pulled it back and continued pushing the broom down the corridor.

Hopefully, the old coot would get a move on and let him be.

"Keep your eye out," Timmons said.

"For what?"

"For dust bunnies—*that's* what!"

"Keep yours out, too," Daniel whispered as the tall, paunchy dirtbag hobbled past.

Daniel reached into his pocket, pulled out one of his tiny "bullets" from his unlimited arsenal and held it in the center of his upturned palm. He blew on it, sending it sailing through the air, until it dropped softly inside the back of Timmons' collar.

Arching his back suddenly and gasping, Timmons began sneezing loudly, one right after the other, spewing spittle and snot. He nearly lost his balance as he hopped on his good leg all the way to the archway, then grabbed the door handle for support.

"*Dang*!" Shaking, the old man sniffed wetly, looking around as if he had no idea where he was.

"What's wrong, Chief?" Daniel kept a straight face as he pushed his broom closer. "Got a cold?"

Timmons sniffed and sneezed again. This one sent a trail of snot in Daniel's direction, until it landed with a *splat*! on the floor a couple of feet from where he was standing. "*Damn*!"

"Two more feet," Daniel said, "and you woulda splashed my shoes."

Sniffing, Timmons pulled a filthy hankie from his pants pocket and blew loudly into it. The noise sounded like the mating call of a moose.

Daniel stopped pushing his broom. "You shouldn't come to work if you're sick, ya know. You might make *me* sick, and then I'd have to call in."

"I ain't sick, dammit." The old man sniffed again. "I just picked up somethin'. It's your fault. You're stirrin' up the air, ya know."

"I thought I was bein' paid to do that…"

"Yeah, whatever." The old man sneezed once more, splashing his sleeve and left shoe. Then he turned and, grumbling, resumed hobbling down the hall.

"Fuck with me and you'll be sorry," Daniel muttered, grinning devilishly. "They didn't send me up here for nothin'."

One hundred and sixty years ago, as an inferior in the Dark Place, he turned himself into a small, innocent-looking dandelion so the supers and subs wouldn't notice him hiding in the Valley of Decay. He would still be hiding as a dandelion if Olivier hadn't been looking for an inferior with power over the poisonous flowers in the Valley.

Back in the early part of the twentieth century, the pandemic flu epidemic in Europe had claimed nearly one hundred million lives. Baphomet, the super demon controlling Europe at the time, used Daniel D. Lyon—the moniker he'd chosen specifically for his skills—for several months to help spread the epidemic. Once Daniel's purpose had been fulfilled, he was brought over to America by Balberith in 1918 to help spread the disease after World War I had ended. He was used in every decade ever since, primarily for outbreaks in everything from measles to chicken pox to polio, and had been particularly active during the last forty years with multiple sclerosis, then in the eighties and nineties, with the AIDS virus, which was developed in a laboratory by one of Balberith's more resourceful subordinates.

Daniel was originally known as the "Defiler"—the demon who could cause sickness or nausea just by touching a mortal with one of the rank dandelion seed-heads he'd brought up with him from the Valley of Decay. It was only natural that he chose his mortal name, Daniel D. Lyon, in honor of his preferred weapon of choice when dealing with mortals.

He'd been making mortals sick and nauseous for a century and a half. Particularly active during the last twenty years, he'd been afflicting mortals in banks and in supermarkets, making them nauseous and light-headed, thus forcing them to suffer countless maladies. He'd influenced people to sneeze on one another in crowded malls and in restaurants, causing major epidemics. He was also responsible for several different strains of flu that had closed down businesses and schools.

Nowadays, Daniel kept a quiet profile working as custodian in the hospital and applying his craft whenever someone from the League called and told him what was needed to be done. It had been several days since his last call, and he'd been getting restless. When he was restless he did things on his own, mostly for his own amusement. He'd been working here for more than a year and had made a lot of kids sick, but he was getting bored and had considered moving to a different place—possibly a town with an amusement park, or major league baseball stadium.

The last time he'd used his skills was about a week ago, when the League ordered him to infect the daughter of a certain Police Sergeant in order to disorient him in the middle of a promotion that could cause complications with the League. He'd simply shape-shifted his form to that of a nurse, gone into the room while the little girl was waiting to see one of the doctors for a routine physical exam, dropped one of his tiny "bullets" down the back of her shirt, then left quietly. Since shape-shifting had always been natural for him, the job was ridiculously easy.

His cell buzzed. The display said M. Murray Robertson III.

Daniel grinned. He had a strong feeling that the time had come for him to do something big. Some things were definitely worth waiting for.

"Daniel Lyon?"

"Speaking, sir…"

"Are you busy at the moment?"

"No siree…"

"We need you to do something for us as quickly as possible."

"All righty…"

"Apparently there's a rogue demon at the hospital as we speak, undoing our work."

"How's that?"

"Judging by what I've just been told, this demon does good work."

"*Good* work?"

"She's good—as opposed to evil."

"She?"

"Apparently she's a very beautiful young lady and has been a rogue for quite a while. It seems as though she and her partner, who happens to be an inferior trickster, has sent one of our inferiors back down to the Dark Place."

"No shit—I mean really?"

"The Postman was sent back."

Daniel knew about the Postman. He'd never met him, but had heard of his work. The dude was a dork, but apparently very good at staging accidents. This was a real shame. Daniel didn't like do-gooders. He especially didn't like it when do-gooders undid the work of demons.

"How'd they manage that?"

"That's not the issue. We need you to find them both and do whatever it takes to send them back down below. Braithwaite called me personally to warn me about these two. He said he'd like them delivered to him in Orlando but will be satisfied if they're sent down to the Dark Place as quickly as possible."

If the Big Man had called, this definitely sounded serious. "Braithwaite, sir?"

"Yes. And believe me, the call was far from pleasant."

"I can imagine."

"No. I don't think you can."

Wow. This *had* to be big—even bigger than what Robertson was hinting at. And a babe was involved.

Daniel sighed. This job might put him on the map and get him that subordinate rating he'd been lusting after the last hundred years. "A babe, eh?"

"Her name is Tiffany, and the way she was described to me tells me she's someone a normal man just can't ignore."

"Tiffany. Figures."

"We'll give you twenty-four hours to do this."

"I prob'ly won't need that long, actually. A babe like that? I'll find her in an hour or so."

"Finding her isn't the problem. Apparently she's much tougher than she looks. As I've already said, she sent the Postman back down. And from what Braithwaite told me, she's done this same thing twice before."

Daniel grinned. "*My* kind of babe…"

CHAPTER 24

At six-thirty, Tiffany and Chip got into Momma's car.

Tiffany was tired. The emotions she'd experienced during the last couple of hours had done her in. She sat back in the seat and closed her eyes as Momma pulled out of their space.

After a minute or so of silence, Momma, staring straight ahead, said,

"That certainly was one terrific performance, you two."

"Thanks, Momma."

"No problemo," Chip said from the back seat.

Momma continued looking straight ahead. "I don't think I've ever seen anything quite like that before."

"It's a gift," Chip said.

"It…seemed…a lot more than that," Momma said softly.

Tiffany could tell something was bothering Momma. However, she knew better than say anything until Momma brought it up.

After a brief silence, Momma said, "Tell me something, baby."

"If I can, Momma."

"How were you able to heal those children?"

Tiffany feared Momma was going to ask them about this when they were alone. She could tell Momma was confused and even a little frightened by what she had seen. But since Momma was extremely bright and perceptive, Tiffany knew to weigh her words carefully.

"I don't know if I actually *healed* them, Momma. I might have made them feel a little better, but that tends to happen at a magic show. Their excitement level seems to take away their pain and discomfort for a little while."

"I'm not sure what happened back there," Momma said after some thought, "but I distinctly heard Doctor O'Hara and two other doctors talking about the monitors the children were hooked up to."

"What about them?"

"Well, they said most of the stats hadn't changed, but a few had, and dramatically. They also said the ones that hadn't changed should have, because the children were showing significant signs of improvement. It just didn't make any sense to them. That's probably why several of them made it a point to question you when you'd finished with the Conlin girl."

"I don't know anything about medical technology, Momma. All I know is that Chip and I used our skills to make them feel better, and it worked. And as I told everyone before we left, it was bound to work because children truly believe in magic. And when you believe in magic, Momma, all things are possible."

"Look at what happened later on," Chip threw in. "Did you see that stethoscope thingy?"

Momma nodded. "I saw it. I just don't believe what I saw."

"Magic is believing what you've just seen even though you know what you've just seen shouldn't have actually happened," he said.

"He's right, Momma. You could say the same about the children. Magic lives in the imagination and is literally mind over matter. I simply used it to make them forget about their illnesses."

"Just how long will this mind-over-matter thing last?"

"That depends on the child, Momma."

Momma glanced at her and said nothing. She turned back to her driving. "Are you *sure* you were using magic, Baby?"

Tiffany didn't like the tone of Momma's last question. "What else do you think it was, Momma?"

Momma didn't reply.

"Momma? *Please* tell me what's really bothering you."

"I don't know, dear. All I know is that my baby daughter left home five years ago, went to Hollywood, did a few commercials, then came back home." When she spoke again, her voice was much softer. "But when you came back…you turned out to be very, very different..."

"Different how, Momma? I'm the same person I was—"

"No, dear. You're not. When you left, you were still a little girl. My little girl."

"I'm still your little girl, Momma…"

"No, dear. You're now a grown woman, and—"

"I'm five years older, Momma. But I'll always be your little girl."

"I know, baby." Momma patted Tiffany's hand. "But that doesn't change what you did back there."

"Chip and I made a room full of sick kids feel better. What's wrong with that?"

"Nothing, dear."

"Then what's the problem?"

"The problem is *how* you did it. Face it, baby, you and Chip did things that literally stagger the imagination. Chip's lamp trick…it was something I still can't believe—even though I actually saw it with my own two eyes."

"It wasn't nothin', Ma'am…"

"Yes it was." Momma remained dead serious. "But that flame thing you did, dear…it was frightening. I can't imagine anyone being able to do such a thing."

"Oh, I'm sure some famous magicians—"

Momma shook her head. "I don't trust them—especially the ones doing those specials on TV. I can't trust anything I see on TV, for one thing. What you did was live. And you used no props. None that I could see."

"As I said, Momma, kids—"

"I know what you said, dear. But I'm an adult. I stopped believing in magic years ago. As you've no doubt discovered for yourself, life tends to take most of the wonderful things you believed in as a child out of you over the years—which is why people stop believing in many things when they become adults. But I saw the same things the children did. So did Abby. So did Doctor O'Hara and all the other adults who were there. They all saw what you two did, and they're all undoubtedly thinking the same thing. They're thinking that everything you did, everything they saw, was literally impossible."

Tiffany didn't reply. She had no idea how to handle this.

"*I don't know what else to say to her,*" Tiffany sent to Chip.

"*Face it, Tifferoo...we were just too damned fantastic.*"

"*That doesn't help.*"

"*Well, short of telling her we're both dead and some unknown force has been making us more powerful, there's nothing else you* can *tell her.*"

"Baby, Abby asked me if I could possibly persuade you and Chip to do a live demonstration on one of the local TV stations for their morning show."

"What?"

"She suggested that the hospital would consider sending the Chief Administrator and maybe one or two of their Pediatric specialists with clips of some of the children who no longer show any signs of illness since your performance."

"*This is terrible,*" she sent to Chip. "*We can't possibly do this on TV*!"

"That's right," he said. "Bummer."

"What was that?" Momma asked.

"Just jitters," he said. "Sorry."

"What do you say, baby?" Momma asked. "Does it sound like something you might want to consider? It could be great publicity for the hospital."

"We can talk about it in the morning—okay, Momma? We're both pretty tired."

"Of course. We'll talk about it over breakfast."

"*Over breakfast*," Tiffany sent to Chip.

"*That means we've got twelve hours to come up with something.*"

"*That's right. Twelve hours.*"

"*And it had better be good. Your mother's a bright lady.*"

"*That's why I'm so nervous*," she replied, sinking in her seat.

***

Daniel D. Lyon spotted the Sedarski place on NE Glen Oak a few minutes after seven o'clock that evening. A silver Honda was parked in front of the garage. The lights blazed behind the windows on the ground floor. He drove on by, stopped at the next block and parked his Challenger in the paved lot of a small strip mall down the street. He killed the engine, doused his lights and sat there, thinking about his strategy.

From what he'd learned at the hospital posing as a visiting doctor, the Tiffany demon and her inferior sidekick had just put on a show for the kids at the hospital. As a result, many of them no longer appeared to be showing symptoms of any signs of sickness.

This in itself made him want to chew on a handful of heavy-duty carpet tacks. It was bad enough that this Tiffany demon did good deeds. But it was even worse that she and her sidekick had undone what Daniel had been doing since he first came to this one-horse town.

Now he knew what all that commotion was about while he was on the second floor, putting up with Old Man Timmons' dust bunny bullshit. He just wasn't prepared for something like this. He hadn't expected any demon, rogue or otherwise, to shit-can what he'd been doing the last twelve months.

He'd also learned that the Tiffany bitch and her inferior buddy were living with Sandra Sedarski on NE Glen Oak, just twenty minutes away. The Sedarski woman worked in the office at the hospital. She didn't seem to pose a problem, but if Daniel had to get rid of the twosome, Sedarski would most certainly have to be eliminated as well.

Either way, he didn't view this job as much of a problem.

He glanced at his watch. 7:18. It would probably be hours before they retired for the night. He wanted to do the deed as soon as possible but realized he might have to wait. He'd always been the quick-results-instant-gratification type of guy. In other words, he hated waiting—especially when it involved performing gratifying demon work. But waiting was often necessary—especially if the job had to be done efficiently. From what Robertson had told him, this Tiffany bitch was dangerous and not to be trifled with.

To Daniel, this one factor made the task much more exciting. His thoughts centered on how his status would improve exponentially once he'd sent the babe and her sidekick back down below.

He'd been told at the hospital that the Sedarski woman was actually Tiffany's mother. He figured that was a lie. It was merely some sort of cover story, obviously. Demons didn't have mortal kin. Tiffany probably chose Sedarski for some practical reason. She probably needed a place to stay so she could be close to the hospital.

She'd certainly made her mark tonight. From what he'd heard, nearly all the infected kids were getting better. Just thinking about this pissed him off even worse. It had taken him many months to infect all these kids. He'd even had to pose as a custodian and put up with that asshole Timmons for eight hours a day just to be able to stay close to his work. If the supers and subs down below heard about what just happened, he'd become a joke.

There was no way Daniel D. Lyon would let a rogue demon babe turn him into a joke. He hadn't spent two centuries in the Valley of Decay collecting poisonous dandelion spores for nothing.

A tap on his window.

He rolled it down.

A tall, dark-haired guy in a custom-made suit stood beside his door, frowning down at him.

Daniel frowned back. "Yeah?"

"You're in my space."

"So?"

"This is my parking space."

"So?"

The man sighed impatiently. "My name is painted clearly on the sign in front of your car." He pointed. "See it?"

Daniel gazed at the sign just a few feet beyond the windshield. Light from the overhead streetlamp lit up most of the area. Sure enough, a black sign painted *MARK PETERSON, M.D.*, showed prominently, in bold white letters. He turned back to the moron in the suit. "You're Peterson?"

"*Doctor* Peterson." The man's glare deepened.

"Whatever."

"Well?"

"Well what?"

"You just saw the sign."

"Yeah, I saw it."

"Move your damned car, then."

"I don't want to."

"Why not?"

"For one simple reason: I don't want to."

"I can have you towed."

"So?"

"Do you know what that means?"

"What? Having me towed?"

"What else are we talking about?"

"Go ahead. Get a tow truck here."

"You don't care?"

"Nope."

The jerk produced a cell phone. "Last chance."

"For what?"

"For having your car towed, asshole."

"Oh. I thought it was yours, dickhead."

"Huh?"

"It's your last chance to walk away healthy."

The man blinked. "Is that a threat?"

"That depends."

"On what?"

Daniel shrugged tiredly. He was getting weary by the moment. This ridiculous arguing was going nowhere. He had important things to do, and this well-dressed moron was distracting him. "It depends on you standing there like a dickhead and not walking away…"

The man crossed his arms defiantly across his chest. "Well, I guess it *is* a threat, then…because I'm not walking away!"

"Okay, then…if you really want to be a dickhead, I won't stand in your way…" Daniel pulled a spore out of his pocket and flicked it in the man's direction. It drifted toward his face and disappeared in his mouth just as the man opened it to reply.

The man began coughing and choking. He clutched his throat. His cell phone dropped, clattering on the pavement. He doubled over and hacked away.

Daniel got out and closed his door. He watched the man gasping and hacking bile. Strings of spittle fell from his gaping mouth, dangling just a few inches from the pavement. "If I were you," he said, tapping the man on the back, "I'd see a doctor about that. It sounds kind of serious."

As the man continued choking and hacking away, Daniel crossed the street and went down the block. It was still early, but he was tired of waiting. He was going to make a killing tonight and wanted to do it while he was all fired up. Luckily, Dr. Dickhead had just fed the flames.

This was the perfect night to make his name with the Royal League of Demons.

CHAPTER 25

At eight o'clock, Tiffany and Chip sat in the living room with Momma, watching TV on her widescreen. Momma and Tiffany sat on the couch, both enjoying a glass of wine. Momma had put on an episode of "*Medium*" from her Netflix queue.

Chip sat in the armchair next to them, having a large glass of orange juice. He'd been silent during the episode but, judging by the way he kept frowning, seemed to be having a problem with it.

"Something wrong?" Momma asked.

"This show's doing a number on me."

"What's wrong?" Momma asked. "Can't you understand what's going on?"

"Oh, I know what's going on…"

"Don't you believe in the afterlife?"

Chip glanced at Tiffany.

"*Be careful...*"

"*No problemo, Muffin.*" To Momma, he said, "Oh, I believe in the afterlife, all right…"

"Then what's the problem?"

"Something about the show just doesn't work for me."

"Such as…?"

"Well, this blond babe dreams a bunch of heavy stuff, and sometimes this stuff really happens, only it might not happen the way she dreamed it. If it does, it might have happened in the past, the present, or the future…or it might not have happened at all—right?"

"Right..."

"So this babe calls her boss, or the cop guy, to tell them her dream so they can solve the really nasty murder case they're working on. They tell her she has to be wrong, but they find out later on that she was right—or pretty close to being right. Am I on-base so far?"

"Yes…so what is it that doesn't work for you?" Momma asked.

"I'm just wondering why the phone is on her hubby's side of the bed. When she has to make a call, she has to crawl over him to get to the phone. I think the phone should be on her side of the bed. It just seems stupid to me."

Momma just smiled.

"Is that it?" Tiffany asked.

"Not really…"

"What else is bothering you?" Momma asked.

"I'm not so sure they got the dead thingy nailed down right, but what do you expect? No one writing or producing the show is dead, so…"

"You know she's a famous medium, don't you?" Momma said.

"I thought the blond babe was an actress…"

"The *real* Allison."

"There's a *real* blond babe? In real life? No shit—I mean really?"

"Yes," Momma said. "She's a renowned medium, and many of these cases have happened during the course of her career." She turned to Tiffany. "Don't you two ever watch TV?"

"We haven't really had the time, Momma."

"The two of you stay in hotels during your travels, don't you?"

"Well yes, but we usually don't have that much time to surf the channels."

"That's a real shame," Momma said. "It doesn't sound like you two have much actual play time."

"It's not from the lack of trying," Chip said with a wink.

"Not much at all." Tiffany said, glaring at him.

Momma had a sip of wine. "Well, getting back to the real Allison… From what I've read, I believe she still works with the Police whenever they need her services."

Chip shrugged. "They still don't have the dead thingy nailed down."

"*Watch it*," Tiffany warned.

Momma seemed confused. "What would you know about the dead, Chip? You can't be much older than what? Twenty-five?"

Chip grinned. "I'm a lot older than I look."

"Thirty, maybe?"

He chuckled. "That's a *little* closer…"

At 9:00, Momma switched on an episode of "*Good Witch*."

A few minutes later, Tiffany began to get a strange feeling. "*I think someone's outside*," she sent to Chip.

"*There are probably a lot of folks outside, Muffin. This is the big city of Peoria in all its splendor, right?"*

"I mean outside this house—idiot."

"Same thing, right? And, by the way, oucherino."

"That's not what I'm getting at."

"Then please explain in graphic detail this sudden attack of acute paranoia."

"I think someone's sneaking around out there."

"Out where?"

Tiffany had some wine to mask her frustration. *"Outside the house—just like I said."*

"Want me to go out there as a firefly so I can fly around in the dark with my tiny flashlight and explore?"

"You can do that?"

"No, but I can make myself darker so no one can see me."

"That would be great--if you could actually do it..."

"I smell a definite but *entering our meaningful discussion."*

"I was just gonna say that I can't see you doing this without Momma getting suspicious."

"You mean because she might notice that I'm not sitting here anymore?"

"Since there are only three of us in this room, it would definitely become an issue of concern."

"Watch me, grasshopper. And observe how the master operates."

"Master?"

"Figure of speech." Chip finished his orange juice, put the glass down and stood up. "If no one minds, I think I'd like to take a little walk out back to stretch the ol' legs."

"Is something wrong?" Momma asked.

"I'm just a tad restless, and would like to fluff the old petals—if you know what I mean." He ran a hand through his thick red mop.

"I understand," Momma said. "Go right ahead. We won't be going to bed for a while—unless you're too tired to stay up much longer, dear."

"I'm fine, Momma."

"All righty-rooty, then. See ya in just a few minutes..." Chip went through the kitchen, opened the back door and disappeared into the night.

***

Momma picked up her wine glass. "How long have you known Chip, baby?"

"Why, Momma?"

"It seems like you two really have a good thing going."

"What do you mean?"

"Well, I've noticed that when you both get quiet, it seems like you're somehow communicating with one another."

Tiffany fidgeted. Once again she realized just how perceptive her mother was. She knew right then that she and Chip should be even more careful. "Whatever would make you think that, Momma?"

"Just a feeling I've had. I felt that way when you two were performing at the hospital. It just seemed as if you both knew exactly what the other was thinking."

"Well, when you spend that much time working closely with someone, you get to know one another's habits and idiosyncrasies..."

"That's probably what I was thinking. How many times have you done that same act?"

“Too many to remember.” She thought it best just to lie and be vague. Otherwise, she’d have to think up a slew of explanations—which would probably lead to even more questions.

“Is the act always the same? Or do you change it from time to time?”

“It’s never the same. We almost always have to go by our instinct and just see what works.” It was time to move on. “Would you like more wine, Momma? I think I’d like another sip or two.”

“That sounds fine, dear. There’s another bottle in the pantry. I’ll get it.” She got up.

“That’s all right, Momma. I’ll get it.”

Momma smiled. “No, dear. You and Chip are my guests.” Without another word, she turned and went back into the kitchen.

Tiffany sat back and concentrated. “*Chip? You okay*?”

No response.

“*Chip?*”

Silence.

No response. This wasn’t good. What bothered her even worse was that she no longer sensed anyone wandering around outside.

Then she noticed that Momma was taking too much time to find another bottle of port wine.

Fearing trouble, Tiffany sat bolt upright. “Momma? Everything okay in there?”

Silence.

“Momma?”

Her pulse fluttering, Tiffany jumped up.

Just then, two figures slipped through the open doorway. Momma was carrying a wine bottle and smiling. Chip trailed behind her.

"Something wrong, dear? You look like you've just seen a ghost."

"Nothing, Momma…" Tiffany sat back down and forced herself not to stare. Something just didn't feel right…

As Momma sat down beside her, Chip returned to his armchair, picked up his empty orange juice glass and held it out as she poured wine for Tiffany and herself.

"Really?" Momma looked surprised. "I thought you drank only orange juice and water."

Chip was silent as he studied his glass. Then he said, "Oh..." He shrugged. "I thought I'd try something different."

Tiffany watched him suspiciously as Momma filled his glass.

Something was *very* wrong. Chip *never* drank alcohol; he said it would wilt his petals. She wanted to send over something to ask if he felt okay, but some inner feeling told her not to say anything right now.

Just then, she heard his voice in her head: "*Tifferoo*?"

She stared at her wine glass. "*Chip*?"

"It's me. What's going on in there?"

In there. What did he mean by that?

The figure facing her was gobbling up the wine in his glass and gave no indication that he was communicating with her.

Her suspicions grew.

"Are you serious?"

"C'mon, Tifferoosky. What's happening in there?"

The figure in the chair lowered his glass and began staring at her. Once again, her strange feeling took hold, turning her insides cold. She could tell that she was in the presence of a shapeshifter. If so, she had to be extremely careful. This shifter was sitting less than two feet from Momma.

Then she wondered if this was the same demon that had been making the children sick.

"I think there's a shapeshifter in here with us," she sent to Chip.

"What's he look like?"

"I thought he was you."

"Just for the record, Babykins, he ain't me. I'm outside. I can't be inside, too."

"I already figured that one out. How'd he get past you?"

"Let's worry about that later and see how we can nail his butt before he does any serious damage in there."

"Where are you?"

"Out back, in the bushes."

"Why's everyone so quiet?" The Chip-figure quickly drained half his glass of wine. "It's like a morgue in here." No one said anything. He tilted his head. Then he nodded. "Yep. A morgue, all right."

"I'm just wondering why you're drinking wine," Tiffany said casually. "It's…well, it's kind of weird."

"You never saw me drink wine before, babe?"

"No."

"Maybe you're just winding down after your show," Momma said.

"That's it. Yep. I'm winding down." He hoisted his glass and drank more. "A wind-down by downing wine." He chuckled. "Really hits the spot." He drained his glass, put it down on the table, picked up the bottle and filled it again.

"My goodness," Momma said. "When you try something different, you really go all out, don't you?"

"That's me, lady. Just call me the All-Out guy!" He grinned and downed nearly half of his fresh drink. "By the way, babe," he said to Tiffany, "didn't we have fun with those sick kids?"

She didn't like his tone, but it convinced her she was right. This was definitely not Chip. "Yes. We did, didn't we?"

"Barrels. A shitload, actually." He shook his head. "They're not sick anymore, are they?"

"I honestly don't know. We were both told that many of them were feeling much better. Don't you remember? You were standing right there beside me."

"Yeah. Guess I forgot." He sighed. "The excitement. The hustle. The bustle. All that sorta crap…"

Momma was gazing at Chip suspiciously. "Is something going on that I—"

"*Chip? You still out there*?" Tiffany felt a wave of panic settling in. "*I think we're going to have to do something quickly. If Momma says the wrong thing, she might—*"

Just then, the doorbell rang.

Momma cringed and checked her watch. "Why, it's almost ten. Who on earth could *that* be?"

The Chip-figure shrugged. "I honestly don't know. I've got sort of a nifty idea about solving the mystery, though. Why doesn't one of us get up and open the door?"

Momma went to the door and checked the peephole. "For heaven's sake..." She pulled open the door.

Abby Turner was standing there, smiling at her. "Hi, Sandra. Sorry to bother you at this late hour, but I have to talk to your daughter and her partner. It's about their spot on the local TV station we mentioned earlier."

Momma turned. "Baby? Abby would like to talk to you and Chip."

"Sure, Momma." Uneasy, Tiffany got up and went over. "Hi, Abby. Is there a problem?"

"Well, no...but there seems to be a snag that just came up, and I wanted to get with the two of you before we made the arrangements for the TV spot. Can we talk? Is that all right with you, Sandra?"

"It's fine with me," Momma said.

"If you don't mind," Abby said, "I think we'd better talk in the kitchen. This could get complicated."

"Oh..." Momma nodded. "By all means." She gestured to the kitchen. "I'll just go back to the couch and watch the rest of the program. Just make believe I'm not here."

Tiffany and the shapeshifter followed Abby into the kitchen.

"What's wrong, Abby?" Tiffany kept her voice low. "And why this secretive stuff?"

"Yeah," the shapeshifter said. "What's all this secret shit? I was all set to start getting a buzz from that second glass of wine."

Gazing at Tiffany, Abby sent over, "*It's me, Tifferoo...get his attention as soon as I wink.*"

It took her only a second to figure it out. It didn't make sense that Chip was able to shape-shift, but that wasn't important right now. They had to take care of the shapeshifter right away, and if Chip could suddenly appear as someone else to make this happen, then so be it.

"Make this quick," the shapeshifter said. "We need to get back. I've got almost half a glass of wine—plus the rest of that bottle—with my name on it."

Abby winked.

"Personally," Tiffany whispered to the shapeshifter, "I think you're drinking entirely too much wine." She moved a little to her right. "I really think you need to cool it."

"Listen, babe…if I wanted advice like that, I'd get my mother here. No offense, but you sure as hell don't look like anyone's—"

Before he could finish his statement, Abby, standing slightly behind him, suddenly turned back into Chip, who immediately transformed into the Yellow Lady's Slipper.

Sensing danger, the shapeshifter glimpsed the incredible sight and gasped. His eyes grew. In that same instant, the flower's petal swayed toward him, brushing his face. Just as he began losing consciousness, he changed into a tall, slender, dark-haired man with rough features and cold, dark eyes. An instant later, he slid quietly to the floor.

Alert for any sign of movement, Tiffany watched him guardedly. There was none.

The flower turned back into Chip.

"That was really close," she whispered, "but I'm glad you were able to—"

"Uh-oh…" Chip stared past her, at the doorway leading to the living room.

Momma stood in the archway holding her glass of wine, her eyes filling the sockets, her mouth wide-open.

CHAPTER 26

"Wh-What on earth… Who is *that?* Wh-what's going *on*?" Momma gawked at the shapeshifter, then at Chip, then Tiffany. "Baby…what in heaven's name *is* all this? What's…going *on* in here?"

"Momma? Are you all right? You're so *pale*…"

Momma couldn't take her eyes off the motionless figure on the floor. She trembled; drops of wine spilled from her glass, forming a tiny puddle on the floor at her feet.

"Momma?"

No reply. Momma began lowering her arm slowly, stiffly. Her glazed eyes remained fixed on the figure lying on the floor.

Sensing disaster, Tiffany rushed over. She took the glass from Momma's grip and set it on the counter. Then she grabbed Momma by the waist. Together, she and Chip helped her back into the living room.

They laid her gently onto the sofa, until she was lying comfortably. Tiffany took the afghan draped over the back of the sofa and covered her with it. She knelt facing her and pushed some of Momma's tousled hair away from her face. "Momma? Are you gonna be okay?"

"Baby?" Momma's eyelids became heavy. In seconds they closed, and she appeared to be sleeping.

"Is she gonna be all right, Tifferoo?" Chip asked, standing behind Tiffany.

Tiffany felt her mother's pulse. It was rapid, but gradually settled down. "I think she's okay. She would have fainted if we hadn't grabbed her when we did."

"We have a shitload of stuff to do, Tifferoo. And we've got to do it pretty damned fast. I suggest we start in the kitchen."

"How much of your special juice did you give him?"

"I gave him the full dose. It should keep him out for most of the night, but that's just a wild guess. He really needs to be moved. He shouldn't be anywhere in the house when your mother comes to … "

"We need to find a place to stash him."

"How about your mom's car?"

She frowned. "That's a terrible idea."

"Can you think of a better one?"

"No…"

"Then, until you come up with a nifty brainstorm, I suggest we stick to my idea—at least, for now."

"All right, but we can't just dump him in the Honda and leave him there indefinitely. Momma might notice—especially when she gets in the car to drive somewhere."

"We'll have to take him somewhere early tomorrow morning. We can give your mom some story, but we don't have to think of that right now."

"I guess we can carry him outside and put him in the back seat, but we've got to come right back.

Yes, this was Momma they were talking about now, and Tiffany knew that she could never do anything to hurt the woman who'd brought her into this world. But she had to face facts. Momma had seen something she shouldn't have, and this alone would make her vulnerable to all the bad things that could happen in a very short time. But since Tiffany was quite possibly the only one on this earth with the power to keep Momma completely safe, she really had no choice.

And although she dreaded doing anything with her mother's memory, she realized that this was quite possibly the only way she could get Momma back.

"I think I can do this," she said—to herself more so than to Chip.

"Before you work your magic on her, keep this in mind. We can't possibly do that TV spot."

"I was thinking the same thing."

"If you find yourself weakening, think of this. We both suspect how the hospital people will react to what we did today. And even if they don't say too much about how we healed all those kids, if we do that TV spot, we'll probably end up as local celebrities. Braithwaite'll hear about it and find us in no time at all."

"I know."

"Keep that in mind, Tiffers. I know you'd like to stay here, but we can't do it. Not yet, anyway."

Chip was right. Sighing deeply, she nodded. Then, focusing on the job at hand, she turned back to Momma.

"Momma," she said softly, "can you hear me?"

Silence. The woman continued sleeping.

Tiffany closed her eyes and focused on sending her deepest thoughts into her mother's consciousness. "*Momma, this is Tiffany. I know you're sleeping, but I also know you might be able to hear me. I want you to listen to me, and I want you to listen carefully. I'm going to tell you some things that might not make sense to you right now, but you have to listen and believe everything I say. I love you with all my heart and would never lie to you, and I would never tell you anything that would hurt you, frighten you, or make you uncomfortable. If you can hear me, please nod.*"

After several moments, Momma nodded very slightly.

Tiffany sighed in relief. "*First of all, I want you to forget everything you thought you saw in the kitchen. I want you to forget all about the flower you might have seen as well as the strange person lying on the floor. You have to forget all about Abby coming to talk to us, because she really didn't come to the house at all. When you came into the kitchen, you saw Chip and me having an argument. That's all. Chip and I are friends as well as partners. We argue all the time. Do you understand?*"

Another slight nod.

"*I have to tell you something else, Momma. Believe me, this is something I don't want to do, but it really has to be done. Chip and I have to leave. We can't stay here, and we can't do that spot on the local TV station. I hope you can understand. We have things we have to do elsewhere, and we can't do them here. But I want you to know that I'll be back. One day very soon I'll come back and stay with you, and we can get to know one another all over again and do all sorts of fun things together. One day...one day we can...we'll...*"

"You okay, Tifferoo?"

"No, but I can do this." Tiffany wiped her wet eyes. The waves of sadness had swept through her, bringing back memories she hadn't thought about for a long time. Images of the three of them sitting at the dinner table, laughing and sharing good times together, rushed past. She also caught flashes of Dad taking her to the circus as a little girl, and the three of them having fun at a picnic at an aunt's house.

There were more, but she pushed them aside. This wasn't the time for such treasured nostalgia. This was the time to fix something that could possibly hurt Momma. Tiffany had to be strong again—strong enough to cast the precious memories aside.

Taking a deep breath, she cleared her mind and turned back to Momma. "*One day we can be together again and share our memories, and I promise that when you're old, I'll be right here beside you to take care of you... And when it's time for you to pass, I promise that I'll be here with you then, too, and I'll go with you and make sure we follow the same road that will lead to where Dad will be waiting for us. I also promise that whenever you need me, all you have to do is think of me and call my name, and I'll come back to you. I'll always come back to you, Momma, because I love you and always will. Do you understand*?"

A nod.

"*One final thing. When you wake up, you're going to feel wonderful. In fact, you're going to feel better than you have in a long time*." Tiffany placed her hands on her mother's hands, visualized one last piece of her heart slipping from her into Momma's hands, and smiled.

Moments later, Momma opened her eyes. Squinting, she looked around. "Did I ...fall asleep?"

"You were tired, Momma. It's been a long, busy day."

Momma blinked. "What's wrong, dear? You look like…like you've been crying..."

"I was just worried about you, Momma. You were sitting there, sipping your wine. Then you just nodded off. You would've spilled your drink if I hadn't been close enough to grab the glass."

"My God…really? I'm *so* sorry, baby… Some host I am!" She sat up. "I could've sworn I went into the kitchen to get more wine, but I guess I was just dreaming. Too much wine, obviously. I really should be ashamed of myself!" She glanced at Chip. "Are you two okay?"

"Yepperino."

"Why, Momma?"

"I have this vague memory of the two of you arguing in the kitchen. I hope it wasn't serious."

"Just business, Momma. We argue all the time."

"Yepperino." Chip nodded eagerly. "All the time."

Momma glanced at the wall clock. "My stars! It's nearly midnight! I think we'd all better call it a night." She shifted on the sofa and stood.

"How do you feel, Momma?"

Momma shrugged and suddenly looked confused. "Actually…I feel wonderful…"

"Really?"

Momma laughed. "As a matter of fact, I don't think I've felt this great in a long time!"

***

Watching the activity from outside the living room window, the well-dressed, gray-haired man crouched behind the rose bush. A moment later, he pulled out his silver cell phone. When he heard his colleague's voice at the other end of the line, he whispered, "Everything seems to be turning out, Albert."

"Do you think you quelled the flames at the hospital?" Albert asked.

"I'm reasonably sure I handled the situation satisfactorily. I intervened with two of the hospital's chief administrators before they were able to get in touch with the wrong people."

"And you think your work there is finished?"

"I'm not quite certain. Something of this magnitude could easily turn bad."

"It generally does when things happen that mortals cannot possibly understand."

"Yes. Especially when their technology does not accept such phenomena."

"This could become a sticky situation, George."

"I'm afraid you could be right. I'll stick around down here for a few days to make sure no other repercussions result from the Limboite's actions. I've heard that the television and news media could become involved."

"That is unfortunate. It could turn into a circus."

"This is why I intend to remain here for a little while and make sure this doesn't escalate. I think I'll be able to contain it if I stay close and keep my ears open. At least mortals are easy to manipulate. Otherwise, we'd be in even worse trouble."

"It is unfortunate you were forced to intervene again on the Limboite's behalf."

"Yes, but judging by what she's accomplished, I consider this sudden trip extremely beneficial."

"I understand she and her partner have actually cured at least three dozen sick children in that city."

"From what I've observed, I believe the actual count is between forty and fifty."

"Very impressive."

"Yes, especially since the children were infected by a dark messenger sent to this city from down below."

"What is the latest on this messenger?"

"He is being taken care of as we speak. You have no doubt also heard that the Limboite has already eliminated another messenger from this city. This one, I have heard, was responsible for more than two hundred and fifty murders."

"Yes. I was given the same information. The Limboite is definitely making her mark."

"This is why I don't mind intervening on her behalf. She has done excellent work since leaving the Dark Place."

"Yes, but we must remember that she might occasionally require a slight nudge toward subtlety. If word gets out that she can actually cure sickness…"

"I understand, Albert."

"And I believe we have recently heard a rumor that she brought a family pet back from near death."

"From what I've heard, she used genuine love to accomplish that feat. I believe this same technique was what she used to cure the illnesses in the hospital. We all know how rare something like that is in the mortal world."

"Of course we do. But as I've just said, subtlety must prevail above all else."

"Yes, but we must not forget the good work she is doing. She is now ridding this town of a second dark messenger. That is impressive, given the fact that she has only been here a couple of days."

"Truly impressive. Even so, her recent actions merely demonstrate that she needs to be monitored—on an occasional basis, of course."

"I concur. As I have stated many times before, she is truly a pure, honest soul. She possesses only goodness in her heart. I sincerely believe this."

"I agree with you. But we still must keep an eye on her."

"You are not suggesting that she might go rogue, are you?" George asked.

"Not at all. We are much more worried about the opposition. The super demon now in charge of things down there seems to be aware of everything she does. His network, unfortunately, is extremely formidable."

"He will not inform anyone about her unless it is to find, subdue, and send her back to the Dark Place. Otherwise, news of her accomplishments will, in his eyes, diminish his power. This super demon possesses a colossal ego. He will not risk his reputation if he thinks the Limboite can outsmart him. This is why he will always send a subordinate to subdue her, and to do it as quietly as possible."

"We cannot let that happen, can we?"

"We cannot prevent it, either."

"Agreed. Our limitations are quite clear. We can only intervene as a last resort."

"In any case, she is doing exemplary work. She is weakening the opposition and giving it a bad name. The super demon would not risk word of this getting out. This would give mortals hope and take away much of the fear they have for demons."

"Duly noted. Resume your work, and keep us informed."

"I shall do that. I might have to change my form from time to time to accomplish this, but if it is necessary, it will be done."

"Good luck."

"Thank you." George pocketed the phone. Once the lights went off in the living room of the

Sedarski household, he slipped away and disappeared in the darkness of night.

DAY FOUR - "DEALING WITH ANOTHER DEMON"

CHAPTER 27

The next morning, as they were having breakfast, Tiffany struggled to stay calm and hoped Momma would not sense her inner turmoil. Neither she nor Chip had been able to look in on the shapeshifter, and she quickly found that she could not keep from worrying about the whole situation. She had visions of him coming out of his unconscious state, getting out of the Honda and returning to his life as a demon.

Then she wondered why he'd targeted her and Chip.

Did this have anything to do with the Postman?

Had Breath Mint heard about any of this? Had he sent another demon after them?

Did this have anything to do with what they'd done at the hospital?

The moment she considered that, the minuscule spore she'd taken from the Conlin girl flashed in her mind like a tiny flare.

Was *that* what this was all about?

Was the demon the one making the children sick?

"Something on your mind, dear?" Momma asked.

Tiffany blinked back into reality. The fog cleared, and Momma suddenly appeared to her across the table. "I'm sorry. What was that, Momma?"

"You seem lost in thought."

Tiffany's head swam. Luckily, she was able to sort it all out. "Chip and I…we have to go into town for a little while, Momma. Will it be okay if we used your car?"

"Of course, dear." Momma spread some strawberry jam onto her wedge of toast.

"You weren't going into work this morning, were you?"

"No, baby. I didn't want to go in while you were staying with me, so I told them I wanted to take off the rest of the week."

Tiffany didn't reply.

Momma nibbled on her toast. "Will you be following up on your appearance on the local TV show?"

"No, Momma…" Tiffany glanced at Chip. "I don't think we'll be able to do the show."

Momma went silent. Tiffany waited tensely for her to say something. Momma sipped coffee. "I understand, dear."

"Really?"

She nodded. "I had this strange feeling when I woke up this morning that you and Chip will probably be leaving soon. I can't explain it, but…" She shrugged. "You have prior commitments, right?"

"Yes, Momma."

"I guess whatever you did last night worked, Tifferoo."

"I didn't think it would work quite this well…"

"Don't question it. Just enjoy your handiwork."

Momma shrugged and had more coffee.

"You're not sad, are you, Momma?"

"Of course I am, dear. But I understand—I truly do. You and Chip obviously can't stay in the same place for very long. Entertainers don't do that unless there's a reason. You and Chip are very special. You're very good at what you do. Based on what you've accomplished here, I'd say that the more you travel, the more people you'll help—and this makes me very proud."

"I'm glad you're proud of us, Momma."

"I'm extremely proud…and I hope you can do the same thing somewhere else. But I am kind of glad you're leaving."

"Why is that, Momma?"

Momma sighed. "What you did at the hospital… I hope you realize that you upset a lot of people there."

"You mean the staff?"

"Well, I heard a couple of the doctors talking about calling someone in to review some of the cases. I've got this sneaking suspicion that they're a bit frightened about the whole thing."

"They probably feel threatened."

"It's more than that, dear. I think they could quite possibly call an emergency meeting with the Board to discuss this."

"Why can't they just be satisfied that the children are feeling better?"

"They're doctors, dear. Scientists. What you did makes no sense to them. They're all about meds and technology and funding and therapy, and when someone enters the picture and alleviates documented suffering with a wave of her hand…" She shrugged. "It baffles them."

"Momma, do I have to worry about you?"

"No, baby. I'll be fine."

"You're sure?"

"The way I see it, they can't really cause much of a negative reaction to any of this without upsetting a lot of people—especially the parents and families of the children. What they'll probably do is engage themselves in restudying the cases individually. I'm sure Abby will tell them that you and I hadn't been in touch with one another in years, so they'll know that I'm just as flabbergasted about all this as they are." She smiled. "Don't worry about me, baby. Just do what you have to do, and when you do come back, I'll be extremely happy all over again."

"Yes, Momma. I just hope you realize how much I'd love to stay here with you."

"I really wish you *could* stay here. But that's not in the cards right now, is it?"

"No, Momma."

Momma smiled. "I have this strong feeling that you'll come back one day, and this time you'll stay forever."

Tiffany smiled back. "Yes, Momma. One day I will definitely come back. It won't be very long from now, and when that day comes, I won't ever leave you again."

Momma placed her hand on Tiffany's. It was very warm, possibly from her coffee cup. "I'll be *so* happy when you do come back, baby. You don't have to make any other promises."

"Whatever you say, Momma..." Once again, Tiffany fought down the urge to cry.

***

At ten o'clock, the shapeshifter still hadn't budged. He lay on his side in the back seat, his eyes closed, snoring steadily.

"I never knew your juice was so powerful." Tiffany was impressed as she got in front, pulled the driver's door shut and fired up the ignition.

"Neither did I..." Chip slid in beside her. "A lot of things have been different lately."

Tiffany backed the Honda down the drive. "You never did tell me what happened out back last night." She put the car in gear and went up to the stop sign at the end of the block.

"I wish I knew. When I went outside, I heard movement in the bushes. Then I saw that guy slipping out from behind a bush. As soon as he saw me, he reached into his pocket and tossed something at me, but in the dark I didn't see what it was. There was some light coming from the streetlamp, but I still couldn't see anything. Whatever it was must've been really small."

"Could it have been some sort of seed? Or spore?"

"You're thinking of that thing you took from the Conlin kid at the hospital, aren'tcha?"

"Exactly."

"Whatever it was, it made me feel kind of queasy. I figured I ought to go down and stay down. The moment I did, I found that I'd changed into my spirit form. Once I'd changed, I no longer felt queasy. I think the change must've done something to break whatever spell he'd zapped me with. Anyway, there I was, standing in one of the bushes about five feet away. I don't think the shifter saw what happened. He just stepped over my human form and snuck into the house."

"He what?"

"Like I just said, he stepped over my human form."

"You said you were standing in the bushes in your *spirit* form…"

"I had no idea what was going on, Tifferoo. I remember watching him sneak inside the house. Then I realized that I was standing in the bushes…but I was also lying on the ground, where I'd fallen."

"You…became *two* spirits?"

"I honestly don't know, Tifferoo."

"What happened next?"

"The moment the shifter went inside, my human form disappeared altogether. It was as if it had become a shadow."

Tiffany went silent.

"Weird, huh?"

She shrugged. "Maybe you slipped out of your human form too quickly."

"That makes no sense. If you remember, whenever I do the change, it's always during an emergency, and I only have a split second to do it."

"Well, whatever happened, I think it's best that we don't question it. It worked. We were able to overpower him. That's all that really matters."

"What about my sudden ability to shape-shift?"

"Like I said, don't question it. Your powers are obviously growing, too."

"It's about time."

"Better late than never, right?"

"Righterino. So where are we going and what do we intend to do with him? We can't just toss him in a dumpster." He tilted his head. "Or *can* we?"

Tiffany stopped at the intersection. When traffic was clear, she pulled out and made the left onto Main Street. "I was thinking that maybe we could do the same thing to him that we did with the mailman."

"You mean take away his powers?"

She nodded. "First thing we have to do is go through his pockets and see what he's got in there."

Chip frowned. "I'm a guy."

"So?"

"Guys don't go through other guy's pockets."

"Cops do it all the time."

"I'm not a cop. I'm a trickster. The bestest of the best in the West. And now that my powers are growing, I guess you could call me the bestest of the bestest—"

"Stick a sock in it. Save the accolades—and please do it for someone who actually wants to hear them."

"You're really cold, girl."

"Someone has to be."

"I can be cold when I wanna be…"

"Does this mean you'll go through his pockets?"

Chip smiled weakly. "I guess I'm not quite in the mood to be cold right now."

"You realize this makes you a sissy boy, right?"

Chip shrugged. "I've been called worse."

"I know."

***

Fifteen minutes later, Tiffany drove past the Marriott Pere Marquette. Taking Fulton, she went down the street that led them to the rear lot of the hotel.

The lot was nearly deserted. She parked in a space at the end of the third row, and she and Chip got out and opened the rear doors. With Chip's help, she pulled the shapeshifter into an upright position on the seat. Chip held him up while Tiffany checked his pockets.

"Be careful, Tiffers. There's no telling what he might have in there."

"I think I found what we've been looking for." She pulled her hand out of his right front pocket and opened it. A tight clump of gray seed-heads about the size of a golf ball rested in her palm.

"What the hell?"

Tiffany brought her hand up to her face and sniffed. The smell was faint—both sweet and sour. She wrinkled her nose. "It smells kind of funky but looks like it might have come from some sort of flower." She held it out to him. "You're a flower. Any ideas?"

Chip sniffed and abruptly pulled away. "Smells like something that's been lying in a box with smelly old socks and tennis shoes. But it sure looks like dandelion spores."

With the index finger of her free hand, Tiffany separated the clump. The seed-heads were clearly visible amongst the tangle. "It looks like what I pulled from the little girl at the hospital."

Chip stiffened. "You mean this asshole's the reason those kids were sick?"

"Could be..."

"Now it's beginning to make sense."

Tiffany was silent for a few moments. "Tell me something."

"Ask away, my delicate flower..."

"How could a *dandelion* make anyone sick?"

"Need you ask? This boy's a demon. If he picked up the spores from the Valley of Decay, they were probably poisoned centuries ago. And since he's a demon, all he has to do is handle them to make them turn deadly..."

"Now I understand."

"All righty-rooty, then, Milady...let's rearrange this asshole's brain cells and park his worthless ass to the curb."

Tiffany pocketed the spores. She moved closer to the unconscious inferior. "Can you hear me in there?"

A nod.

"Tell me your name."

"Daniel D. Lyon."

"What's the D stand for?"

"Nothing. It's just part of my mortal name. Dan D. Lyon is kind of a joke."

"You're quite the comedian. The trouble is, you don't make people laugh, you make them sick. You've been making them sick for how long now?"

"For more than a hundred and fifty years—ever since I was brought back up here. It's what I do, and I'm good at it."

Tiffany forced herself to stay focused. "How long have you been in Peoria?"

"A year and some change."

"And you've been making people sick since you've been here?"

A nod.

"You're the one responsible for making the children sick at the hospital?"

A grin. "That's me."

A flash of heat flared up her back, settling between her shoulder blades. She wanted to turn this jerk into a slime ball and pour him down a storm drain.

But that wasn't the way she did things.

Not *a demon*...not *a demon*...

"From now on, your days of making people sick are gone—understand?"

No reply.

"I took away your spore supply. In other words, you can no longer use them. You'll need to find another hobby from now on—stamps, or maybe baseball cards. Do you understand?"

A nod.

"Do you have any more spores hidden somewhere?"

Another nod.

"Where are they?"

"In my apartment."

"Where, exactly?"

"Under the rug in my living room."

Tiffany closed her eyes and concentrated on the demon's thick skull. "*No more spores...no more sick children...and no more shape-shifting...*"

She opened her eyes. "Did you hear what I just told you?"

Another nod.

"All right. Where are the rest of your spores?"

No response.

"Did you hear me?"

A nod.

"Where are they?"

"I...don't know..."

"You're sure?"

A nod.

"In other words, you no longer know anything about spores, where they are, or what you've been doing with them. Got it?"

Another nod.

"One other thing—"

"Tifferoo?"

"Chip, I'm working here!"

"I really think you need to take a break and check out the scenery."

"And why would I want to do that?"

"Three words: We've got company."

Tiffany reluctantly pulled her gaze from the inferior and turned in the seat.

A police cruiser was pulling up to the space behind them.

CHAPTER 28

Tall and broad-shouldered, the driver carefully squeezed out of the cruiser. He watched them as he put his service hat on. Then, squaring his shoulders, he walked right over.

Tiffany got out and watched him approach. She remembered having seen the man before. She was nervous at first, but his beaming smile suggested they had nothing to fear.

Then she remembered: the hospital. She had seen him in the room with Mandy Conlin. He was standing behind the chair where Mandy's mother sat.

He stopped about five feet away and tipped his hat. "Morning, Miss Sedarski." He nodded to Chip.

"Good morning." Tiffany smiled back at him. "You were at the hospital, weren't you?"

He looked surprised. "I didn't think you'd remember—not with everything going on all at once. I'm Sergeant Harry Conlin. I was making my rounds when I noticed your mother's car and decided to come on over and see if everything was okay. I've seen the car several times at the hospital."

"How's Mandy doing?"

"She's doing just fine, thanks to you two." He nodded briefly to Chip. "As soon as I saw it was you in the car, I knew I had to come over and thank you personally. I couldn't do it at the hospital. As I said, it was kind of hectic, and…well, we were a little overwhelmed after your visit."

"It *was* kind of crazy, wasn't it? But it's really okay. We're both glad she's doing well."

"So are many of the other kids, from what I hear…"

"We're happy we could help."

He went silent. He seemed to be staring past her, at the car. Tiffany realized right then that he was looking at the inferior. She had to think of something quickly.

"Friend of yours?"

"Actually, we just found him…he was wandering around in sort of a daze. We picked him up and put him in the back seat, and then he just collapsed. We've been trying to revive him, but he seems…we don't know if he's drunk, unconscious, or hallucinating. I'm really glad you came over. Chip and I don't live here and have no idea what to do with him."

Sergeant Conlin marched right over and cautiously approached the open rear door of the Honda. He laid his service hat on the roof of the car and bent for a closer look. "Sir?" He nudged the man, who still didn't move.

Tiffany glanced at Chip. "*Bring him back.*"

"Tifferoo, I'm sure this dude would notice a flower slithering into the back seat of the car. You'll have to do the honors."

She closed her eyes and focused. "*Wake up. You won't remember anything. All you'll know is that you're confused. You've been wandering around, trying to figure out who you are.*"

"Sir? You all right?" The cop shook him more vigorously.

"He's not dead, is he?" Chip asked.

Tiffany gave him a look.

He returned her look. "*Just trying to add a touch of authenticity to the moment, dearest.*"

"No." Conlin moved closer. "He does smell strongly of wine…" He straightened, grabbed his radio and called it in. Then he backed away from the vehicle, talking very softly but not taking his eyes off the suspect in the back seat. He turned to Tiffany and Chip. "They'll be sending a unit for him directly. I could do it, but I've got to be somewhere else in a few minutes."

"Thank you."

"No problem." He grabbed the groggy inferior by the arm and pulled. The man opened his eyes, shook himself and looked around. "Where…what…who the fuck are *you*?"

"Seriously?" Conlin scowled. "Doesn't this uniform tell you anything?"

"Fuck. Yeah, it tells me…*fuck*!" The inferior tried pulling away.

Conlin was much bigger and stronger, and in much better condition. He pulled the man out easily and held him up until he could stand on his own. Then he coaxed him over to the police cruiser and made him stand facing it.

The inferior tried pulling away again. "What the fuck…what're you *doin',* man? Am I…am I under arrest?"

"For now, you're being detained, sir…" Conlin pulled the man's arms behind him and cuffed him.

"What the fuck for?"

"Sir, don't resist. I'll be forced to taser you—"

"I didn't do a fucking—"

"I smell wine on your breath."

"So? I wasn't even drivin'! Did anyone see me get out of a fuckin' *car*? Don't ya need to be drivin' a fuckin' *car* before you can be pulled over and—"

"How'd you get here, then?"

The man looked around. He noticed Tiffany and Chip and squinted at them both, as if trying to remember them. After about ten seconds, he shook his head. "I don't…*you* brought me here, didn'tcha? You! Bitch! Did *you* bring me here?"

"Sir, I'd watch my language if I were you…"

"Fuck you!"

The big man squinted. "That's not exactly the right way to go about watching your language..."

"Damn you, bitch! Fuck you and that faggy weirdo with ya!"

"Me? A *fag*?" Chip scratched the back of his neck. "I do admit that I've been overwhelmed in the past by Clark Gable and Cary Grant movies…but a *fag*? I'm slightly insulted…and somewhat offended…"

"It's probably the wine," Tiffany said. "I don't think he actually meant that."

Sergeant Conlin stepped subtly in the way, blocking the inferior's view. He had his hands ready to search the man's pockets. "Sir, do you have any sharp objects on you that might poke or cut me?"

"Man, this really sucks! I didn't do a fuckin' thing! *Not a fuckin' thing*! Those two over there…what the fuck are *they* doin', standin' there, lookin' at me like that?"

"They picked you up. You were wandering around and didn't seem to know where you were going. They were going to take you to a hospital. They had no idea what else to do."

"I wasn't wanderin' around…I was…"

The cop finished searching the man's pockets. He found a wallet and keys. "You were what?" He held up the ring of keys. "And what does this look like?"

He blinked. His jaw lowered. "They're…*keys*…"

"To a *car*, maybe?"

"Wait a minute, now. Those keys don't mean nothin'. I tell ya, I *wasn't drivin'*! I was—"

"Then what *were* ya doing?"

"I was…" He turned and gazed at Tiffany again, then Chip. He began shaking his head. "I must be really fucked up, man. I don't remember *what* the fuck I was doin'—"

"Then ya might have actually been driving after all?"

"Listen, man—"

"We'll take you in and find out what's going on. For all we know, you might have suffered a concussion." He opened his rear door, placed his hand on the inferior's head and helped him safely into the back. "Don't go anywhere, now." He closed the door and came right back. "Like I said, we'll take him in and find out what's going on. We'll take good care of him."

Tiffany stared at the shadow in the back seat of the cruiser and forced herself to stay calm. She thought of all those sick kids and once again considered turning the inferior into sludge. *I'm* not *a demon... Besides, I fixed the situation—in more ways than one*.

Anyway, they would soon take him to the Police Station and he would have his comeuppance. And she reminded herself that if things followed their natural course, the town of Peoria would no longer have to worry about this inferior.

"Can we go now?" Chip asked.

The cop nodded. "Once again, I'd like to thank both of you for what you did at the hospital."

"It was really nothing," Chip said. "All in a day's work."

The cop shook his head solemnly. "It was a lot more than nothing, believe me. You gave us back our little girl."

Tiffany smiled. "It was a pleasure."

Conlin turned serious. "While we're talking about this, I think I'd better give you two a heads-up. No one seems to know what exactly is going on at the hospital, but I've heard through the grapevine that some of the board members are skeptical and extremely confused about the whole thing."

"We understand," Tiffany said.

"Well, I feel it only fair to tell you that talk of some sort of investigation was in the works, but you probably won't have to worry about it now."

"Why not?" Chip asked.

Conlin shrugged. "It was hushed."

"By who?" Tiffany asked.

"There are a lot of things flying around in the rumor mill, but what I got was that several Board members with many high-powered connections want this kept quiet."

"That makes sense," Tiffany said. "It's strange, but it makes sense."

"In other words," Chip said, "they don't want this getting out."

Sergeant Conlin nodded. "I don't know exactly what's going on, but we've seen this sort of thing before. It all boils down to the same thing: someone with a bunch of clout was embarrassed or slighted by something and wants to save face by keeping it buried."

"*Whaddya think, Tifferoo*?" Chip sent over.

"I think we've stepped on Breath Mint's toes and he's telling the Diocese to keep this quiet so word doesn't get out that someone's undoing their work."

"*Sounds good to me*."

Conlin smiled and tipped his hat. "Anyway, that's how things are. And in my opinion, that's how they should stay. My wife Felicia and I—and also Sonya, our other daughter…well, we'll never forget what you did."

"Officer?" Tiffany said.

"Yes?"

"Off the record…what do *you* think about all this?"

"About what you did?"

She nodded.

He went silent for a few moments. Then he shrugged. "You gave us back our little girl. I honestly don't care who you are, what you are, what you did or how you did it, and I'm sure the other parents feel the same way. The only thing we truly care about is that our kids are no longer sick."

"Then what we did—it didn't seem weird or strange to you?"

He went silent for a few moments. His brows pushed together. Tiffany caught a glimpse of something in his thoughts that made her shudder. When he spoke again, he said, "Miss, I'm a cop. Believe me—I've seen a *lot* of strange things, most of them bad. But when they turn out good, that's when I find that even a little over thinking of the situation might be a bad thing." He tipped his hat and went back to the cruiser.

Tiffany and Chip got back in the Honda. Before she could pull out of their space, a police van pulled off Fulton, heading straight for the rear lot.

"What was that look he gave us that seemed to freak you out?" Chip asked.

"I caught an image of the postman in his thoughts. Sergeant Conlin saw him die and disappear in traffic. It probably happened after I took away his powers."

"Then the postman went back down." Chip grinned. "Cool beans!"

"Yes. One less demon for us—or anyone else—to worry about."

"The butt-kicker lives!"

CHAPTER 29

M. Murray Robertson III got the call at precisely nine o'clock the next morning, as he entered the bank and went down the long hall leading to his office. The call was from Orlando, Florida. Robertson knew damned well that the caller was Braithwaite and that the super demon was calling about what happened at Children's Hospital two days before.

His pulse racing, Robertson collapsed in his chair and took a few deep breaths before picking up the phone. He wanted to be comfortable when the super demon got on the line. The filleting he was bound to endure was going to be excruciating.

"Mr. Robertson?"

"Yes?"

"This is Daniel Grove calling on behalf of Mr. Waite. I'm about to put him through."

Click.

"Robertson, you know why I'm calling, don't you?"

Waite's voice was so loud that it made Robertson's eardrum crackle. Gasping, he pulled the phone away from his ear.

"Robertson? You there?"

While waiting for the ringing to subside, he cautiously brought the phone back to within a few inches from his ear. "Sir, I'm right here… And I can hear you perfectly."

"I want you to tell me what's going on. Last we talked, you told me you were going to send another one of your boys after that blond bitch and her stinkweed friend. By my estimation, forty-eight hours have passed since our talk. She and her buddy are not only still there, but, judging by a phone call I just received, she's still doing her shtick, and doing it quite well. My contact told me she's now healing sick kids, and these kids were made sick by another one of your inferiors. I was also told that this inferior is nowhere to be found. Just what the fuck is happening there?"

Robertson shuddered in his chair. This was horrible news. The day before, he was told by Ron Alsworth that the super demon had heard what happened at the hospital, and that a whole bunch of heavy-duty shit started flying and would undoubtedly linger heavily in the air for a long time to come.

Unfortunately, that wasn't *all* the news, and Robertson dreaded having to tell Waite the rest of it. "Well, sir, there was some sort of…well—"

"Some sort of, well, *what*?"

"Well, sir—"

"The way you're stumbling around, stepping all over your tongue, I've got this nagging suspicion that what happened in that piss-ass town happened without your knowing anything about it. I also have this feeling that you're about to tell me something else I'm not gonna like. Does this sum it up in a nutshell?"

"Well, sir—"

"Will you *for Christ's sake* cut the "well, sir," shit out of this conversation and grow a pair before I reach through the fucking phone line and strangle your pitiful neck with that hundred-dollar tie you're wearing?"

Robertson swallowed. He was about to speak when something the super just said nagged at him. *Hundred-dollar tie.* He looked down. Then he lowered the phone and brought it a little closer to his face. He stared at it in amazement—as if it was something he'd never seen before. Then he jerked it away—as if it was a poisonous snake. How on earth could Braithwaite know what he was—

"Well? I'm waiting…"

Focus... He could worry about the tie thing later. Right now, there were more important things to address.

He should have known the super demon would find out what happened. Most of those sick children had been made sick by Lyon on orders from the League. Many of those orders came directly from Robertson's peers while others were executed indirectly, for other various reasons.

But the fact remained: the blonde undid more than a year's worth of the League's efforts in just one hour. As a result, a handful of extremely rich, extremely powerful and well-connected League members were chomping at the bit.

Robertson had not slept at all the previous night. Once the phone calls had stopped, his brain started up and he spent most of the night trying to figure out what had gone wrong. It just didn't make sense that an inferior of Lyon's caliber would fail. All Lyon had to do was nab the blonde and her partner. From what Robertson had seen during the last year, Lyon was a master at what he did. He could shape-shift and make people sick at the drop of a hat. He'd been working alongside Balberith, making people sick for the last century—what was so difficult about going up against a dead blonde and an inferior?

How the hell could someone who wasn't even a demon match up to a shapeshifter?

"I'm waiting, Robertson. By the way, here's a news flash. I *detest* waiting. But the good thing is that I usually don't *have* to wait. Such clout comes from being a super demon. In other words, if you don't start telling me what the hell happened up there, I'm liable to pay a surprise visit and let that League of yours know just what I think of them and their—"

"She g-got him, sir." Robertson shuddered the moment he'd said it.

"How's that?"

"The blonde. She…got him."

"That's all you can say that will explain what happened?"

"That's all I really know, sir. She went into the hospital, cured nearly fifty kids, left, and got Lyon the same night."

"Lyon's the shapeshifter?"

"Yes, sir."

A pause. "You realize how this sounds, don't you? You're telling me the blonde managed to undo a year's work of hexes from a demon and send *both* of your inferiors back down to the Dark Place. Is *this* what you're telling me?"

"No, sir."

"Then tell me what I just said that wasn't exactly accurate."

Robertson sighed. "She didn't send the shapeshifter back down, sir."

"Then where the hell *is* he? You'd *better* not tell me she turned him into a Christmas ornament and left him hanging in a shop window..."

"Last I heard, sir, he was taken in to the Police Station."

"For what?"

"I was told he'd been drinking, and one of the charges was vagrancy."

"Vagrancy? You can't possibly be serious!"

"I'm afraid I am, sir."

"Is he still there?"

"As far as I know, sir..."

"Why the fuck hasn't he left? He's a damned *shapeshifter*! He can appear as the Chief of Police—or the Mayor—and just walk right out the fucking door!"

"Apparently—that is, judging by what I was told—he has no idea he *is* a shapeshifter, sir..."

"Now how is *that* possible?"

"He has no idea who or what he is, sir."

"You're telling me he doesn't even *know* he's an inferior? *Or* a shapeshifter?"

"He...seems to have total amnesia, sir..."

Waite went silent.

Robertson continued trembling.

"You know what this means, don't you?"

"Sir?"

"The blonde. She not only got him, she also destroyed him."

"I'm afraid so, sir."

"Those two went to your damned hospital, made the sick kids well, sent one inferior down to the Dark Place and destroyed the other. You know how this makes us look, don't you?"

"Yes, sir."

"You also know what's being done about this, right?"

"Not exactly, sir. I've talked to several of my colleagues, but they've all been told to keep this quiet."

"Of *course* we have to keep this quiet, you dumbass! Don't you know what this will turn into if word gets out? Once the news hounds get wind of it, it'll turn into a three-ring circus! CNN will run with it. It'll hit all the Cable news networks in minutes and be all over the globe in an hour! We can't possibly let the fucking world know what those two have been doing. Do you have any idea how this'll look if the supers running the other countries find out what's happening over here? I'll be a laughing stock. I'm a *super demon*, goddammit! Do you really want to know what will happen to you and that piss-ass town of yours if I even suspect I've become a laughing stock?"

"I can only imagine, sir."

"Then I don't need to explain anything else to you. I don't need to explain why your League was given strict orders to drop this subject cold, and why no word of this will leak anywhere—and *I mean anywhere*!"

"Yes, sir."

"I've instructed every single League member to do whatever is necessary to quash this mess, and that means forking over whatever money is necessary to the fucking hospital and the medical profession itself to keep a tight lid on this."

"Yes, sir."

"If that means stepping on certain doctors' toes, then so be it."

"Yes, sir."

"As I've told everyone else, you've all got plenty of money. Use it for whatever means necessary."

"Yes, sir."

"I don't want those two getting away with this, but I want this taken care of quietly."

"Yes, sir."

"This means I'll have to send one of my subs after them, and he'll probably have to round them up once they leave your stupid town. I don't want anything else happening in that town. Understand?"

"Yes, sir." Robertson suddenly realized he was sweating. Very carefully, he found his silk monogrammed handkerchief and dabbed at his forehead and mouth.

"When you've finished wiping the sweat from your brow," Waite finally said, "I want you to do something for me."

With a shaky hand, Robertson dropped the handkerchief in his lap. He stared at it and suddenly began feeling faint. As he struggled to determine just how the super demon could possibly know what he was doing, Waite said, "I want this done as quickly as possible, and I want it done without any further fuckups. Understood?"

"Yes, sir."

"Find out where the two of them are and what they're doing."

"That's all you need, sir?"

Waite chuckled. "It doesn't sound like much, does it?"

"Well, no, sir—"

"Judging by your past performances, this is probably all you can handle. I'll call back in twenty-four hours, and if you fuck this one up, the two of us will definitely be locking horns. And here's another news flash. My horns stand up to anything. Understood?"

Click!

DAY FIVE - "LEAVING HOME AGAIN"

CHAPTER 30

The next morning, Tiffany decided she and Chip should leave town. She'd wanted to stay a little longer but realized that would be unwise. Judging by what Sergeant Conlin had told them the day before, she knew things wouldn't turn out as badly as she'd originally expected, but she still believed that staying longer would only complicate things. The last thing she wanted was to make things worse for anyone.

And, of course, for Momma.

Although she was pleased that she'd finally been reunited with her mother, she had to face facts. She had unwittingly brought two demons into Momma's house. She and Chip had destroyed both demons, but that didn't matter in the great scheme of things. As long as Tiffany and Chip stayed visible, the chances of more demons coming around were much too great to dismiss.

The three of them sat at the dining room table, saying very little. Tiffany sipped her coffee and ate her scrambled egg and toast while Chip drank his orange juice and nibbled on an eggshell from the napkin in his lap whenever Momma wasn't looking.

Since Tiffany had communicated mentally with Momma two nights before, she knew Momma was aware of what was going to happen. She just didn't know how she could discuss it rationally. She'd been looking forward to this reunion for a very long time. Now that their visit was coming to an end, she didn't think she was strong enough to go through with it.

But she had to do this. Momma didn't know Tiffany was dead and that was how it had to stay. If Tiffany remained here with Chip, it would be only a matter of time before Breath Mint sent more demons after them. Tiffany knew she and Chip weren't powerful enough to handle more than one or two at a time. She had little doubt that Breath Mint would hear about what happened at the hospital. He probably already knew that she and Chip were responsible for sending the Postman back down, as well as stripping the dandelion guy of all his powers.

Tiffany cared only that Momma stayed safe. That meant she and Chip had to leave before some other demon showed up at her door.

"The two of you are awfully quiet this morning." Momma watched them both as she sipped her coffee.

"I know, Momma."

"You have to leave, don't you?"

Tiffany stared at her half-eaten scrambled egg.

"Baby…" Momma placed her hand over Tiffany's. "You can tell me."

Tiffany sighed. "Yes, Momma."

Momma smiled. "You told me you'll be back, didn't you?"

"Yes, Momma. Of course I'll be back."

"Then there's no reason to be so sad, is there?"

"No, Momma."

Momma kept her smile. Tiffany realized right then that she could never forget her mother's beautiful face when it was all lit up. It had never failed to lift her spirits and would always remain etched deeply in her heart.

"Do you have any idea where you'll be going from here?" Momma asked. "You're going to continue doing your act, I hope."

"Yes, Momma. But we don't really know where we'll go from here." Tiffany thought it best if she didn't tell Momma anything that could put her in jeopardy.

"Do *you* have any ideas?" Momma asked Chip.

"Moi?" He put down the orange juice carton and grinned. "Tifferoo's the brain here. I just go where she goes, and hope that wherever she goes doesn't wilt the ol' petals."

Momma watched them in silence. Tiffany could tell she was trying to determine what was really going on. "Are you *sure* there's nothing I need to know about you two?" she finally asked.

"Like what, Momma?"

"You two aren't…well, you're not—"

"It would simplify things," Chip said, grinning. "For me, anyway."

"No, Momma. We're just partners."

"Friends, too, right, Tifferoo? You told me just the other day—or was it last week—or maybe it was last month. I can't remember because I've got a lot of other nifty stuff on my mind—and because I've got a bad case of ADD. It's probably because I get distracted a lot. All it takes is—" He stopped when Tiffany glared. “Anyway, whenever it was, you said, Chip, you and I are friends. Remember that, Tifferoosky?”

Tiffany knew he was only trying in his own crude way to keep her spirits up. “Yes, Chip, we’re friends.” She smiled at Momma. “We’re partners and friends, Momma.”

“I’m also her sidekick. Isn’t that right, too, Tifferoosky?”

“Yes, Chip. You’re my sidekick.”

Momma just smiled.

***

Momma drove Tiffany and Chip to the Greyhound Bus Station on SW Adams Street at one o’clock, after they’d finished lunch.

A slew of memories rushed past, and Tiffany found herself weakening again. This was where she’d come to leave home just five years earlier, when dealing with Jack Phillips became too much. This was where she’d come to leave her hometown forever so she could make a name for herself in Hollywood. This was where she’d come to begin a new life—to travel to the place that led to her untimely death.

This was also the place that would take her back—where she would hunt for the man responsible for her death.

And then what?

Once again, she caught herself facing the same terrifying question.

What will you do when you find him again?

She didn't know. She only knew that she had to track him down, look him in the eye and tell him who she was.

After that, she had no idea *what* would happen.

"This is it, then?" Momma turned in her seat. Her wet eyes glistened in the glare of the afternoon sun.

"I guess so, Momma…"

Tiffany gazed at her mother. She wanted so much to go back in time…to become a little girl once again, when Dad was still alive, and they were the happy family they'd once been.

But she knew better. You could go back home, but you just couldn't rewind time. Time wasn't a clock; it didn't do what you wanted it to. You could save it, waste it and keep it. You could even slow it down if you knew how… But you couldn't put it in a jar and take it out later on, when you wanted to fully appreciate it. Time passed, and along with it, so did the memories one made and cherished. You could hold on to the memories; you just couldn't hold on to time.

Now, as she gazed at her mother, she couldn't help wishing that everything would go back to how it once was. But it just couldn't happen that way. She was dead. So was Dad. Momma was getting older and would eventually grow old and die, too.

"I think I'd better go on in and buy some tickets," Chip said, opening the back door.

"Make sure you actually *buy* them," Tiffany said, still gazing at Momma. "No illusions—or jokes—this time."

"You're no fun at a party." Then he got out, closed the door, and skipped off to the front entrance.

"Sometimes he charms his way to get what he wants," Tiffany said.

Momma was silent for a few moments. Tiffany could tell something was on her mind. "You're not going to tell me, are you, baby?"

"Tell you what, Momma?"

A deep sigh. "What's *really* happened to you…"

Tiffany searched her mother's eyes. She didn't want to drift inside Momma's brain and see what was going on in there. Somehow, that didn't seem proper. Injecting her own thoughts into Momma's consciousness to protect her was one thing—sneaking in there to snoop was a totally different matter. "Whatever do you mean, Momma?"

"I've noticed things ever since you and Chip got into town, baby…things that just didn't make sense to me. They still don't make sense."

"Tell me what doesn't make sense, Momma…"

"It's the magic between you and Chip…and how people react to you…and how you and Chip communicate without actually talking…" Momma smiled. "And, of course, those shoes…"

Tiffany swallowed. "What shoes, Momma?"

Still smiling, Momma shook her head. "Baby, let's not get too worked up about the shoe issue again, okay? We both know what we're talking about. Even when you were little, you were always changing them, decorating them, asking us to take you to the store to buy you a new pair. Then you grew up and became enamored with Marilyn Monroe, and when you read in a magazine what she once said, it made you think you actually *were* Marilyn…"

Tiffany nodded. "Give the girl the right shoes, and she can conquer the world."

Momma's eyes glistened. "I've noticed that you've changed your shoes at least a dozen times since you've been here, and I also know that you didn't take all those shoes from that bag in the back seat. You know how I know that?"

She was afraid to ask. "H-How, Momma?"

"Those bags are empty, aren't they?"

Tiffany looked down. She'd always known how perceptive her mother was; she just didn't think Momma would figure things out so easily.

"Momma…"

"And while you're at it, would you mind telling me why Chip sneaks eggshells and coffee grounds from the garbage? And why he insists on putting the regular food back?"

Tiffany just sighed; her thoughts raced.

"Am I right, baby?"

In spite of her intentions, Tiffany knew she was going to have to go right on in there and work her magic again. It wasn't because Momma had things figured out; that was only part of it. Tiffany realized she couldn't leave town without keeping Momma safe. The Diocese—as well as the League of Demons—lurked everywhere. She and Chip had cleansed Peoria of two inferiors. The word was probably already out, and the path would eventually lead to Momma. And there was no way Tiffany would leave Momma at risk.

"Baby? *Please* tell me what's going on…"

Tiffany placed her hand on Momma's forearm and closed her eyes. *"Momma,"* she thought, *"you're better off not knowing about me or what I've become. I'm your daughter and always will be, and I love you and will come back to you when the time is right. I have one last errand to do, and when I've finished doing it, I will come right back home. In the meantime, I must leave you safe from all the evils in the world. To do that, I have to take all the good I can find inside me and transfer it to you, and when I'm finished, no bad or evil will be able to enter your being. If someone asks about me or where I've gone, just tell them Chip and I have gone back on the road. And if someone tries to cast a spell on you, it will automatically reverse itself back to the person casting the spell and they will walk away, totally clueless of what happened. And please don't worry about us. Chip and I will be just fine. But this time I promise to keep in touch, and as I told you before, whenever you need me, just think of me, and I'll know instantly. I love you, Momma. I always will, and when I come back home again, it will be forever."*

Tiffany opened her eyes. "I don't think you should worry about the bags, Momma."

Momma looked around. "The bags? You're not taking your bags?"

"We're taking them, Momma."

Momma wiped her eyes. "My baby's leaving me again, and I'm talking about those stupid bags—as if they're actually important."

"I'm leaving you, Momma, but as I told you before—"

"I know you're coming back, baby."

"I promise I will, Momma."

"I know." Momma smiled through her tears. She pulled her close, and they hugged each other until they both began sobbing quietly.

A couple of minutes later, Chip came back with the tickets. Momma stepped out of the car and hugged him, and then she and Tiffany hugged again.

Momma got back in the Honda. Tiffany waved as Momma eased away from the curb and joined the flow of passing traffic.

"You okay?" Chip asked.

Tiffany sniffed and wiped her eyes. "No."

"Let's get rid of these bags and get on the bus, then. These are first-class tickets. We get to sit behind the driver."

"First-class tickets? On a *bus*?"

He shrugged.

"Did you do something that's going to get us in trouble?"

"Moi?"

"Yes. And cut the crap."

"I have absolutely no idea what you mean, sweet cakes."

"You know exactly what I mean." She grabbed both suitcases, went over to the wall near the corner of the building and set them down. The moment she left them on the pavement, they turned back into the same white boxes they were when Brad had given them to her at the Marriott. Then she straightened.

Someone behind her said, “Hi, Tiffany…”

She turned. It was the cute little girl with chestnut hair she’d seen in Mandy’s room. She was wearing a dark-blue tee shirt, jeans and a pair of run-down tennis shoes. She stood there stiffly, staring dumbly at the boxes. Tiffany thought she’d say something about it, but she didn’t. She just watched Tiffany and her pretty green eyes grew moist. “You really *are* someone very special, aren’t you?” she said softly.

Tiffany suddenly remembered who she was. “Vicki?”

She nodded. “You saved my dog.”

“I remember. How’s Toby doing?”

“He’s doing just great—thanks to you.” She glanced at the boxes again. “H-How did you—“

“That’s good, Vicki. Give him a kiss from me when you get back home.”

Vicki gave the boxes one last glance. “Is it true? You really *are* leaving?”

“Yes, Vicki. We have to go now—“

“Do you really *have* to?” Vicki’s smile instantly vanished. “I mean, can’t you stay a *little* while longer?”

“I wish we could, but…” Tiffany shrugged.

“I so *totally* wish I could say something right now to tell you how I feel,” Vicki said.

“Your smile already told me.”

“Mandy’s my best friend. I’ve been worried sick about her.”

"Well, you can stop worrying now."

Vicki blinked. "She'll really be all right, then? She won't be sick anymore?"

"She won't be sick anymore."

"You saved my dog…and then you saved my best friend. How can you possibly understand what you've done for me?"

Tiffany began to feel her composure crumbling steadily.

"I'll never forget you, Tiffany. Never *ever*!"

"I know."

"And there's nothing I can say or do to get you to stay longer?"

"I'm afraid not." Tiffany wanted to take the sadness from the little girl's face. *I've done so much here in the last few days. Surely, making a little girl smile should not be much of a problem for me…*

Vicki sniffed. "Like I said, I'll never forget you, or what you did for me, for Toby, and for Mandy. And for all the other kids who aren't sick anymore. I wanted to catch your act at the hospital, but I didn't find out about it in time, and by the time I did, I couldn't get in there because I wasn't sick. But I did manage to get in to see Mandy. And when I did, I got to see you again…and I got there in time to see you work your magic again."

"I'll be back, you know."

"Really?" Her eyes lit up. "When?"

"It won't be very long."

"How long? *Please* tell me it won't be very long!"

"I'm not exactly sure, but I promise we'll be back long before you know it."

"I can't wait! I'll be here. Promise you'll stay longer when you come back?"

"I will." Tiffany glanced at the little girl's shoes. The stitching had loosened in some places and the seams had already split. Her toes were nearly visible. It wouldn't be long at all before the shoes would fall apart. "Your tennies look…well, pretty tired. It's really not good for your feet."

Vicki smiled sheepishly. "It's all right. Really. Mom says I have to save up my money because I go through them so fast. Dad…well, Mom always has a rough time finding him, so we don't have enough money for new shoes right now…" Her cheeks flushed. "My feet are so…so *big*…"

"What's your favorite color?"

"What?"

"For tennis shoes. What color do you like?"

"Well…light-blue, but—"

"Close your eyes."

"Huh?"

"Close them tight, now." Tiffany placed her hand on Vicki's head. "I want to give you something before I leave."

Excited, Vicki closed her eyes.

Tiffany focused. Vicki's shoes suddenly turned light-blue and brand-new again, with tiny silver stars forming a V near each toe.

Vicki's eyes shot open. She looked down. Then she looked at Tiffany again. Her eyes were enormous. "H-How did you…h-how did they—"

"I just made a few adjustments. Your feet are very important. When they don't feel good, the rest of you doesn't—"

Without warning, Vicki wrapped her arms around her and hugged her tightly. Tiffany closed her eyes and struggled to keep from crying again.

When she pulled away, Vicki's eyes gleamed in the afternoon sun. But she was smiling brightly. "I was right," she said softly.

"What do you mean?"

Vicki sniffed. "You really and truly *are* an angel!"

Tiffany couldn't reply.

"Well, you are, aren't you? Look what you've just done. And the hospital thing…and Mandy…and Toby…and—"

"Go home, Vicki." Tiffany brushed some of the girl's heavy chestnut hair away from her face and wiped away a tear. "Kiss Toby for me and tell him he's a good puppy. And stay happy."

"You'll come back, right? You just said you would. *Please* don't lie to me. *Please* come back!"

"I wouldn't lie to you, Vicki."

"I know you wouldn't. Angels don't lie, do they?"

Tiffany sighed. "I'll definitely be back, Vicki."

"Promise?"

"Yes. I promise."

EPILOGUE

Once the bus got moving and crawled up to the intersection, Tiffany turned in her seat. Lowering her voice, she said, "Now you can tell me how you *really* got those tickets."

Chip's eyes sparkled. "Did you really have to do the shoe thing with that little girl?"

"Yes. And stop changing the subject."

"She'll tell everyone what you did—"

"So? She tells a few of her friends I changed her shoes for her. What's the big deal?"

"You don't think the magic thing will come up in the conversation?"

"You can't be serious…" Sometimes she didn't believe what came out of his mouth.

"Me? Serious? Surly you joist…"

"The magic thing? Really?"

"You don't think it takes a little magic to change someone's footwear, precious?"

"That's not exactly the point."

"There's a *point* here?"

"Well, yeah…even you raise a valid point once in a while."

His tiny green eyes twinkled. "How about that? I've actually raised a point!" Then, suddenly confused, he scratched the back of his neck. "What exactly is my point, Tifferoony?"

"The point is this. Didn't we do a whole bunch of other magic at the hospital? You changed into a lamp, remember? And don't forget my disappearing act. And then there was that thing with the giant wrist watch on your arm… And don't forget that light bulb you made appear over your head. Then we did that stethoscope-appearing trick after the show—"

"But changing her *shoes* in front of her like that? Don't you think you went a tad overboard?"

"You said that same thing when I brought her dog back."

"I guess so…but the *shoe thing*? *Really*?"

"Didn't you see what she was wearing? Those shoes were awful. They would have ruined her feet."

"I still think you went overboard."

"Good shoes are very important, you know."

"Tifferoo—"

"Besides, I'm sure she probably already told a few of her friends what I did with her dog. What harm will any of that do?"

"This kind of stuff is bound to get back to Braithwaite." He whispered the name.

"You don't think he's already heard about what we did at the hospital?"

"That's what's worrying me, angel. If he's already heard about it, he probably already sent someone else sniffing around."

"Don't you like irritating Breath Mint? *I* certainly do…"

He sighed. "Of course I do. And it's *Braithwaite*." He whispered the name again. "But if he gets upset enough, you know what'll happen."

"He'll throw a tantrum."

"Precious, you know damned well that his tantrums are just a tad worse than your average—"

"I know, I know."

"Don't forget, he loves explosions."

"How can I possibly forget that?"

"He likes blowing up mortals, too."

"So what? He's been looking for us ever since we left Florida. We're still here, aren't we?"

"He's bound to get lucky one of these days."

"Maybe he will, maybe he won't. Until then, I don't think we should waste time worrying about it. Let's get back to my original question. How did you get those tickets?"

"Would you believe—"

"No."

"All righty-rooty… How's this? I was standing behind this really weird-looking guy with a three-day growth of beard, and when he turned around, I saw that it was really a woman, and—"

"That won't get you anywhere, either."

"Tifferoo, how can I explain myself if you won't let me explain myself?"

"Because you're in one of your silly moods. Nothing you say makes sense, and I have to assume that you're just being funny to disguise what you've actually done."

Chip pushed his lower lip forward and pouted.

"Pouting won't work, either." She turned back to the window and watched more of her hometown passing behind them. "I'm really not in the mood."

"I was trying to snap you out of it."

She remained staring out the window. "It won't work. But thanks anyway."

"We did a lot of good here, Tifferoo."

"I know."

"And you got to see your mom."

Tiffany sniffed back a tear.

"We also got rid of two more badasses."

A nod.

"And you know we'll be back, righterino?"

Tiffany forced a smile. "Righterino."

Chip grinned. "I knew *that* would bring you out of it."

Tiffany sat back. "You know your powers really are growing, don't you?"

"Are you referring to what happened outside your mom's condo?"

"You couldn't have done that before."

"Split into two spirits? I doubt it."

"You also shape-shifted."

"You noticed."

"Of course I did. I was right there when you came back and turned into your flower thingy."

"But why now? And why in *Peoria*, of all places?"

"It happened when you needed it to happen, didn't it?"

"You've definitely got a point there."

"And it helped us nail the jerk making all those kids sick, right?"

"Right."

"Then don't question it." Tiffany closed her eyes and tried to relax, but all she could think of was Momma and when she'd get to see her again.

"You miss her already, don'tcha?"

A nod.

"How long do you think it'll take for us to take care of business in good ol' Hokeywood?"

Tiffany thought about the wolf guy…and the Dark Place…and the Meddaworld…and the Valley of Decay…and the Castle of Demons. She thought about everything that had happened to her since the party at Johnny Rock's. A fresh batch of seething hot anger sliced through her when the face of the man who'd killed her flashed in front of her eyes. He was tall and dark and clean-shaven and as good-looking as they came…and just as cold-blooded and evil as any of the demons she and Chip had dealt with.

When she thought of that, she realized at that moment that Hollywood was quite possibly the most evil place on the face of the earth. And it also made her realize that when she died and went to the Dark Place, she'd actually left another dark place in the process.

"Tifferoo? You in there somewhere?"

"I'm here."

"Well? How long do you think it'll take?"

"Only as long as it takes for us to find the guy who gave me that drink," she said softly.

"And then?"

"I really don't know."

"You're not a demon, Tifferoo."

"I know."

"But something tells me you're thinking like one right now."

"Let's find him first."

"And after that?"

"I go back home."

Chip blinked. "Alone?"

"Unless you want to come with me…"

"I thought we were buds, Tifferoo." He looked hurt. "Partners."

"We are."

"Then I guess I'm going back to Peoria with you when we've finished balancing the scales of justice in good ol' Hokeywood."

Tiffany closed her eyes. The man's face returned, and the heat drifted though her again. *Not a demon*, she reminded herself. *You've just healed dozens of sick kids, saved the life of a dead dog, sent a demon back to the Dark Place, put the other one out of commission, and gave a little girl a brand-new pair of comfortable shoes. And you've done all of this in less than a week. You are definitely* not *a demon.*

But sometimes a girl had to resort to extreme measures to undo a horrible act…

Especially if a very bad man had to be taken down in the process.

ALSO BY DAVID BERARDELLI

THE APPRENTICE
THE WAGON DRIVER
DEMONCHASER I
DEMONCHASER II
STEPPING OUT OF MY GRAVE
ESCAPE CLAUSE
FATAL INNOCENCE
THE FUNNY DETECTIVE
JUST A SIMPLE ERRAND
COLORS
WORKING FOR A MOB BOSS
AND DARKNESS FELL
AFTER DARKNESS FELL
DEMONCHASER III
IN ANOTHER REALM
BEYOND RECOGNITION
THE NIGHTMARE COLLECTOR
HIDDEN
BEYOND GUILT
A RIPPLE IN TIME

www.ingramcontent.com/pod-product-compliance
Lightning Source LLC
La Vergne TN
LVHW030909080826
845145LV00010B/2820

* 9 7 8 1 7 8 6 9 5 6 6 8 2 *